"THERE'S THREE OF US, AND ONLY ONE OF HIM."

Mitchell hesitated. From what he'd heard, this man could take out all three of them without working up a sweat.

"I ain't got all day," the newcomer informed them.

Telford stupidly made the first move. He tried to bring his M-16 up, envisioning the great reward he would receive if he killed the man in buckskins.

But he never lived to claim it.

The newcomer's right hand flashed to his right holster, his motion a streak as the pearl-handled revolver cleared leather.

Mitchell saw Telford's head snap backward as the revolver boomed, a portion of the upper rear of his cranium exploding outward in a geyser of blood, brains, and other bits and pieces. He was slammed to the asphalt by the impact.

Also in the ENDWORLD Series:

DAVID ROBBINS

ENDWORLD

DENVER RUN

LEISURE BOOKS   NEW YORK CITY

A LEISURE BOOK

Published by

Dorchester Publishing Co., Inc.
6 East 39th Street
New York, NY 10016

Printed in the United States of America

Dedicated to

Judy and Joshua
and
to the memory of Sparta and the Spartans,
especially Leonidas and the 300 at Thermopylae;

to the memory of Crockett, Bowie, and Travis,
and the other defenders of the Alamo;

to the memory of Lt. John Chard, Lt. Gonville
Bromhead, and the garrison at Rorke's Drift;

to the Japanese samurai;

and to the military men and women everywhere,
and to all veterans:

we have nothing to be ashamed of.

1

The wind from the north was bitterly cold.

"Hurry it up," groused the tall soldier, his brown eyes scanning the surrounding countryside, his cheeks stinging from the icy gusts, as he stamped his booted feet again and again in an effort to keep the circulation going.

One of the two troopers engaged in changing a rear tire on their jeep glanced up at the speaker, scowling. "If you think you can do any better, big mouth," he snapped, "be my guest!"

The first soldier shook his head. "You're doing just fine. What are you getting so touchy about? I'm freezing, is all."

"And you think we're not?" demanded the second trooper, an older man with a protruding paunch.

The third soldier looked up, glaring at both of them. "Will you two shut the hell up? We'd get done a lot faster if you would stop your damn bickering!"

"I just don't see why Brandon can't help," complained the second soldier, arching his back to alleviate a cramp in his right hip as he crouched next to the jeep.

"Somebody has to keep watch," stated the third trooper, removing the punctured tire and placing it on the highway next to the lug nuts.

"Why can't I be the lookout?" demanded the second soldier.

Sighing, his black hair whipping in the breeze, the third soldier stared at the second. "What the hell is the

7

matter with you, Telford? You whine more than anyone else I know. If you moved your arms as much as you flap your gums, we would have been done by now."

Telford grunted, reaching for the good tire lying on the road next to his left leg. "I didn't mean anything by it," he said in justification of his griping.

"No," the third soldier cracked, "you never do."

"Let's just get it changed, Mitchell," Brandon remarked, "and get the hell out of here."

"I'm with you," Telford chimed in. "I don't like being left out here in the middle of the boonies."

Mitchell, the youngest of the trio, took the spare tire from Telford and positioned it on the hub.

"I still don't see why the captain had to go and leave us here," Telford went on while Mitchell worked at replacing the lug nuts.

"You know the answer to that one as well as we do," Brandon commented while watching a stand of trees on the other side of Highway 81. "Speed and surprise are essential to our mission. He couldn't afford to wait while we fixed the flat."

"I wish I was an officer," Telford said longingly.

Brandon chuckled. "You? An officer? Don't make me laugh. You'll always be a private, lunkhead, just like the rest of us."

Mitchell was working on the last of the lug nuts. "It won't take us long to catch up with the others."

Telford snickered, his expression slightly sinister. "Won't the Family be in for a big surprise!"

Brandon cocked his head to one side, listening. "Do you guys hear something?"

"I don't hear anything," Telford responded.

Mitchell slowly stood, the lug wrench clasped in his right hand. He stared to the west, back the way they had come, and focused on the distant horizon. Highway 81 stretched for as far as the eye could see in a westerly direction, sections of the road buckling or cracked from age and neglect, a rarely traveled reminder of the technological status of civilization before World War III. "I hear it," he confirmed.

"Sounds like a truck to me," Brandon commented,

clutching his M-16 a bit tighter.

"I hear it too," Telford finally affirmed. "What do you think we should do?" he asked nervously.

Mitchell dropped the lug wrench on the ground and walked to the driver's door. He opened it and removed a pair of M-16's from the jeep. "Here." He tossed one of the weapons to Telford.

The three of them, the lanky Brandon, the cranky Telford, and Mitchell moved behind the vehicle and spread out along the highway. Mitchell took the center of the road, Brandon stood to his right, and Telford edged to his left.

"Maybe it's one of ours," Telford said hopefully.

"It probably is," Mitchell stated.

"Nobody else uses these roads," Brandon mentioned.

The noise of the approaching truck grew louder and louder. A black speck appeared on the horizon, then grew larger and took on a distinct form as the vehicle drew nearer.

Brandon recognized it first. "It's a troop transport!" he exclaimed in relief. "It's one of ours!"

"I wonder what it's doing way out here," Mitchell speculated aloud. He knew the troop transport wasn't part of the special force sent to eliminate the detested Family. Their jeep had been the only vehicle to suffer a breakdown, and the remainder of the convoy would be miles ahead of them by now. Maybe the transport had been sent to join the expedition. Then again, it really didn't matter. At least the occupants would be friendly, fellow members of the Army of the Civilized Zone.

Soon, Mitchell mentally told himself, the Family would learn an important lesson: it wasn't smart to mess with the Civilized Zone. One hundred years after the horror of World War III, the Civilized Zone embraced what was left of the former United States of America. During and after the nuclear conflict, the Government had evacuated thousands upon thousands of citizens into the Midwest and the Rocky Mountain region. Martial law had been declared, and the once-proud people of the United States had found themselves living under a military dictatorship. The former states of Kansas, Nebraska, Colorado, New Mexico, most of Wyoming, eastern Arizona, and Oklahoma, the northern half of Texas, and most of Montana had been incorporated into the Civilized Zone and were currently ruled with an iron fist by Samuel II. His father, a man named Samuel Hyde, had been the Secretary of Health, Education, and Welfare at the outbreak of the war. He was attending a speaking engagement in Denver when the war broke out, and assumed the reins of government after the President, the rest of the Cabinet, Congress, and the Supreme Court had been obliterated in a preemptive strike on Washington, D.C.

The troop transport was barreling toward the jeep.

Telford lowered his M-16 and scratched the stubble on his pointed chin. "I hope they've got a drink with them," he remarked.

"You know we're not allowed to drink on duty," Brandon reminded him.

Telford deliberately belched. "Who's going to know?" he demanded. "The captain and Brutus are way up the road, and Sammy is probably playing with himself back in Denver."

"Don't you have any respect for your superiors?" Mitchell inquired, peeved, as always, by Telford's abysmal lack of decorum.

"Of course I do," Telford retorted, snickering. "When they're within earshot."

Mitchell decided to ignore him and concentrated on the rapidly approaching truck. He found himself reviewing the sequence of events leading up to his present situation.

A century after the war, Samuel II had decided the time was ripe to commence reconquering the territory outside the Civilized Zone. His forces defeated the Flathead Indians at Kalispell, Montana, and then prepared to attack a large company of superb horsemen known as the Cavalry based in South Dakota. Before the assault could be launched, and while the Army was in the process of assembling its tactical units at Cheyenne, Wyoming, for the big drive into neighboring South

Dakota, something unthinkable happened.

Someone used a thermonuclear device on Cheyenne.

Samuel II was furious. And so was Samuel's associate, a brilliant scientist known as the Doktor. The Doktor suspected that a small clan known as the Family was responsible for the nuking of Cheyenne. Without advising Samuel II, the Doktor dispatched 2000 soldiers, the majority of whom had been enroute to Cheyenne when it was struck, to the Family's compound in Minnesota. This 30-acre compound, called the Home by the Family, was situated in northwestern Minnesota. Under the command of Captain Luther and Brutus, the special force had one mission only: to raze the Home to the ground.

The troop transport was 40 yards from the jeep and beginning to brake.

"Maybe the truck is carrying munitions," Brandon guessed.

By the time it was 20 yards out, the truck had slowed to a crawl.

"I'll bet the driver is as surprised to see us as we are to see him," Telford commented.

Mitchell attempted to see the driver, but the truck's windshield was caked with dirt and grime. He could distinguish nothing more than a blurred form behind the steering wheel.

The troop transport stopped ten yards from the three troopers.

Brandon took a step toward the truck.

Mitchell abruptly, inexplicably, was filled with premonition of impending danger. He'd felt it before, during the campaign against the Flatheads, and had learned to trust his instincts.

But what could be wrong now?

The driver's door on the transport was flung open, and a lean, blond, buckskin-clad figure jumped to the asphalt. His blue eyes were dancing with mirth, and his blond mustache and lips were curling upward in a wide grin.

"You!" Mitchell cried in alarm.

"Howdy, gents," the newcomer offered in a friendly

manner, his tone belied by the proximity of his hands to
the pearl-handled revolvers strapped around his narrow
waist.

Mitchell glanced at his two companions. From the
shocked expressions on their faces he knew they also
recognized the man with the fancy handguns.

"I'm afraid I'm gonna have to ask you boys to drop
your M-16's," the man in the buckskins stated.

Telford licked his dry lips. "And what if we don't?"
he demanded.

The newcomer chuckled. "That suits me right fine,"
he said. "But it would be a heap healthier for you if you
did drop 'em."

Brandon gazed at Mitchell and Telford. "There's
three of us and only one of him."

Mitchell hesitated. From what he'd heard, this man
could take out all three of them without working up a
sweat.

"I ain't got all day," the newcomer informed them.

Telford stupidly made the first move. He tried to
bring his M-16 up, envisioning the great reward he
would receive if he killed the man in the buckskins.

But he never lived to claim it.

The newcomer's right hand flashed to his right
holster, his motion a streak as the pearl-handled
revolver cleared leather.

Mitchell saw Telford's head snap backward as the
revolver boomed, a portion of the upper rear of his
cranium exploding outward in a geyser of blood, brains,
and other bits and pieces. He was slammed to the
asphalt by the impact.

Brandon attempted to bring his M-16 to bear, but
compared to the gunman he was moving in slow
motion. A bullet from the revolver caught him between
the eyes and twisted his body to the left. His brown eyes
locked on Mitchell and he blinked once, his face reflecting his shocked disbelief, before he groaned and
crumpled to the highway.

Mitchell found himself alone, his M-16 held at his
side, staring down the barrel of a pearl-handled
revolver.

"What's it gonna be?" the gunman questioned him.

"Do I have a chioce?" Mitchell asked, his tone strained.

The passenger door on the troop transport suddenly snapped open and a stocky man dressed all in green, with a green long-sleeved shirt and green fatigue pants, dropped to the ground and ran around the front of the truck. His appearance presented quite a contrast to the gunman's. He was shorter in stature than the gunman by at least half a foot. His black hair was cropped short, barely covering his ears, whereas the guman's blond locks descended to his shoulders. While both men might accurately be called handsome, the man in green had broader facial features and brown eyes. In his hands was an FNC Auto Rifle. Under his right arm in a shoulder holster was a revolver. And tucked under the front of his leather belt was a tomahawk.

"Drop it or die," the gunman said to Mitchell.

The trooper debated his prospects. He could comply with the gunman's command, or he could try to kill the gunman, an act equivalent to certain suicide.

Mitchell released the M-16 and it clattered as it struck the surface of the road.

The gunman grinned. "Smart move!"

The man in green glanced at the gunman. "I thought I told you to wake me up if we ran into trouble."

The gunman shrugged. "There wasn't any trouble."

"Oh?" The man in green nodded in the direction of the two bodies. "What do you call this?"

The gunman chuckled. "A piece of cake, pard," he replied.

"One day," the man in green predicted, "your arrogance will be the death of you."

"Worrywart!" the gunman retorted, and laughed. He casually reloaded his right revolver from his cartridge belt, then twirled the handgun into its holster.

The man in green covered Mitchell with the FNC.

"So what do we have here?" the gunman inquired. He sauntered up to the soldier. "What's your name?" he demanded.

"Mitchell," the trooper hastily blurted out. "Arthur

Mitchell.''

"And what are you doing here, so far from the Civilized Zone?" the gunman queried.

Mitchell swallowed hard, but refused to respond.

"We'll get to that in a moment," the gunman stated ominously, his hands resting on his pearl-handled revolvers. "I noticed you recognized me when you first saw me."

Mitchell nodded. "You're Hickok."

"How'd you know who I am?" Hickok asked.

"We know about the Family," Mitchell revealed. "And we know about the Warriors."

The man in green stepped closer. "Then you must know who I am as well."

Mitchell shook his head. "Sorry. I can't quite place you."

Hickok cackled.

"Don't let it go to your head," the man in green said to the gunman.

Mitchell was astonished by their cool composure. What were they going to do to him? Kill him? Were they playing some kind of game? Was that it? How could they make jokes at a time like this? Hickok had just slain two men, yet he was engaging in light-hearted banter as if nothing had happened. What kind of men were these Warriors?

Hickok indicated the man in green with his right hand. "This is my pard, Geronimo. Geronimo, meet Arthur Mitchell."

"I heard him say his name," Geronimo remarked.

"Why do you have such strange names?" Mitchell ventured to inquire, hoping if he kept the conversation going, if he kept them talking, they might delay doing whatever they were going to do to him.

"Strange?" Hickok repeated. "What's so strange about our names?"

"I've never heard of anyone called Geronimo before," Mitchell explained.

Geronimo straightened. "I selected my name in honor of a great Indian who lived long, long ago in prewar times."

"You picked your own name?" Mitchell questioned in disbelief. "You Family types sure are weird!"

"I thought you said you knew about our Family," Geronimo reminded the youthful soldier.

"I know you have your compound in northwestern Minnesota," Mitchell divulged. "We were told you're a pack of filthy degenerates, renegades intent on murdering everyone in the Civilized Zone. The officers also told us about the Warriors, about how you've slaughtered innocent woman and children and done all kinds of terrible things."

Hickok gazed at Geronimo. "Is this bozo for real?"

Geronimo's brow was furrowed in thought. "Evidently, the officers have told the lower ranks lies about us."

"Why would they feed the troops a bunch of bull about the Family?" Hickok asked, puzzled.

"Obviously, they want to insure that their troopers will hate us so much, will consider us so despicable, so vile, we'll be shot on sight, no questions asked," Geronimo reasoned.

"Mighty clever of the rascals," Hickok commented.

Geronimo stared at Mitchell. "It would seem you have a lot to learn about our Family."

"I already know all I need to know," Mitchell responded defiantly.

"Which reminds me," Hickok stated. "There's something I need to know from you."

"I won't tell you a thing!" Mitchell declared.

"I think you will," Hickok disagreed. His left hand slowly drew his left revolver and raised the gun until the barrel was touching Mitchell's nose. He cocked the hammer. "I want to know what you're doing here, and I want to know now."

"You'd better tell him," Geronimo offered.

"And if I don't?" Mitchell boldly asked, as if he didn't already know the answer.

"Well, then, Arthur," Hickok said, grinning, "I reckon I'll ventilate your nostrils wth my Python."

Geronimo grimaced and took a step backward. "Just don't splatter his blood all over me! These are clean clothes I've got on!''

Hickok's steely blue eyes bored into Mitchell's. "What's it gonna be?''

Mitchell gaped at the gleaming metal barrel of the Colt Python and felt a shiver rack his body.

"I'm gonna count to three,'' Hickok announced. "One.''

Mitchell's mind was racing. He knew it would be tantamount to an act of treason to disclose the information the gunfighter wanted.

"Two.''

Mitchell's mouth was abnormally dry. He wasn't a coward, but he disliked the prospect of dying needlessly. What purpose would it serve to be—

"Three,'' Hickok finished his count.

Before Mitchell could find his voice, the Warrior pulled the trigger. The blast was deafening.

Geronimo shook his head and sighed. "Now look at what you've done.''

Hickok's moccasined right foot flicked out and nudged the form at his feet. "Kind of pitiful, ain't it? They sure don't make soldiers like they used to.''

2

Where had they all gone?

The huge man stood on the crest of a low hill, in the very middle of U.S. Highway 287, and gazed to the south. In the distance could be distinguished the outskirts of Fort Collins, Colorado. His scouts had just informed him the city was deserted, utterly devoid of life, abandoned.

What the hell was going on?

Despite the freezing temperature, the big man was only wearing a black-leather vest and fatigue pants, as well as a pair of moccasins, the traditional Family attire. His arms, both bulging with extraordinarily massive muscles, seemed impervious to the frigid conditions. Piercing gray eyes surveyed the terrain ahead. The wind stirred his dark hair, causing his bangs to fall down above his right brow. His brawny hands rested on the handles of his matched set of Bowie knives, one knife on each hip, the sheaths attached to his brown deerskin belt.

Why would they do it? Evacuate an entire city?

The sun was poised in the eastern sky, heralding the dawning of a new day. A flock of sparrows frolicked in a field to his right, chirping happily, enjoying the November morning.

Was it a ploy? Were they trying to lure him into a trap?

He glanced over his right shoulder at the convoy waiting on the highway below: 3 jeeps, a half-track, and

15 troop transports. The 3 jeeps, the half-track, and 2 of the troop transports had been confiscated from soldiers in the Twin Cities. The remaining vehicles had been appropriated after the battle in Catlow, Wyoming, the conflict referred to as ''Armageddon'' because of its significance to the Freedom Federation.

The Freedom Federation. He faced front, reflecting.

Initially, the idea for the Freedom Federation had been proposed by the Leader of the Family, the wise and wizened Plato. The Family couldn't hope to oppose the Civilized Zone on its own. Fortunately, the Family knew of three other groups, three other organized, or partially organized, outposts of humanity struggling to make a go of it amidst the rubble and ruins of a once-mighty civilization. One of these groups, called the Moles, lived in a subterranean city 50 miles east of the Family. The second group, now known as the Clan, had once dwelt in the Twin Cities of Minneapolis and St. Paul. With the Family's assistance, the occupants of the Twin Cities migrated to a small, desolate town in north-western Minnesota that had been known as Halma. This town was only 8 miles southwest of the Home, the walled compound occupied by the Family. The third group in the Freedom Federation, controlling the territory once known as eastern South Dakota, was the association of superb horsemen called the Cavalry. These three groups, in cooperation with the Family, formally signed a peace treaty governing their relations with each other as their first official act. Their second official act was to declare war on the Civilized Zone.

And here I am, the big man told himself, leading an invasion of the Civilized Zone, our column hundreds of miles inside the enemy province, driving toward Denver, Colorado, the capital and administrative seat of power for Samuel II.

The man with the Bowies frowned, displeased. Why couldn't someone else be here instead? Why couldn't he be back at the Home with his beloved wife, Jenny? Why didn't Plato—

''We are ready to move out,'' someone said behind him, interrupting his reverie.

The big man turned. Parked ten yards to his rear was the SEAL.

Three men stood not five feet away. The speaker was a small man, not much over five feet in height, dressed in black, baggy clothing and holding a katana, a Japanese sword, by its scabbard in his right hand. His Oriental features displayed a degree of concern for the man with the Bowies. "Is anything wrong?" he inquired. "You appear troubled, Blade."

Blade shook his head. "I'm fine, Rikki," he lied.

Rikki-Tikki-Tavi didn't believe Blade was telling the truth, but he tactfully refrained from making an issue of it. If something was bothering the chief of the Family's Warriors, then Blade would divulge it in his own good time.

The man on Rikki's right pointed at Fort Collins. "Do we go in today?" he asked his leader. This man was almost as large as Blade. He wore an unusual seamless dark-blue garment sewn together by the Family Weavers. Stitched on the back of this garment was the ebony silhouette of a skull. His hair and his mustache were both a peculiar, distinctive shade of silver, the hair cut short and the mustache drooping around the corners of his mouth. He carried a Wilkinson "Terry" Carbine in his right hand. Under his left arm was a Smith and Wesson Model 586 Distinguished Combat Magnum in a shoulder holster; under his other arm was a Browning Hi-Power 9-millimeter Automatic Pistol. A curved scimitar was in a leather sheath strapped to his belt and angled along his left thigh.

"Yes, Yama," Blade replied. "We go in shortly."

"Why do you suppose we haven't encountered any opposition?" asked the third man. He was of average build, and dressed all in green, his attire custom-made by the Weavers and patterned after the illustrations of medieval apparel contained in several of the books in the Family library. His blond beard was neatly trimmed, jutting forward on his pointed chin. Because he wore his hair long, he tied it into a ponytail using a six-inch strip of leather. He clutched a compound bow in his left hand, and a quiver full of arrows was affixed to his brown belt and slanted across his right hip.

"I wish I knew," Blade told Teucer. "I can't imagine why Samuel hasn't launched a counterattack."

"Possibly he has heard about the Doktor," Rikki remarked.

Blade nodded. The Freedom Federation Army had confronted the nefarious Doktor in Catlow, Wyoming, and emerged victorious. He stared at his "army." Filling the troop transports below were 200 fighters from the Clan and 150 Moles. In a field to the east of the highway, mounted and ready to go, were 484 members of the Cavalry. Not much of an army, numerically speaking, but it had proven itself against the Doktor's forces.

The head of the Warriors mentally tallied the total: 834. A considerable quantity, to be sure, but the army of the Civilized Zone had to be much larger. Even allowing for massive casualties after Cheyenne had been nuked, the Civilized Zone's military force still had to outnumber the Freedom Federation's fighters by at least three to one.

So where were they?

Why hadn't Samuel II's army appeared?

Blade gazed at his companions, all Warriors like himself, the only representatives of the Family. Originally, 6 Warriors had departed the Home as the Family's contribution to the Federation's fighters, but he had been compelled to send Hickok and Geronimo back to the Home. So he was left with 4 Warriors, counting himself. Compared to the Cavalry's contribution, 4 seemed like such a paltry number. But since the Family only had 15 Warriors to start with, 4 was more than a fair share.

A tall horsemen in buckskins, the typical attire of the postwar frontiersman, broke away from the Cavalry ranks below and rode his magnificent palomino up the hill. He reined in and swept the four Warriors with a questioning glance. His hair was a light brown tinged with gray streaks along the temples. Clear blue eyes, deep-set in his rugged features, settled on Blade.

"Is something wrong? What's the holdup?" inquired

the rider in a husky voice.

"What is this?" Blade snapped. "The question of the day? I don't see why everyone thinks there's something the matter!"

The rider shot a quizzical gaze at Rikki-Tikki-Tavi, who simply shrugged and shook his head.

Blade was glaring in the general direction of Fort Collins. "Since everyone is so all fired up to get going," he stated, "get the column moving!"

"As you wish," the rider said stiffly. He wheeled his mount and galloped down the hill.

Yama and Rikki exchanged knowing looks. Yama nudged Teucer's left elbow, and the two of them turned and headed for the convoy.

Rikki waited until Yama and Teucer were out of earshot. He walked up to Blade and touched his right arm to get his attention.

"What is it?" Blade asked him absently.

"That was no way to address Kilrane," Rikki mentioned.

"He should have waited below like I told him to do," Blade declared.

"Kilrane is the leader of the Cavalry," Rikki noted. "He has a legitimate right to express his concerns."

Blade sighed and ran his right hand through his tousled hair. "I know," he said wearily. "I'll apologize to him the first chance I get."

"Do you want to tell me about it?" Rikki prompted his friend.

"It's the same old story," Blade commented.

"Enlighten me," Rikki goaded him.

Blade frowned and squatted on his haunches. He idly poked his right index finger into a small hole in the road.

Rikki-Tikki-Tavi waited patiently, wishing Hickok and Geronimo were still with the column. They were closer to Blade than anyone else, with the possible exception of his wife, Jenny. Geronimo in particular was adept at cracking Blade's laconic shell when the hulking Warrior was in one of his infrequent moody spells.

"You know," Blade said slowly, "that Plato wants me to become Leader of the Family after he passes on to the higher mansions."

"Of course," Rikki confirmed. Plato's selection of Blade as his intended successor was common knowledge in the Family.

"And you've probably heard I don't want the job," Blade remarked.

"There is speculation to that effect," Rikki admitted.

"Have you ever wondered why I don't want to become the Leader of the Family?" Blade asked.

"I assume you have a good reason," Rikki responded diplomatically.

"As you well know," Blade said in a reserved tone, "my father was the Family's Leader before Plato."

"Yes," Rikki affirmed.

"And I saw what it did to him," Blade continued. "I saw how much strain he was under. Having the responsibility of safeguarding the welfare of so many people is an awesome burden."

"But don't you already have such responsibility?" Rikki interjected. "As the leader of the Warriors?"

Blade shook his head. "Being leader of the Warriors and the Leader of the Family are two entirely different posts. As the top Warrior, I'm responsible for protecting the Family and preserving our Home. My duties are strictly military in nature. But once I agree to become Family Leader, providing the Family goes along with Plato's recommendation and elects me to the position, the scope of my duties would expand.

"Ultimately, every aspect of our life would depend on me. How much food should we grow to see us through each year? How large a stockpile should we keep on hand to see us through the rough times? What if our supplies run low? How do we go about replenishing them if we can't manufacture what we need? If the children didn't have enough to eat, it would be my fault. If the climate should take a drastic turn for the worse, as it's been known to do from time to time, I would be accountable for insuring we have enough food and clothing. The fate of the Family would rest in my hands." Blade stopped and looked up at Rikki. "It scares me," he revealed.

"I've never known you to be scared of anything," Rikki noted.

"Oh, sure," Blade went on. "I can face any opponent in combat. But that type of courage is different from the kind a person must have if they're going to shoulder the responsibility for over eighty people."

"You think you lack such courage?" Rikki asked thoughtfully.

"I don't know," Blade honestly confessed.

"Then why dwell on it?" Rikki asked.

"Because of what happened in Catlow."

"Catlow?" Rikki didn't understand. The battle with the Doktor had been a resounding victory for the Federation.

"I made too many mistakes," Blade stated.

"What mistakes?"

"I should have taken more fighters into Catlow," Blade reprimanded himself. "I should have deployed our forces differently."

"But the losses we sustained were minimal," Rikki pointed out.

"The loss of even one life is one too many," Blade philosophized.

Rikki pondered Blade's words. Something didn't quite fit. Suffering casualties in a war was inevitable. Blade knew that. And the strategy they had employed in Catlow had worked remarkably well. Blade knew that too.

So what was really troubling him?

The head of the Warriors stood. "Let's go," he said. "We'd better join the column."

"Wait a minute," Rikki advised.

Blade stared at the Family's supreme martial artist. "What is it?"

"I've been listening to your words," Rikki stated slowly, "and they don't ring true. They don't jibe with the Blade I know."

"We can finish this discussion later," Blade suggested, starting to walk off.

"Let's finish it now," Rikki recommended. "We should clear the air before you inadvertently insult one of our friends again."

"I've said all I'm going to say," Blade stated impatiently, obviously reluctant to continue their conversation.

"Then allow me to have my say," Rikki countered, hoping his insight was correct.

Blade folded his muscular arms across his expansive chest. "Go ahead. Speak your piece."

"I may not know you as well as Hickok or Geronimo," Rikki began, "but I've known you since our childhood. I think I can accurately gauge your motives in this instance."

"You think so, huh?" Blade interjected skeptically.

"Hear me out," Rikki urged. "I don't think you're afraid of the responsibility a Family Leader must shoulder. After all, you've been the top Warrior for, what, four years? If you couldn't handle responsibility, you would have resigned your post a long time ago. Next to being the actual Leader of our Family, the position of chief Warrior entails the most responsibility of any other vocation. No," Rikki concluded, "it's not the responsibility."

"Then what is it?" Blade asked quietly.

"Why did you become a Warrior in the first place?" Rikki inquired, and then proceeded to answer his own query. "You became a Warrior because you felt the Spirit was guiding you to use your skills to protect our Family. Am I right?"

Blade nodded.

"You can't stand the thought of any of our loved ones coming to harm, and you have devoted your life to insuring they can live in peace, free from the constant fear of being attacked, of being injured or killed. Am I right?" Rikki asked again.

"I became a Warrior for the same reason you became a Warrior," Blade said. "And the same reason Hickok, Geronimo, Yama, Spartacus, and all the rest became Warriors. The Spirit blessed us with certain unique talents, and we've decided to use our talents to protect the Family."

"True," Rikki conceded, "but in your case I think it goes deeper than that."

"I don't follow you," Blade commented.

"Don't you?" Rikki studied Blade's features. "Let me put it to you another way. Hickok, like ourselves, is a Warrior."

"One of the best the Family has," Blade noted.

"I concur," Rikki said. "But if one of our Family was killed by a scavenger or a mutate, how do you think Hickok would react?"

Blade didn't have to formulate a response; he automatically knew the answer. "Hickok would seek out the scavenger or mutate and blow it away."

"Precisely," Rikki agreed. "And how do you think Hickok would feel about the departed Family member?"

"He'd be upset about it, naturally," Blade responded.

"Naturally. But he wouldn't dwell on the death. He wouldn't blame himself for what had happened."

"So?"

"So there is the difference between Hickok and you," Rikki elaborated. "Hickok, and the rest of the Warriors, would accept the reality and inevitability of the death. All of us, Blade, die. Sooner or later, the Grim Reaper catches up with all of us. Our Elders have taught us to view death as the technique for passing on from this world to one of the mansions on high. Death is a step in our spiritual growth. All of us have accepted this fact, all of us except you."

"I know we all die," Blade said testily.

"But you don't accept the act of dying," Rikki remarked. "You blame yourself when others die, even if you can not prevent them from dying." Rikki paused. "It isn't the responsibility of leadership you fear. It's the prospect of others dying because of your fallibility. You've always been hard on yourself when it came to making mistakes. You dread the fact others might die because of one of your mistakes. It's not the responsibility," Rikki reiterated, "not the mistake itself, but the dying you can't tolerate."

Blade gazed at the ground, his brow furrowed as he contemplated Rikki's words.

"I may be taking a stab in the dark," Rikki went on, "but I think it has something to do with your father."

Blade's head snapped up. "My father?"

"Your father was killed about four years ago by one of the Doktor's monstrosities," Rikki said. "This next may be too personal, and I apologize in advance if I'm overstepping my bounds, but I wonder if you've ever come to grips with your father's death. I wonder if you blame yourself because you weren't with him that day, because you weren't there to stop that mountain lion from slaying your father. I wonder if the shock of your father's death hurt you so much, affected you so profoundly, you can't face the likelihood of other loved ones passing on. You don't want to be caught in such a situation again. It's ironic, isn't it? You're a Warrior, and you dispense death to anyone or anything threatening our Family. But you can't accept the act of dying. You can dish it out, Blade, but you can't take it."

Blade averted his eyes. He turned and watched the column begin its climb up the hill.

"I'm sorry if I hurt your feelings," Rikki offered.

Blade didn't respond.

"Don't take what I've said too seriously," Rikki suggested.

Blade mumbled a few words.

"What did you say?" Rikki asked.

"I said," Blade stated heavily, "you were right on the mark. It's about time I owned up to it. I never did adjust to my father's death. I've even had nightmares about it. I . . .." He hesitated, his voice lowering. "I loved my father very much."

"Healing takes time," Rikki observed. "When you can face up to your father's death," he predicted, "you'll be able to accept your destiny as Leader of the Family."

Blade glanced at Rikki, his features downcast. "I pray you're right." His eyes conveyed his inner torment. "Dear Spirit, how I pray you're right!"

3

"It looks like wimpy is finally comin' around," the gun-fighter declared.

The trooper groaned and slowly opened his brown eyes. For a moment, he stared around in confusion at the interior of the truck cab. "Where am I?" he wanted to know.

"You don't remember?" Geronimo prodded him.

The soldier was confused. He was seated in a troop transport, wedged between an Indian on his right and a man in buckskins driving the vehicle, on his left.

"Come on, Arthur Mitchell," the blond man said. "Don't tell me you've plumb forgotten our little chit-chat already?"

In a rush, Mitchell recalled everything. The gunman. Brandon and Telford. The Family. The Warriors. The revolver barrel pressed against his nose. "I'm still alive!" he exclaimed in amazement.

"This boy is bright," Hickok quipped.

"You didn't shoot me?" Mitchell queried in astonishment.

"What was your first clue?" Hickok retorted, chuckling.

"I thought I was dead!" Mitchell marveled.

"Hickok turned the barrel aside at the last instant," Geronimo explained.

"But what happened?" Mitchell asked.

"You went and fainted," Hickok informed the trooper.

"I fainted?"

"Dropped like a rock," Hickok said.

"I don't get it," Mitchell remarked, bewildered. "Why didn't you kill me?"

"I ain't partial to blowin' away wet-nosed kids," Hickok mentioned.

"I'm not a kid!" Mitchell bristled. "You aren't much older than I am. What are you, twenty-five?"

"Thereabouts," the gunman admitted.

Mitchell glanced at Geronimo. "But they told us you would kill us. They said you've murdered woman and children."

"You can't believe everything you're told," Geronimo said. "You always have to consider the source, and if they might have an ulterior motive."

"But you shot Brandon and Telford," Mitchell stated lamely.

"Give me a break!" Hickok rejoined. "They were aimin' to put holes in my new buckskin shirt. My missus would have a fit!"

"You're married?" Mitchell's mouth fell open.

"Didn't you see the ball and chain on my left leg?" Hickok responded.

Mitchell gazed at the highway ahead, scarcely noticing the scenery they passed as the troop transport lumbered along at 40 miles an hour. "I'm so confused!" he muttered.

"While you're tryin' to collect your marbles," Hickok said, "I'm gonna give you the rules."

"Rules?" Mitchell stared at the gunman.

"Yep. In case you ain't noticed, we didn't bother to tie you up. But I gotta warn you, just in case you get an itch to make a break for it, that Geronimo and I can take care of ourselves real good, with or without our irons. We may not be Rikki-Tikki-Tavi, but we can—"

"Who?" Mitchell interrupted.

"Rikki-Tikki-Tavi," Geronimo replied. "He's a fellow Warrior."

"Rikki-Tikki-Tavi?" Mitchell shook his head, perplexed. "Did this Rikki-Tikki-Tavi pick his own name, like you told me you did?"

"Rikki chose his own name," Geronimo answered.

"Where did he ever get a name like that?" Mitchell inquired.

"From a book."

"A book? You guys get your names from books?" Mitchell asked.

Geronimo smiled. "Perhaps it would help if I provided some background. The man we call the Founder of our Family, the man who built the Home prior to World War III, wanted us—"

"What was this man's name?" Mitchell asked.

"He was called Kurt Carpenter," Geronimo disclosed. "He was a survivalist, a man who thought a war was inevitable and who decided to do something about it. He was very wealthy, and he used his money to buy a plot of land near what was once known as Lake Bronson State Park in northwestern Minnesota. Carpenter personally directed the construction of his survival site, and called it the Home. He decided to call his followers, the people he invited to the Home before the war erupted, the Family. He was worried the Family might forget about the history of society, about the factors leading up to the cause of the war. So he initiated a special ceremony he termed the Naming."

"The Naming?" Mitchell repeated, fascinated by this glimpse of Family history.

"Carpenter left a diary behind," Geronimo detailed. "In it, he said he was worried the Family wouldn't learn from the mistakes humanity had made. He was afraid we would disregard our 'historical antecedents,' as he called them. So, to foster an understanding of history, Carpenter encouraged every Family member, when they reached the age of sixteen, to select the name of a historical figure they admired as their very own. This practice goes on even now, a century after the war. It's not a mandatory requirement, but most Family members follow it. Now, though, we take names from literature and other sources as well as the history section of our library."

"You have a library?"

"Carpenter left us hundreds of thousands of

volumes," Geronimo said. "We have books on every conceivable subject."

"And you can read any of the books you want?" Mitchell inquired.

"Certainly."

"We have to get a permit to take a book from a library," Mitchell said, "and even then we're only allowed to read government approved books."

"The Civilized Zone is ruled by a dictatorship," Geronimo observed. "They control every aspect of your life. The Family is different. We can read any book in our library we want, and all of us are pretty avid readers." He paused, smirking. "Except for Hickok, of course. He's illiterate."

Hickok pretended to glare across at Geronimo. "Don't listen to that mangy Injun. I can read and write as good as him. I went to the same school he did."

"The Family has a school?"

"Yep," Hickok replied. "Our Elders teach the youngsters everything they know."

Mitchell stared from Hickok to Geronimo and back again. "You mean to tell me you both went to the same school?"

'Same school, same teachers," Hickok answered. "But we didn't wear the same britches!" He grinned at his own joke.

Mitchell faced Geronimo. "It's not possible."

"What's not possible?" Geronimo asked him.

"How could you both have gone to the same school?" Mitchell demanded. "You talk like any normal person, but he," Mitchell jerked his left thumb in Hickok's direction, "talks so . . . so . . . so . . ." He couldn't seem to find the right word.

"Weird," Geronimo finished the sentence.

"You got it," Mitchell said. "How come?"

Geronimo chuckled. "Hickok took his name from his childhood hero, a man who lived way back in the old Wild West days."

"What's the Wild West?" Mitchell asked.

"An early period in American history," Geronimo elaborated. "There was a famous gunfighter by the name of James Butler Hickok. The idiot driving this truck thinks James Butler Hickok was the greatest man who ever lived. Consquently, he dresses like the books say Hickok dressed. Unfortunately, he even talks like he believes the Hickok of old talked. You know he sounds ridiculous, and I know he sounds ridiculous, and I've tried to convince him of this fact many times. But have you ever tried to reason with a man who has the intelligence of a turnip?''

Despite his situation, momentarily forgetting his predicament, Mitchell laughed.

Hickok wisely concentrated on his driving, ignoring the barb.

Mitchell abruptly stopped laughing. "What am I doing?" he asked aloud. "I'm as crazy as you guys! Here I am having a good time with the enemy!"

"We're not your enemies," Geronimo said, disputing him. "We're opposed to Samuel the Second and anyone who sides with him, but we're not an enemy unless you want us to be."

"This doesn't make any sense," Mitchell remarked. "You guys aren't anything like what I expected."

"It's nothing to get all bent out of shape about," Hickok declared, noting how perturbed the soldier appeared.

"If you only knew," Mitchell said glumly.

"What's botherin' you, buckaroo?" Hickok inquired.

Mitchell looked at Geronimo. "You really don't plan to kill everyone in the Civilized Zone?"

"How many times do I have to tell you?" Geronimo shook his head. "Besides, how could we? There are thousands and thousands of people living in the Civilized Zone. The Family only has about eighty or ninety members." He paused and glanced at Hickok. "How many do we have? I've lost track. We've been adding new members so fast lately, I can't keep count of them all."

"Well, there's Sherry and Cynthia," Hickok enumerated, "and Tyson and Cindy, and Gremlin and Lynx, and—"

"There's something I need to say," Mitchell blurted.

"What is it?" Geronimo asked.

Mitchell's features reflected an intense inner turmoil. He opened his mouth to speak, then closed it again.

"Spit it out, boy," Hickok exhorted him.

"Are there a lot of women and children at your Home?" Mitchell queried.

"We've got a passel of young'uns," Hickok replied. "About twenty or so, I reckon."

"And the Family has close to thirty women members," Geronimo divulged. "Why?"

"All those women and children!" Mitchell stated, horrified.

Hickok slowed the truck. "What's eatin' at your innards, boy?"

"It's about why I'm here," Mitchell said.

"I asked you that before," Hickok reminded him.

"Do you know who the Doktor is?" Mitchell questioned him.

Hickok and Geronimo exchanged knowing glances.

"We know about the Doktor," Geronimo replied, not bothering to disclose the part they had played in the battle with the Doktor in Catlow, Wyoming.

"The Doktor hates the Family," Mitchell said.

"Tell us something we don't know," Hickok cracked.

"Did you know the Doktor blames you for the nuking of Cheyenne?"

"He blames the Family for that?" Geronimo asked.

"So I was told," Mitchell responded. "That's why I'm here."

"Be specific," Geronimo directed him.

"The Doktor wants your Family wiped off the face of the earth," Mitchell informed them.

"That'll be the day!" Hickok declared.

"That day might come sooner than you think," Mitchell said. "The Doktor has sent a large force to destroy your Home."

Hickok slammed on the brakes so hard the troop transport slewed to an abrupt stop.

"What the hell is going on up there?" shouted someone from the back of the truck.

"Who was that?" Mitchell inquired, glancing over his shoulder. The view afforded by the small window located in the rear panel of the cab only permitted him to see the canvas-covered bed of the truck. "Is there somebody riding in the back?"

"Never mind them," Hickok said brusquely. "What large force are you talking about?"

"The Doktor was so mad when Cheyenne was hit," Mitchell explained, "he sent out a strike force under the command of one of his trusted officers and one of his freaks. I was part of the convoy until my jeep broke down."

"Where is this strike force now?" Geronimo asked anxiously.

Mitchell pointed directly ahead. "Up there, somewhere."

"How many are there?" Geronimo pressed him.

"Two thousand."

"Two thousand!" Geronimo leaned forward, staring through the dusty windshield.

"Are they all regular Army troops?" Hickok inquired.

"Except for Brutus," Mitchell answered.

"Brutus?" Hickok repeated.

"Brutus is one of the Doktor's genetically produced creatures," Mitchell said. "We call them freaks."

"Two thousand troops," Geronimo stated, his mind boggled by the number.

"Two thousand troops," Mitchell affirmed, "a convoy of trucks to carry them, and the tank."

Hickok reached out and gripped Mitchell's left arm. "Tank?"

Mitchell tried to pull away. "Hey! You're hurting me."

Hickok disregarded the plea. "Did you say a tank?"

Mitchell nodded, frightened by the sudden gleam in the gunman's eyes. "Yeah. A tank. One of the few still functioning. The Doktor told us he wanted your Home reduced to a pile of rubble."

Geronimo, his face pale, looked at Hickok. "The Family won't stand a chance!"

4

He wondered if he was going to have a heart attack.

The elderly man stood on the rampart above the lowered drawbridge and watched the stream of evacuees pouring into the Home. Men, women, and children, but mostly women and children, were hurrying within the walled confines of the Home as rapidly as their legs could carry them.

As if the 20-foot-high brick walls topped with barbed wire would withstand a determined assault!

The gray-haired man on the rampart turned and gazed over the Home itself. Kurt Carpenter had planned the compound with an eye to practical utility. A plot of 30 acres was enclosed within the square configuration of the walls. The eastern half of the Home was devoted to agricultural production or preserved in its natural state. Situated in the center of the compound, forming a line separating the eastern half from the western, were the cabins reserved for the married couples and their children. The western portion of the Home contained the Blocks. Carpenter had had six concrete structures constructed in a triangular formation. Each Block was designated by a letter. The Family armory, stocked with every conceivable weapon, was called A Block and was the southern tip of the triangle. Northwest of A Block and 100 yards away was B Block, the Family sleeping quarters for single members. Another 100 yards to the northwest was C Block, the infirmary managed by the Family Healers. D Block, the spacious workshop, was

100 yards east of C Block. And 100 yards east of D Block was E Block, the giant library. E Block was the eastern point of the triangle. Finally, 100 yards to the southwest was F Block, used for farming and gardening purposes. Positioned in the middle of the western wall was the only means of entering and exiting the Home: a large drawbridge. Carpenter had seen fit to provide one additional line of defense. A stream entered the compound under the northwest corner of the wall, via an aqueduct. The water was diverted along the base of the wall in both directions. It formed an inner moat, completely surrounding the compound, and flowed from the Home under the southeast corner.

All of these features were reviewed by the gray-haired man as he surveyed the commotion below. The gusty breeze was lashing his long hair and beard. A brown wool shirt and a pair of faded, patched beige pants covered his stooped, frail frame. His face was lined with creases. As he scanned the frantic crowd the worry in his blue eyes deepened.

"Any orders, Plato?" asked someone to his right.

Plato turned.

The speaker was a tall blond man, his hair styled in a crew cut, his blue eyes alert and clear. He wore a blue shirt well past its prime, and buckskin pants and moccasins. A wide leather belt encircled his waist, and attached to the belt was a long scabbard containing a genuine broadsword, one of the numerous exotic weapons Kurt Carpenter had stockpiled in the Family armory.

"Any orders?" the speaker repeated.

"How far away do we estimate them to be?" Plato inquired.

"Four Clan hunters spotted them about four miles south of Halma," the man with the broadsword stated. "Their convoy was stopped. I suspect they will stay encamped for the night." He gazed up at the late afternoon sun. "It's already close to dark, and I doubt they'll try moving at night."

"I pray you're correct, Spartacus," Plato said.

"If their convoy starts out early tomorrow morning,"

Spartacus went on, "they probably won't arrive here until noon or so. They'll travel slowly this close to the Home."

"Why?" Plato questioned him.

Spartacus stared out over the field in front of the western wall. The Family deliberately kept the area outside the walls cleared of vegetation. For 150 yards in all directions, the Family diligently removed any sprouting trees or growing shrubs, anything a potential enemy could use for concealment, an essential defense against a possible surprise assault.

More members of the Clan were flocking into the Home.

"They might be expecting us to counterattack," Spartacus commented. "They'll come in slow, prepared for trouble."

Plato gazed at a young mother hastening her two small children across the drawbridge. "We were fortunate those hunters saw the convoy," he remarked.

Spartacus nodded. "The Clan would have been wiped out. The hunters guessed there must be a couple of thousand troops."

Plato grimaced as a lancing spasm rocked his left leg. His body was deteriorating rapidly, all due to the accursed senility. For some unknown reason, the Family Elders were afflicted with a form of premature senility, aging years in mere months. Although the cause hadn't been determined, a section of the Doktor's notebooks dealt with the senility and was in the process of being deciphered by the Healers.

Did the notebooks hold the answer, not just for the senility, but for the presence of the force from the Civilized Zone? Did the Doktor know the Family possessed his notebooks? Had he sent the convoy to reclaim them? Was the Doktor still alive? Had Blade failed in his mission to Catlow? Or had Samuel II simply decided to eliminate the Family?

Plato thoughtfully stroked his bushy beard. This was all his fault; he alone could accept responsibility. It had been his idea to send one of the Warriors, Yama, to the Cheyenne Citadel on the spying assignment. While there, Yama not only stole the Doktor's four notebooks describing in minute detail every experiment and project the Doktor had ever devised, he also assisted Lynx in destroying the Doktor's headquarters with a nuclear-tipped missile known as a "thermo." Regrettably, the Doktor wasn't in his headquarters at the time. He would want his four blue notebooks back at any cost.

Was that why the troops were approaching?

Or was it because Samuel II and the Doktor were tired of the Family's interference in their affairs? After all, the Family was responsible for assisting the residents of the Twin Cities in escaping from the Civilized Zone's army and relocating them in Halma. The Family had also forestalled Samuel II's attempt to overrun the Cavalry. Had the dictator elected to remove a perennial thorn in his side?

Plato realized the Family's situation was extremely precarious. Of the 15 Family Warriors, 6 were gone, part of the Freedom Federation's force invading the Civilized Zone. The Family divided its Warriors into 5 sections for organizational purposes. Each section was comprised of 3 Warriors apiece. They were designated as Alpha Triad, Beta Triad, Gamma Triad, Omega Triad, and Zulu Triad. Each Triad had an appointed section leader. Blade, the commander of all the Warriors, was also the head of Alpha Triad. With Blade and the other Alpha Warriors, Hickok and Geronimo, gone, the command of the Warriors would normally pass to Rikki-Tikki-Tavi, the Beta Triad head. But Rikki and his Beta companions, Yama and Teucer, were also gone. Next in the chain of command was the leader of Gamma Triad: Spartacus.

Plato found himself wondering whether Spartacus was capable of directing the defense of the Home. During peaceful periods, the Family Leader was in charge of the Home. But when an emergency arose, the Warriors automatically assumed command. The Warriors were skilled at their craft, but none of them had ever confronted a crisis of this magnitude. In its entire 100-year history, the Home had never been subjected to a mass onslaught.

If only Blade and the others were here!

Plato consciously suppressed his trepidation. He

would have to have faith in Spartacus.

The long line of Clan refugees extended from the drawbridge, across the field west of the Home, and into the forest beyond. Some of them waved up to Plato and Spartacus as they entered the compound.

Plato felt an odd pain in his chest, and wondered again if he were on the verge of a heart attack. Was contemplating the impending attack too much of a strain for his weakened physique? He disregarded the discomfort and decided to take stock of the Family's options.

The Freedom Federation was composed of four factions: All four of the groups had committed a large percentage of their fighters to the force invading the Civilized Zone. The Freedom Federation Army was hundreds of miles distant—in either Wyoming or Colorado, if Blade had adhered to the invasion strategy —too far away to be of any assistance to the Family in its time of need. None of the four factions had sent all of their fighters on the invasion. The Family still had 9 Warriors left, plus 34 men and 31 women; Tillers, Empaths, Weavers, Metalworkers, and the like. True, the other men and women weren't as skilled as the Warriors in the martial arts, but they all took annual refresher courses in the use of firearms and would fight to preserve the Home.

What about the other factions?

The Cavalry was based in eastern South Dakota. Getting word to them would take too much time.

The Moles lived in an underground city approximately 50 miles to the east of the Home. They probably had about a hundred fighters on hand to safeguard their city while the rest were away with the expedition. Their ruler, Wolfe, was unreliable. Plato didn't know whether Wolfe would send help or not.

Which left the Clan.

The former residents of Minneapolis and St. Paul numbered 543. With 200 of its ablest fighters gone with the invasion force, the Clan was left with 343 members, the majority of them women and children. How many fighters did the Clan have on hand?

"I've called a meeting of the Warriors and the Clan leaders," Spartacus mentioned, shattering Plato's introspection.

"Excellent idea," Plato remarked. "I'd like to attend, if you don't mind."

"Why would I mind?" Spartacus asked.

"I don't want to impede your performance," Plato stated.

Spartacus grinned. Leave it to Plato and his grandiose vocabulary! Anyone else would have said, "I don't want to get in your way."

"It appears most of the Clan have arrived," Plato remarked.

There was now a gap between the end of the line and the edge of the trees.

Spartacus nodded in satisfaction. When the runner from the Clan had arrived earlier in the day, bringing word of the presence of the military convoy, Spartacus had sent word to the head of the Clan, a man named Zahner, and advised him to evacuate Halma and march to the Home as rapidly as possible.

The compound below was crammed with people, the Clan congregating with the Family in the open space between the concrete blocks. Their voices rose in a noisy tumult.

Spartacus waited until the last of the Clan entered the Home, and then he signaled to the four men manning the drawbridge mechanism. They immediately proceeded to raise the drawbridge.

"Let's get to it," Spartacus commented, and led the way down the flight of wooden stairs. Supported by enormous beams, the stairs were positioned to the south of the drawbridge and traversed the moat.

Plato followed the Warrior to the base of the stairs.

There was a reception committee waiting for them below. Eight Warriors stood in a straight row, their eyes on their temporary chief.

Spartacus, his left hand on the hilt of his broadsword, slowly walked along the line of fellow Warriors, nodding at each of them in turn.

Seiko was first in line, attired in loose-fitting black

clothing similar to the apparel worn by Rikki-Tikki-Tavi. Both were Family members with Oriental blood. Both were devoted martial artists. Seiko was five inches taller than Rikki, and his facial features were broader. Because Kurt Carpenter had seen fit to stock only one katana in the Family armory, and because by mutual agreement Rikki possessed it, Seiko had dedicated himself to mastering several other Oriental weapons, his personal preferences being the nunchaku and the sai. And, like every Warrior, he was competent at using many of the varied firearms in the armory.

Second in line was Shane, the youngest Warrior. Only recently having turned 16, he had become a Warrior primarily because his hero, Hickok, was a Warrior. Shane had proven himself in combat, and was one of the fastest gunmen in the Family. He proudly wore a Llama Comanche .357 Magnum on his right hip. The Family Weavers had, at his request, sewn together a black Western-style outfit, using photographs in some of the reference books in the library as guidelines. Shane's brown eyes lit up as Spartacus passed by. He was excited at the prospect of some action. His brown hair, worn long in imitation of Hickok, stirred in the breeze.

Both Seiko and Shane were members of Gamma Triad.

Next came the head of Omega Triad, a strapping Warrior with curly blond hair and penetrating green eyes named Carter. In a holster on each hip was a Guardian-SS Auto Pistol, made of stainless steel, with a narrow trigger for quick firing and Pachmayr grips. Carter wore brown pants and a light brown shirt, both specially made by the Weavers, both insulated against the chilly weather.

After Carter came another Omega Triad member: Ares. He was one of the tallest Warriors, standing six feet, three inches. His attire was a peculiar leather affair, with a dark-brown one-piece shirt and short leather breeches cut off above the knees. Another distinctive feature about Ares was his haircut. He had shaved his hair off on both sides of his head, but left a trimmed red crest running from his spine to the center of his sloping forehead. A short sword was attached to his belt, angled across his left hip. He held a Colt AR-15 in his arms. It was common knowledge he had taken his name from the ancient Greek god of war. Many felt his name was highly appropriate; Ares could be blood-thirsty when aroused.

Gideon was next in line. He was a short, stocky man with black hair and brown eyes. He wore his hair down to his broad shoulders and braided in a single tail. His square features were tense but firm. He wore a green wool shirt and brown trousers. A large military-style knife was strapped to his left hip. He clasped an Uzi Carbine in his left hand.

There was only one Triad remaining.

Crockett was the head of Zulu Triad. A lean, wiry man with high cheekbones, a prominent nose, and keen brown eyes, he wore buckskins and carried a Remington Model Four Auto Rifle. A bandolier of cartridges crossed his chest from left to right. "I hear we're going to have some visitors," he casually mentioned as Spartacus came abreast of his position in line.

"That we are," Spartacus said.

"Don't those Civilized Zone types know it's not polite to pay a visit uninvited?" Crockett asked sarcastically.

Spartacus kept walking.

The next Warrior was Samson. He was one of the few men in the Family with a build almost as powerfully developed as Blade's. He had light brown hair and brown eyes and his hair was worn long, draping to the center of his back. Like his Biblical namesake, Samson had never allowed his hair to be touched by a scissors or razor. He wore a camouflage outfit constructed by the Weavers. On either hip, snug in their carefully crafted swivel holsters, were a pair of Bushmaster Auto Pistols. In Samson's right hand was a Bushmaster Auto Rifle. He used the Bushmasters for two reasons; they were deadly pieces, and their ammunition was interchange-able.

Finally, Spartacus came to the last Warrior.

This one was unique.

This one was a woman.

In the hundred-year history of the Family, there had been four female Warriors. Only five months ago, the previous female Warrior had been slain in savage combat. The current woman Warrior was named Sherry, and she was exceptional in two ways. First, she was from outside the Family, a Canadian, the first non-Family Warrior ever appointed. Second, she was Hickok's wife, a matter of considerable importance to Spartacus. He knew she was a new addition to the Warrior ranks and quite inexperienced. She would need looking after.

Sherry was a statuesque blonde with striking green eyes. She was tall, about six feet, and almost skinny, with a slim waist and small feet. Not particularly fastidious concerning her clothing, she wore a brown, patched blouse and baggy green pants a size too large. She had a stately demeanor, a high forehead, full cheeks, and thin lips. A Smith and Wesson .357 Combat Magnum was in a holster on her right hip.

Spartacus nodded at Sherry and walked back to the middle of the line. He scanned them, his expression earnest and grim. "All of you know an enemy force is approaching the Home," he began. "We are undermanned because six of our fellow Warriors are absent, but we can rely on the assistance of the rest of our Family and we'll have help from the Clan. As soon as I know how many fighters we have at our disposal, I'll divide them up and give them their assignments." He paused. "As far as we are concerned, we have a slight tactical problem. We have four walls to cover, and only three Triads on duty. Consequently, I've decided to oversee the defense of the western wall myself—"

"Just you alone?" Seiko interrupted.

"And my share of the other combatants," Spartacus replied.

"Is such a course of action wise?" Seiko asked, pressing the issue.

"We have no choice," Spartacus responded. "If any of you find your walls are not being attacked, you are free to render help where necessary."

Seiko frowned, but didn't say anything else.

"As I was saying," Spartacus resumed, "Seiko and Shane will direct the defense of the north wall. Carter, Ares, and Gideon will handle the defense of the south wall." He looked at Crocket. "You, Samson and Sherry will have the east wall. Any questions?"

Crockett stepped forward. "Since the only way they can get into the Home is through the drawbridge, wouldn't it make more sense to concentrate the Warriors on the west wall? Why go it alone?"

"I won't be alone," Spartacus reminded him. "I'll be dividing up the other combatants and assigning them to each wall."

"I wish Hickok was here," Shane absently interjected.

Spartacus noticed Sherry glance at the drawbridge, her face troubled.

"How soon will we know the enemy strength?" Ares inquired.

"Soon," Spartacus promised. "I'll be sending out a scouting party shortly."

The November wind was picking up.

"A few other items," Spartacus mentioned. "I know each of us tends to prefer certain weapons over others, and you can use your favorites as you see fit. But each of you will go to the armory and, if you don't already have one, get an automatic rifle or machine gun and all the ammunition you can carry."

"When should we report to our posts on the walls?" Shane asked.

"As soon as you've picked your weapons," Spartacus instructed him. "Any questions?"

No one spoke.

"Hop to it!" Spartacus directed them.

The eight Warriors wheeled and headed toward A Block, the armory.

Spartacus saw four men approaching from the north.

The first man was of average height, and he was wearing tattered jeans and a blue shirt. He had fine brown hair, parted on the left and styled so it draped over his ears. His eyes were a sharp blue. In his 30s, he still retained a youthful appearance. There was a distinctive cleft in the center of his upper lip, and he had been graced with a classic square jaw. He was the type of man you knew you could trust at first glance. His name was Zahner, and he was the head of the Clan.

On Zahner's right walked a giant black man. He wore green fatigue pants and a fatigue jacket, both taken from dead soldiers in the Twin Cities. His features were prominent: a large forehead, a wide nose, and thick lips. He wore his hair in a curly Afro. In his hands was an M-16. His name was Bear, and he was one of Zahner's lieutenants.

Keeping pace on Zahner's left was his other lieutenant, a man dressed in conservative black clothing, except for a thin white collar around his neck. He was on the lean side. The lower half of his face was covered by a bristly brown beard. He was known as Brother Timothy.

The fourth man was a few feet behind the trio of Clansmen. This one was tall, and he moved with the grace and controlled power of a mountain lion. He wore buckskins, and they fit his tall frame as if he had been poured into them. A .44 Magnum Hombre single-action revolver was in a holster on each hip. His brown shoulder-length hair swayed as he walked. The man was called Boone, and he was one of the Cavalry, second in command to Kilrane himself. Because six of the Warriors had left the Home as part of the invading force, Kilrane had decided to leave Boone and 20 other riders at the Home to compensate for the Warriors being undermanned.

Spartacus didn't waste any time. "Are all of your people inside the Home?" he demanded.

Zahner stopped, nodding. "All of the Clan are accounted for." He frowned. "We were working on repairing the dilapidated buildings in Halma, getting them ready for the winter. We'll never finish them before the first snow now."

"We'll help you after this is over," Spartacus promised.

Bear snorted. "I heard of lookin' on the bright side, but you're crazy, Sparty-baby! Ain't you heard the news? There's thousands of them suckers out there!''

"The Lord will preserve us," Brother Timothy interjected.

"How many fighters do you have?" Spartacus asked Zahner.

"About two hundred and twenty," Zahner answered, "counting men and women. The rest are too young."

"That's more than I thought you'd have," Spartacus said. "It's good news."

"Maybe not," Zahner remarked. "We don't have many guns. What good is it to have two hundred and twenty fighters if you can't arm them?"

"We can arm them," Spartacus stated. He pointed toward the armory. "Have your people, the ones who can fight, line up in front of A Block. We'll pass out weapons to them."

"Do you think you have enough?" Zahner queried.

Spartacus shrugged. "Don't know for sure. Kurt Carpenter, our Founder, stocked our armory with hundreds of weapons. He said in his diary he knew civilization would decline after the Big Blast, and he wanted us to be able to protect ourselves."

"What's the Big Blast?" Brother Timothy asked.

Spartacus grinned. "It's how we refer to World War III."

"Cute," Brother Timothy said.

"Get your people lined up," Spartacus reiterated to Zahner. "I'll divide them up among the four walls. As for the children and other noncombatants, put them in F Block. It's furthest from the walls. If they won't all fit, then put the rest in D Block."

"Will do," Zahner said and turned. He hurried off, Bear and Brother Timothy in tow.

Boone, his thumbs looped under his brown belt, strolled up to Spartacus. "Kilrane told me to put myself and my men at your disposal. What would you like us to do?"

"Can you have your men ready to leave before dark?" Spartacus inquired.

"We're ready to go anytime," Boone replied. "We're Cavalry," he added proudly.

"Good. I want you to get as close to the enemy

convoy as you can. See if you can get a reliable count on their number, and find out if they have any artillery with them.''

Boone beamed. ''Some action, at last! We're on our way!'' He ran off.

Spartacus heard a slight cough behind him and turned.

Plato was standing a few feet to his rear, his hands clasped behind his stooped back, smiling.

''What's so funny?'' Spartacus inquired, puzzled.

''Oh, nothing,'' the Family Leader responded. ''I'm merely happy to perceive the Family is in such capable hands.''

Spartacus glanced around to insure they were alone. ''Don't tell anyone,'' he said softly, ''but I've never been so nervous in my life!''

''That's encouraging,'' Plato stated.

''Encouraging?'' Spartacus repeated. ''Why?''

''It would be extremely unusual if you weren't nervous,'' Plato said. ''Being nervous at a time like this is normal. If you weren't nervous, I'd begin to suspect something was wrong with you.''

Spartacus stared at the drawbridge, then scanned the rampart above it. ''I can hardly believe the Home is going to be attacked.''

''It is,'' Plato declared. ''Which reminds me. Where do you want the Family's noncombatants?''

''I'd say B Block,'' Spartacus answered, ''but I think it's too close to the west wall. How about putting them in the cabins in the middle of the compound?''

Plato nodded. ''A commendable choice. Where do you want me?''

''In the cabins with the older men and women and the children.''

Plato's eyebrows arched upward. ''What?''

Spartacus cleared his throat. ''In the cabins,'' he repeated.

''I can still handle a firearm,'' Plato said with a trace of indignation.

Spartacus walked up to Plato and gently placed his right hand on the Leader's left shoulder. ''I know you can. I don't mean to hurt your feelings. But I can't allow anything to happen to you. We really won't need you on the walls."

"I will not tolerate any special treatment," Plato declared testily.

"Plato," Spartacus said tenderly, "you are the heart and soul of our Family. The Family would go to pieces if you died—"

"Nonsense!" Plato snapped.

"I'm doing what I think best for the Family," Spartacus told him. "Blade would do the same thing if he were here."

"I won't hide in the cabins!" Plato countered.

"I'm not asking you to hide," Spartacus informed him. "Making sure the women and children remain as calm as possible is an important task. You won't be alone. Ten of the men will be assigned to defend the cabins to their dying breath. You will be in charge of them."

"I will?"

"You will," Spartacus affirmed.

"Well, in that case," Plato reluctantly concurred.

"I'm going to be busy at the armory," Spartacus mentioned. "Would you take care of getting the women and children to the cabins?"

"I would be delighted," Plato said, and walked off.

Spartacus turned and surveyed the frantic activity taking place in the compound. Was there anything he had missed? Boone and the other Cavalrymen were preparing to depart on their reconnaissance patrol. Plato was going to make sure all of the Family's children and other noncombatants took shelter in the cabins. The Clan's children, some of their women, and their few elderly would be somewhat secure in F Block.

So what did that leave him?

He could expect 220 fighters from the Clan, women and men. If he took 10 of the Family's men and assigned them to protect the cabins, he was left with 55 men and women from the Family capable of manning the walls. Not counting the Warriors or the 21 Cavalrymen, he had 275 combatants at his disposal.

No!

Wait!

About ten of the Family's members were too old. He would need to put them in the cabins, as he had told Plato he would.

Spartacus completed his mental calculations. If he had 265 fighters, and there were four walls to man, he could position 66 on each wall.

Only 66! Was that all?

Spartacus, like every member of the Family, had been raised in a deeply religious environment. The Founder, Kurt Carpenter, had advised his followers to cultivate an abiding spiritual faith in their offspring. Carpenter maintained that a strong faith was essential for the development of noble character and wisdom. He instructed all parents to promote their children's spiritual inclinations. Carpenter firmly prohibited the establishment of an official Family religion; each individual was free to select whatever theology he or she wanted. Consequently, it was with complete reverence and respect that Spartacus gazed skyward, trying to compose his racing thoughts and offer a heartfelt prayer to the Spirit.

But try as he might, there was only one plea he could think of.

One simple word.

Help!

5

"What the blazes are we gonna do now?" the gunman demanded.

"You're the one who wanted to come this way," Geronimo retorted. "I said we should swing to the north, but nooooo! Mr. Know-It-All had to do it his way!"

Hickok pounded the dashboard in frustration. "How the heck was I supposed to know they'd be here! They could've gone another way, you know?"

"Oh, yeah? With all the trucks they've got? And a tank? Did you expect them to take a back road?"

The troop transport was parked on the shoulder of U.S. Highway 59, slightly over four miles south of Halma. The road ahead curved around a wooded section. Camped a quarter of a mile beyond was the Civilized Zone convoy.

Sitting on the seat between the two Warriors, his hands and feet bound and a cloth gag jammed into his mouth, was Mitchell.

Hickok glanced at the trooper. "We're gonna have to leave you for a spell." He opened the driver's door. "No hard feelings about this?" He leaned over and groped under the seat for a moment. Smiling, he straightened, holding a rifle in his right hand.

Geronimo opened his door and dropped to the road.

"I hope you don't have to tinkle anytime soon," Hickok said to Mitchell. He winked and jumped to the ground, closing the door behind him after he landed.

Geronimo walked around the front of the troop transport. "So what's your great plan?"

"I don't have one," Hickok admitted, wiping a dirt smudge from the stock of his Navy Arms Henry Carbine.

Geronimo hefted his FNC Auto Rifle. "No plan, huh?"

"Nope." Hickok grinned. "I'll do what I always do."

"Which is?"

"We'll play it by ear," Hickok said. "Trust me."

"I was afraid you'd say that," Geronimo stated.

Hickok walked to the back of the truck, Geronimo on his heels. The gunman drew aside the canvas flap and peered inside. "How's everybody doin'?" he inquired.

There were three occupants of the rear section. One was a short man in his forties. He wore buckskins and carried a large brown-leather pouch. He was balding, had puffy cheeks and an oval chin. His name was Morton, and he was a Cavalryman. He was also skilled in the healing arts, and his services were sorely needed because of the condition of the other two occupants; one of them, a lovely black woman, was in critical condition, while the second, a man, was in serious condition.

"They're still alive," Morton said in a raspy voice.

Hickok climbed up onto the bed of the transport and walked to the woman. She was lying on a makeshift bed of blankets, her black hair cradled on a white pillow appropriated from the garrison in Catlow, Wyoming. Hickok knelt alongside her and tenderly touched her right cheek. "Bertha? It's me, Hickok."

"She can't hear you," Morton advised him.

Hickok frowned, his mind flashing back to the battle in Catlow. Bertha was a fighter from the Clan, and one of the dearest friends he had outside of the Family. She had fought valiantly against the Doktor in Catlow, and during the course of the conflict had taken three hits. The ones to her right thigh and the left side of her head weren't life-threatening. Her third wound, though, was another story. Bertha had been shot in the left side of her chest.

"Why have we stopped?" Morton asked. "How soon before we reach this Home of yours?"

Hickok glanced at the Cavalryman. He was glad Kilrane, the Cavalry leader, had agreed to send Morton along. Bertha required skilled medical care, and Blade had ordered Hickok and Geronimo to transport her to the Home so the Family Healers could properly take care of her. "We stopped because we got some bad hombres up ahead," he told Morton. "Don't know how soon we'll get to our Home."

Someone groaned to Hickok's right.

Hickok twisted.

Lying three feet from Bertha was a lean man with long brown hair and a lengthy beard. Like Bertha, he was swaddled in green Army blankets to keep his body temperature elevated. Unlike Bertha, his injuries weren't due to gunshots. His name was Joshua, and he was recognized as the most spiritual member of the Family.

The Doktor had crucified him.

"How's Josh doin'?" Hickok inquired.

"Joshua sustained severe wrist and ankle wounds," Morton replied. "He has a high fever, but he's in much better shape than Bertha is. We must get both of them to your Home as fast as we can."

Hickok nodded in agreement and stood. "We're workin' on it. Geronimo and I gotta scout ahead. We left that soldier boy tied up in the cab. You might want to check on him now and then."

"I will," Morton said.

Hickok walked to the edge of the truck bed.

Evening was descending.

Geronimo had overheard Morton's words. He studied Hickok's face, striving to read his reaction. "Bertha will pull through," he offered by way of encouragement.

"She'd better!" Hickok stated, his tone low and gravelly. He dropped to the ground. "Let's go."

The two Warriors crossed the highway and entered the woods beyond.

Geronimo was picturing their position in his mind. They were on U.S. Highway 59, south of Halma.

Between them and Halma was the army convoy from the Civilized Zone. A mile north of Halma, the Family had cleared a direct path from Highway 59 to the Home, driving several troop transports back and forth to flatten any weeds or bushes while four men with axes walked ahead of the transports and chopped down all intervening trees. This had been accomplished immediately prior to the departure of the Freedom Federation's invasion force.

How were they going to get past the Army convoy?

The sky progressively darkened as the two Warriors cautiously moved nearer to the enemy camp.

Hickok slowed as the vegetation ahead thinned out. The sounds of a large encampment filled the cool air: the subdued jumble of hundreds of voices participating in restrained conversations; the crackle of branches and logs burning in a dozen campfires; the clink of metal against metal as many of the troopers savored their evening meal, field rations consisting of baked beans and midget hot dogs; and dozens of other normal camp noises, the belching and burping and laughing which usually accompanied the congregation of so many people in one spot.

Geronimo stopped behind a tree trunk and glanced at the gunfighter.

Hickok was standing with his arms folded, studiously scrutinizing the camp.

"Should we risk getting any closer?" Geronimo asked in a whisper.

"We've got to get a heap closer than this," Hickok replied.

"What does that pea-sized brain of yours have in mind?" Geronimo inquired.

Hickok glanced at Geronimo and grinned, his teeth, a white patch in the gloom of twilight, "Infiltratin'!" he said excitedly.

Geronimo walked over to his friend. "What?"

"You heard me," Hickok declared. "We'll do some infiltratin'!"

Geronimo stared at the camp for a bit, noting the brightness of the campfires, the number of the enemy, and the merits of Hickok's idea. There was only one logical reaction. "Are you nuts?" he demanded.

"It'll be a piece of cake!" Hickok assured him.

"Sure it will," Geronimo retorted.

"It will!" Hickok insisted. "We'll tippy-toe in, mosey around for a spell, and see what we can learn about their plans."

"I'd like to tippy-toe on your head," Geronimo grumbled.

"If you don't like the idea," Hickok said stiffly, "just say so."

"Do you want me to engrave it on your forehead?"

"So what's the matter with my plan?" Hickok demanded.

"For starters," Geronimo pointed out, "won't we be just a little bit conspicuous walking around in these clothes?"

"I've already thought of that," Hickok stated.

"You can think?"

Hickok started to move toward the camp. "If you don't want to come, fine! I'll go it by my lonesome."

Geronimo prayed to the Great Spirit for guidance, and promptly caught up with the gunman. "Why do I have the feeling I'm going to be sorry about this?"

"SSSssshhh!" Hickok hissed.

Geronimo resisted an impulse to kick Hickok in the seat of his pants.

Somewhere to their left, in the dark depths of the forest, an owl hooted.

They reached the final row of trees before the camp. The outer perimeter of the encampment was only 15 yards from the woods. When it had come time to stop for the night, the convoy had simply braked to a halt in the middle of the road. The soldiers had pitched their tents around the trucks and other vehicles, serving as a buffer in case the convoy should be attacked. Guards had been posted at 20-yard intervals. A ring of alert soldiers completely encircled the encampment.

Hickok knelt on the turf, scratching his head.

Geronimo, sheltered behind a nearby tree, spotted a guard about ten yards to their right, slowly walking in their direction. Another sentry was the same distance to their left, drawing nearer. He shook his head, discouraged by the setup. There was no way they would be able to take out any of the guards without being seen by some of the soldiers in the camp.

Hickok must have reached the same conclusion. He was carefully backing away, his Henry at the ready.

Geronimo dropped to his hands and knees and crawled up to the gunman. "Any more bright ideas?" he whispered.

"Where there's a will, pard," Hickok quipped, "there's a way. What say I amble to the right and you take the left? Scout around a bit. See if there's a way in. Maybe we'll get lucky."

Before Geronimo could offer an objection, Hickok, bent over at the waist, jogged to the right and vanished in the undergrowth.

Just great!

Geronimo rose and moved to the left, treading cautiously, watching for limbs in his path or objects underfoot. The darkness made a silent passage all the more difficult. One snap of a twig might apprise the sentries of his position.

The owl wanted to know who was there.

Years of training and discipline, combined with his finely honed instincts and a lifetime spent in the wild, had sharpened Geronimo's senses to the keenest possible level. He felt the breeze on his skin and detected the pungent scent of the pine trees and the rich earth. His ears distinguished the faintest rustling of branches overhead as nervous birds stirred at his passing. He was primed for anything out of the ordinary.

Consequently, he heard the muted voices long before he spotted the speakers.

Geronimo crouched and eased forward, avoiding protruding twigs and circumventing dry bushes.

What was this?

Two men were outside the camp, beyond even the sentries, standing near the forest. From their postures and gestures, it was evident they were arguing.

Odd.

Geronimo eased onto his stomach and inched ahead. A small pine provided an ideal place of concealment only two yards from the duo. He slid under the lowest branches and strained his ears.

" . . . called you out here because I don't want the men to hear what I have to say. It wouldn't be good for morale."

"Screw morale!" snapped the second speaker.

Geronimo twisted to his left, risking a glance upward. The first speaker was an officer, judging by the insignia on his green uniform. He was about six feet tall, his lean frame straight as an arrow, his brown hair cropped close to his head. His hands were on his narrow hips, his angular chin protruding in a defiant posture. "The morale of my men is important to me," he coldly informed the second speaker.

The other man snickered. "The only thing important to me, and the only thing the Doktor will care about, is whether you do as you're told and achieve our objective. We were told to destroy the Family, and that's what we're going to do."

"Don't lecture me about my duty, Brutus!" the officer said harshly.

The second man stiffened. He was well over six feet in height, and even in the subdued light from the campfires his body emanated raw power and . . . something else. He was solidly built, his brown shirt and pants scarcely able to contain his rippling muscles. A sneer twisted his bestial features as he glared at the officer. His hair was black, his eyes smoldering pools of an indeterminate color. "I'll lecture you, Captain Luther, whenever I feel like it!" he stated in a guttural growl.

Captain Luther wasn't intimidated. "I'll remind you for the last time, Brutus. The Doktor put me in charge of this mission, and I'll thank you to stop giving orders to my men!"

Brutus laughed, a peculiarly ominous sound. "Are you threatening me, Luther?"

"What if I am?" Captain Luther countered.

Geronimo saw the one known as Brutus reach out with his right arm. His huge right hand closed on the officer's shirt, clamping down with the tremendous force of an iron vise. He raised his arm straight up, his elbow slightly bent, and lifted Captain Luther from the ground.

"Let me go!" the officer ordered, striving to pry those stony fingers from his shirt.

"Don't ever threaten me," Brutus warned, his tone low and grating. "I won't tolerate being threatened. If you do it again," he said, and paused, glaring into the officer's eyes, "I'll rip your heart from your chest and eat it raw."

"Let go of me!" Captain Luther cried, enraged by the humiliating treatment he was receiving.

"As you wish," Brutus remarked.

The hulking psychopath grinned and released his grip.

Captain Luther dropped to the grass, stumbling and almost going down on one knee. But he recovered his balance and stood erect, glowering up at Brutus, refusing to be cowed. "I am in command of this strike force," he snapped, "and you will obey my orders or else! The Doktor sent you as an adviser—"

"The Doktor sent me to keep my eyes on you," Brutus said, correcting the officer. "And that's exactly what I'm going to do. If you don't like it, tough!"

"You can keep an eye on me all you want," Captain Luther stated. "Just don't let me hear of you countermanding an order of mine again!"

"I did what I thought was best," Brutus said.

"You ordered a patrol out without my approval," Captain Luther declared, "and knowing damn well I had already said we weren't going to send one out!"

"We should check up on the Family," Brutus rejoined, "and see what they're doing."

"They're waiting for us to attack," Captain Luther mentioned crisply. "What else do you think they would be doing?"

"They could be preparing a surprise for us," Brutus commented.

"What can they possibly do against all of us?" Captain Luther demanded.

"You never know," Brutus said.

Captain Luther snickered. "We have two thousand men and a tank, not to mention the other goodies I brought along. By this time tomorrow night, the Home will be a pile of rubble and the Family will all be dead." He chortled. "I can't wait! We'll destroy them!"

"I hope so," Brutus stated, "for your sake. The Doktor will be furious if we fail, and you know what he does with failures."

"I know," Captain Luther said, a tinge of fright in his voice.

"It's strange we haven't heard from the Doktor by now," Brutus noted in a calmer voice.

"He should have contacted us," Captain Luther agreed. "He might simply be busy with other matters."

Geronimo was surreptitiously studying Brutus. The man's high, sloping forehead, extremely bushy brows, and protruding lips all combined to lend a sinister aspect to his appearance. A sudden flaring of one of the nearby campfires caused Brutus to be bathed in a glow of reddish-orange light. For a brief moment, his face was vividly illuminated.

Geronimo was riveted by the bizarre sight.

Brutus was an ogre. His eyes were unnaturally large, giving him a popeyed countenance. The tip of his nose slanted at an abrupt angle, decidedly snoutish in its shape. Two of his teeth, the incisors, extended from under his upper lip. And his skin had a queer pitted quality about it, as if its texture were as rough as the trunk of a tree.

Geronimo recognized Brutus for what he, or it, was.

One of the Doktor's genetic deviates.

The infamous Doktor had refined a technique for altering a human embryo in a test-tube. He had perfected a method of restructuring the genetic code, of producing outlandish animalistic humans, monstrosities part human and part . . . thing. The Doktor had been one of the world's leading genetic engineers. But instead of devoting his skills to the benefit of humankind, he had used his warped genius to create a corps of personal assassins with superhuman strength.

Brutus was obviously one of the Doktor's killers.

Captain Luther and Brutus had calmed themselves considerably. Apparently, the officer wanted to stay on the best possible terms with Brutus despite their disagreement.

"Do you ever wonder what this Family is like?" Captain Luther asked.

"Who cares?" Brutus retorted.

Brutus certainly is the intellectual type, Geronimo thought.

"Don't you ever think about what life would be like outside the Civilized Zone?" Captain Luther inquired.

"Such thoughts are dangerous," Brutus reminded the officer. "They can get you in a lot of hot water."

"Then you've never considered it?" Capture Luther pressed him.

Brutus fidgeted uncomfortably. He unconsciously ran his left hand along his neck, stroking a thin metal collar he wore.

"Don't worry," Captain Luther said, laughing. "The Doktor can't hear you with that monitoring collar of his."

"What?"

"How can he eavesdrop?" Captain Luther queried. "All of his equipment, including the satellite link, was destroyed when Cheyenne was nuked. There's no way he can hear us."

"I don't know," Brutus said doubtfully.

"Suit yourself," Captain Luther stated, and shrugged. "But I can't help but wonder what these people are like. We know a lot about them, like why they call themselves Warriors and Tillers and Healers and such, but—"

"Why do they?" Brutus interrupted.

"It has something to do with the man who started the Home," Captain Luther revealed. "He was a believer in 'social equality,' so he began this nonsense about having every member of the Family receive a title. He thought it would make everyone socially acceptable. You wouldn't have anyone looking down their nose at someone else just because of the job they did."

"Sounds pretty weird to me," Brutus said.

"They're a weird bunch," Captain Luther concurred. "When I learned I was coming here," he elaborated, "I consulted the records on this Family. I wanted to learn their strengths and their weaknesses."

"What did you find out?"

"You'd be surprised how much data we've accumulated over the years with out listening posts," Captain Luther remarked. "Samuel had a great idea there. By periodically setting up our sensitive microphones outside isolated communities, we've been able to keep taps on them." He paused, staring at the encampment. "This Family isn't all that strong. They have a dozen or so warriors who are responsible for protecting their Home. They also have a well-stocked armory. But that's about it. Nothing we can't handle."

"We'll crush them like bugs!" Brutus predicted.

"We haven't spied on them in months, though," Captain Luther went on, "so we don't know what they've been up to lately."

"It doesn't matter," Brutus opined.

"The Doktor gave me the impression he thought they might have had something to do with the nuking of Cheyenne," Captain Luther said.

"The Family?"

"I know it's hard to believe," Captain Luther stated, "but that's the impression I received."

"Do we leave at first light?"

Captain Luther gazed at the stars. "At first light," he confirmed. He looked at the camp again. "I still can't believe the Doktor gave command of this assignment to me."

"Most of the senior officers were killed when the headquarters in Cheyenne went up in smoke," Brutus pointed out. "Besides, the Doktor trusts you."

Captain Luther smiled slyly, as if the unsuspecting canary had swooped within range of the cat's claws. "Then why don't you?"

"It isn't that I don't trust you," Brutus began lamely.

"Then why do you keep butting in?" Captain Luther demanded.

"I need to insure we succeed."

"We will," Captain Luther promised. "Don't worry."

"I can't help but worry," Brutus declared. "If we don't do as the Doktor wants, I could wind up being the course of instruction in one of his anatomy classes."

"If you're—" Captain Luther started to say, then abruptly stopped.

The sharp crack of gunfire erupted from the east side of the encampment.

Captain Luther and Brutus took off at a brisk clip.

Geronimo crawled from under the pine tree and stood.

It had to be Hickok!

What had the big dummy done and gone now?

Geronimo turned and jogged to the south, moving as rapidly as feasible. The trees were giant black sentinels in the night, their limbs ready to gouge or ensnare him if he blundered into one of them.

The shooting had ceased.

What if the soldiers had killedl Hickok?

Geronimo increased his pace, taking senseless risks, darting between and around trunks and other obstacles at a reckless speed.

He should never have let Hickok go off by himself!

They should have stayed together!

Some shouting broke out, off to the east.

Geronimo ran between two trees and artfully skipped to his right to avoid a big bush.

That's when it happened.

His left foot caught in something, an exposed root or a low limb, and before he could break free and right himself, he stumbled forward, headfirst, his arms outstretched.

He never saw the tree trunk.

Geronimo felt an excrucating pain lance through his head. He fell to his knees, dazed, struggling to retain his consciousness. Bright white stars exploded before his eyes, and he collapsed on the musty ground.

In the distance there was more shooting.

6

Hickok traveled in a circular pattern after leaving Geronimo. He stayed clear of the camp, swinging to the east as he searched for a weak spot.

He had a terrific idea.

If he could somehow sneak into the enemy camp and find the head honchos, he'd up and blow 'em away. Maybe, if these wimps were deprived of their leaders, they'd hightail it back to the Civilized Zone and leave the Family in peace.

He grinned at his brainstorm.

True, it might be smart to try and overhear what the bigwings were talkin' about, to see what they had in mind. And there was a prime drawback to his scheme to perforate their noggins; the other troopers would probably gun him down on the spot.

But it would be worth it, he told himself, if it stopped the attack on the Home.

The gunman was a hundred yards along the eastern perimeter of the encampment when he detected the flaw in their sentry arrangement.

Bingo!

There were two of the guards, posted as the others were, 20 yards apart. Behind these guards, lined up single file, was a row of troop transports. Beyond the trucks were several campfires surrounded by soldiers. But the troop transports effectively blocked off the light from the campfires. The area between the two sentries was plunged into darkness.

Hickok smiled as he advanced through the trees for a closer look-see. What a bunch of cow chips! They hadn't spotted the weakness in their perimeter and taken appropriate steps to recify it. These Civilized Zone goons sure were amateurs!

This would be a piece of cake!

The gunman reached the last tree before the camp. The guards were about ten yards off, one in each direction. They appeared to be bored by the sentry detail; at least they weren't actively scanning the woods for any indication of a threat.

That was their second mistake!

Hickok eased onto his stomach, cradled the Henry in his left elbow, and started to crawl from cover. He hesitated. The rifle would only slow him up, and a stray streak of light from the fires might glint off the gun and give him away. He couldn't take the risk. Reluctantly, he placed the Henry at the base of the tree.

He still had his Colt Pythons.

Hickok slowly inched into the open. Neither of the guards paid any attention.

Heh-heh-heh!

The gunman almost giggled aloud at their stupidity. He moved toward the troop transports.

One of the troopers in the camp began singing at the top of his lungs.

Off-key, yet.

Hickok thanked the Spirit for the noise and crawled a mite faster, confident the pair of sentries wouldn't hear him.

The guard to his left coughed.

Hickok froze and peered at the sentry. The man was sniffling. Poor baby! He must have a cold!

There was an unusual hissing sound to his right.

Hickok glanced in that direction.

The other sentry had unzipped his fatigue pants and was taking a leak.

Somebody sure did a lousy job of training these nitwits!

Hickok scrambled under the first truck and paused. The singer was entertaining his companions with a song about a soldier, a barmaid, and leather and lace.

Hickok kept going, always keeping to the shadows. He could see dozens of soldiers on the other side of the truck.

A pair of black boots unexpectedly appeared to his right, near the vehicle. The boots walked from right to left and disappeared from view behind the left rear tire.

Hickok waited until he was certain the boots weren't going to return, and then crawled behind the left front tire.

So far, so good.

Now where the blazes were the officers?

Hickok peeked around the tire and watched the assembled troopers go about their business of eating, cleaning their weapons, and engaging in idle chatter. Some of them were playing cards.

But there was no sign of the officers.

The troop transports were lined up from north to south, with the cabs positioned facing due north, the direction in which they had been driving when the convoy called it quits for the night.

Hickok decided to crawl under the next truck in line. There was a narrow space between the trucks, but no one was looking his way. He carefully moved from under the first truck.

"What the hell are you doing?" demanded a stern voice overhead.

Hickok, startled, glanced up.

A soldier was perched on the fender of the troop transport. The hood of the truck was propped open, and he was leaning on the radiator, a large crescent wrench in his right fist.

Blast!

Why hadn't he seen the mechanic?

"Over here!" the man bellowed, and dived at the intruder.

Hickok rolled, hearing the crescent wrench thud into the ground an inch from his right ear. He was forced to roll into the camp to escape the mechanic, and as he lunged to his feet there were other loud cries of alarm.

Just great!

Some of the troopers were going for their weapons.

Hickok, cornered, grinned and drew his Colt Pythons, the .357 Magnums flashing from their holsters. He snapped off two shots.

A pair of soldiers clutched at their heads and toppled to the turf.

Hickok whirled, just in time.

The trooper with the crescent wrench was a foot behind the gunman, the big wrench uplifted for a crushing blow.

Hickok shot him in the right eye.

The trooper jerked backward, a crimson spray erupting from the rear of his head. He slammed against the cab of the truck and fell to the earth.

Several M-16's were firing from the direction of the nearest campfire.

Hickok spun and blasted the Pythons four times.

Four soldiers were struck in the head, two of them screaming as they fell to the ground.

More M-16's opened up.

Time for Mamma Hickok's only son to make for the hills!

Hickok wisely retreated, knowing he was hopelessly outnumbered. There was no way he could surprise the officers now.

Blast!

The dirt at his feet flew in all directions as a burst from an M-16 missed him by inches.

Hickok ran between the two trucks behind him, making for the open stretch beyond and then the forest. If he could reach the trees, he felt confident he could escape.

The pair of sentries he'd bypassed earlier were hastening toward the encampment.

Hickok's Pythons boomed.

The guard on the right catapulted to the grass.

The sentry on the left twisted to the left as he was hit in the face. He shrieked as he staggered to his knees, then fell forward.

A veritable clamor rose from the camp.

"Get the son of a bitch!"

"He went this way!"

"Sound the alarm!"

Hickok raced toward the tree line.

Three soldiers skirted the cab of one of the troop transports, spotted the gunman, and began firing.

Hickok threw himself to the right. He landed on his right shoulder and rolled, coming up on his knees, his Pythons held at waist level.

The trio of troopers charged.

Hickok's Pythons bucked, spitting lead and death.

Almost as one, the three soldiers went down.

The Pythons were empty!

Hickok rose and ran into the woods.

"There he goes!" someone bellowed.

"After him!"

Hickok jogged due east, wanting to draw his pursuers away from Geronimo and his injured friends in the truck.

Dozens of soldiers crashed into the undergrowth behind him.

Hickok stopped, getting his bearings and listening to the noisy sounds of the troopers.

The soldiers had fanned out in a skirmish line and were advancing, coming his way.

Time to whittle down the odds some more.

Hickok crouched behind a towering pine and quickly reloaded the Pythons, replacing the spent cartridges with new rounds from his gunbelt.

All set!

"Where the hell did he go?" a soldier demanded.

Hickok peered around the tree.

There was a shadowy form not ten feet off.

Hickok planted a slug in the middle of the form. He turned and ran at top speed.

The pine tree shook as round after round of M-16 fire poured into its branches.

Hickok heard the faint buzzing of stray bullets as they tore through the forest.

"This way!" a man yelled.

Busybody!

Hickok altered his course, bearing to the north.

The troopers did likewise.

There had to be a way to shake 'em!

Hickok detected the inky contours of a low hillock ahead. He swung to the right, intending to put the hillock between himself and the soldier-boys.

The vicinity of the hillock was especially dark and murky, obscuring all landmarks.

Something snorted off to his right.

Hickok stopped and crouched, scanning the gloomy vegetation for the source of the snort.

Was it a mutate?

Or worse?

The gunfighter cautiously moved forward.

The . . . thing snorted again.

There was a familiar quality to the noise.

What was it?

Hickok could hear the soldiers clumping through the woods behind him.

Terrific!

Here he was, caught between the troopers and an unknown menace!

Hickok backed up, seeking cover at the base of a huge boulder.

There was a barely audible scratching from the top of the boulder.

Hickok glanced up.

A billowy black shape was dropping toward him.

Hickok tried to bring his Pythons into play. His fingers were tightening on the triggers when the black figure engulfed him. A clinging material enveloped him, pinning his arms to his sides. He surged against the material, struggling to free his arms.

What the blazes was it?

He had to bust loose!

A sharp blow landed on his right temple.

Hickok reeled, stunned. He turned to the right, still striving to extricate himself.

The bulky material was constricting around his body as pressure was applied from the outside.

What the hell was happening?

Hickok thrashed and kicked in a vain effort to

dislodge his assailant.

The constriction had spread from his arms, over his waist, to his legs.

Was it a snake?

Or one of the radiation-induced deviates?

Hickok tripped and fell onto his stomach. Before he could assess his situation, he was grabbed and lifted from the ground. He could feel his body being carried.

Had the soldiers caught him in some type of net?

A blanket?

That was it!

Some type of heavy blanket!

Someone had taken him unawares. They were transporting him some—

His body was suddenly shifted and elevated. His mid-section made contact with another surface.

Now what?

He abruptly began moving, his torso bouncing up and down with the rhythm of whatever he was on.

A horse?

Was that it? Someone had captured him and was carrying him on a horse?

Brother! Were they in for a surprise! They'd neglected to take his Pythons.

As soon as they freed his arms they were dead meat!

7

The Freedom Federation Army was camped for the night on the northern outskirts of Loveland, Colorado. The fighters from the Clan, the Moles, and the Cavalry were in exceptional spirits. Another day in Colorado, proceeding toward Denver at a turtle's pace, and still no evidence of hostilities from the forces of Samuel II. Some of them discussed the matter as they sat near their campfires to ward off the cold night air.

Why? they wondered.

And they were not alone in their speculation.

Standing alone on the southern edge of his encampment, his immense chest and black-leather vest covered with an ill-fitting fatigue jacket, Blade brooded on the same subject.

Why?

First Fort Collins, and now Loveland. Both cities deserted, abandoned by their citizenry. Neither defended by the military.

None of it made sense.

Blade frowned, bothered by the persistant thought it might all be a trap. Why else would Samuel II let them have Fort Collins and Loveland unopposed? Why—

There was someone behind him.

Blade's keen instincts sensed a presence even though his ears had not registered the slightest sound. He spun, his hands dropping to his Bowies.

The diminutive figure three feet to his rear smiled.

"Rikki!" Blade snapped. "What do you think you're

doing, coming up on me like that? If I were Hickok, you'd have a bullet in your brain right now."

Rikki-Tikki-Tavi stepped closer. He shook his head. "Hickok would have heard me. And so would you if you weren't so preoccupied. What is it? Are you still concerned about the prospect of becoming Leader of the Family?"

"No," Blade said, facing south again. "I'm puzzled as to why Samuel hasn't made a move against us yet. Fort Collins, Loveland, and every spot in between have been handed to us on a silver platter. Why?"

Rikki, his ever-present katana in his right hand, stood alongside Blade. "You are in command of this expedition. What do you think?"

"There are several possibilities," Blade stated.

"I'd like to hear them."

"It could be a ruse to suck us into an ambush," Blade said. "But why would Samuel go to all the trouble of evacuating the populace for that?"

"What else?" Rikki probed.

"They don't have as many troops and armaments as we believed they did," Blade continued. "We already know the war severely impaired their industrial production. Most of their munitions, their vehicles, weaponry, and ammunition are antiquated. The geographical area they control lacks crucial natural resources. Either they lost most of their men in Cheyenne when Yama and Lynx used that thermo on the Doktor's headquarters, or their army is off somewhere else. If so, where?"

"What other reasons might they have for not engaging us?" Rikki inquired.

"They may have heard about what we did to the Doktor in Catlow," Blade remarked, "and they're afraid to take us on. But I don't see that as very likely."

"There's one thing you missed," chimed in a newcomer.

Blade and Rikki-Tikki-Tavi turned.

He was four feet tall, this newcomer, dwarfed even by Rikki-Tikki-Tavi. Only four feet tall, weighing 60 pounds, he was the size of a child with the power of a giant. His wiry body was covered with thick, grayish-brown fur. His only clothing was a leather loincloth.

"What do you mean, Lynx?" Blade asked.

Lynx came closer. His gleaming green eyes, his pointed ears and pointy chin, and the reddish nails on the tips of his thin fingers all conspired to produce an inhuman appearance. As well they should. Lynx was one of the few surviving members of the Doktor's Genetic Research Division, the Doktor's personal assassin corps developed through his experiments in genetic engineering and his manipulation of test-tube embryos. Lynx had rebelled against the Doktor and joined the Freedom Federation's cause.

Rikki-Tikki-Tavi stared at the creature, perplexed. He hadn't heard Lynx approach. How was that possible?

"I may have a clue as to why Sammy's got the heebie-jeebies," Lynx offered in his high-pitched voice.

"The heebie-jeebies?" Blade repeated.

"I think it has something to do with the thermo," Lynx said, ignoring the interruption.

"The thermo?" Blade reiterated.

Lynx squinted up at Rikki and held his right hand cupped around his tiny right ear. "Is there an echo here or what?"

Rikki grinned.

"When we were busting heads in Catlow," Lynx detailed, "the Doc said something real strange to me. The dork wanted to know what I did with the rest of the thermos."

"The dork?" Blade absently interjected.

Lynx gazed up at the huge Warrior. "Are you on drugs or something?"

"The Warriors do not contaminate their bodies with pollutants," Blade replied stiffly.

"Hey! Listen up, Dimples!" Lynx said. "I was only yanking your jock strap."

"My jock strap?"

Lynx reached out and tapped Blade's knee with his right hand. "Are you trying to drive me wacko?"

"Why can't you speak simple English?" Blade

countered.

Lynx shook his head. "Whatever you say. But pay attention. You know I used a portable tactical thermonuclear unit on the Doktor's headquarters, right?"

"Right," Blade confirmed.

"And you know we call these units thermos?"

"I know that."

"Well," Lynx elaborated, "the Army had a bunch of thermos near the Doc's headquarters. They were blown all to hell when the HQ went up. But I don't think they know that. I don't think Sammy knows they were destroyed."

"Do you mean Samuel thinks we have some of these portable nuclear devices with us?" Blade asked.

Lynx looked at Rikki. "There's hope for the big guy after all."

Blade's features lit up. "That would explain it! That would explain everything! Samuel believes we have a thermonuclear device. He's afraid we'll use one against his army or on his cities. That's why they haven't hit us yet!"

"It's a logical deduction," Rikki concurred.

"This is great news!" Blade declared.

"I'm glad I made your day," Lynx quipped.

Blade impulsively grabbed Lynx and lifted him from the ground, laughing all the while.

"Put me down!" Lynx demanded, squirming in Blade's grasp.

"I could kiss you!" Blade exclaimed happily.

"You do," Lynx warned, "and I'll bite your lips off!"

Blade deposited Lynx on the grass. "Don't you see what you've done?"

"I told you something I thought you should know," Lynx responded. "Big deal."

"But it is!" Blade stated. "You've given me the answer."

"The answer to what?"

"The answer to how I'm going to defeat Samuel the Second," Blade said, beaming.

Lynx leaned toward Rikki. "I don't care what he says," he remarked conspiratorially. "Either he's on drugs or he's been hitting the brew. What do you think?"

"I think I would like to ask you a question," Rikki mentioned.

"Sure, Rikki-Tikki," Lynx said. "What is it?"

"What exactly is a dork?"

8

It was the middle of the night. A chill wind from the north blew across the ramparts, causing several of the Family's sentries to stamp their feet in an effort to keep warm.

One man, standing by himself in the center of the western rampart above the drawbridge, was immune to the cold. He stood with his right hand on the hilt of his broadsword, dressed in his blue shirt, buckskin pants, and a brown-leather jacket constructed by the Weavers from deer hide.

Spartacus was uneasy.

Had he done all he could possibly do?

His mind was racing a mile a minute. He had tried to get some sleep, but had tossed and turned until, exasperated, he had risen, donned his jacket, and walked from B Block to the western rampart.

Was there anything he had missed?

Spartacus was troubled to the depths of his soul. The Family's very existence depended on his judgment in the crises ahead. If he failed, if he let them down, they would all perish.

A sobering thought if ever there was one.

Spartacus reviewed the steps he had taken so far. The Clan's noncombatants had been placed in F Block and D Block. The Family's children and elderly were in the cabins in the middle of the compound. Weapons from the armory had been distributed. Theoretically, he had done all he could to prepare for the assault.

A skeleton crew was manning the ramparts during the night. At first light all of the fighters from the Family and the Clan would be on their assigned walls. Then would come the hard part.

The waiting.

How long would it take the enemy convoy to reach the Home? Probably by midmorning their vehicles would be within sight of the walls. Would they launch their attack in the afternoon, or wait another night?

Spartacus glanced to his right. One of the Tillers was on guard duty, a lean youth who nervously hefted the Iver Johnson M1 Carbine he was carrying. The Tillers weren't accustomed to handling firearms; working with a plow, reaping a harvest from the soil, was their stock in trade. Spartacus realized the M1 must feel as alien to the young Tiller as a plow would to him. Unlike the Tiller, he considered weapons a fundamental part of his life.

Like his broadsword.

Spartacus gazed down at his cherished blade. It hadn't been his first choice; initially, he'd wanted to own the short sword. Unfortunately, the short sword had already been in the possession of Ares. Because the Founder, Kurt Carpenter, had only stocked one of each type of sword, Spartacus had been compelled to substitute the broadsword for the short sword. Now, years later, he wouldn't part with the broadsword for anything; it had become an extension of his arm, of his personality. He looked down near his feet, at the Heckler and Koch HK93 leaning against the parapet. Spartacus had used it on many occasions on the Family firing range in the southeastern corner of the Home. But he lacked the sentimental attachment for the HK93 that he had for the broadsword. Guns were too impersonal. He couldn't understand how someone like Hickok could prefer a pair of Colt Python revolvers to a trusty sword. A bladed weapon enabled you to—

What was that?

Spartacus glanced up and out over the field in front of the western wall.

There it was again.

A dull rumbling sound of some sort.

"Horses are coming," the young Tiller announced.

Spartacus grinned. There were certain advantages to working with horses and a plow after all. He bent over and retrieved his HK93. Approaching horses undoubtedly meant Boone and the Cavalry riders, but he couldn't afford to take chances.

The pounding of heavy hooves drew nearer.

Spartacus peered into the darkness. A vague, swirling mass became visible in the field, making a beeline for the drawbridge. He waited until he was certain the riders were all wearing buckskins, then he moved to the top of the stairs. "Open the drawbridge!" he shouted to the three men below.

Boone was at the head of the column of riders. They reined in, constraining their mounts until the drawbridge was fully lowered.

Spartacus hurried down the stairs to greet them.

Boone urged his steed forward, its hooves thumping on the wooden bridge as he crossed and entered the compound.

"How'd it go?" Spartacus inquired.

Boone grinned and jerked his right thumb over his shoulder. "See for yourself."

The rider behind Boone was carrying an extra load. The indistinct form of a man was lying on his stomach across the horse's rump, his body completely enveloped in a bulky brown hide. Loops of rope restrained him from his shoulders to his knees. Only his moccasin-covered feet protruded from under the hide.

"What's this?" Spartacus asked.

Boone slid to the ground as his men milled about. "We were working our way to the Army camp when a lot of shooting broke out."

"Were they shooting at you?" Spartacus queried.

"Don't think so," Boone answered. "There was a lot of lead flying around. It was too dark to tell what the fracas was all about. One of my men saw this one sneaking through the trees and pounced on him."

The figure in the hide was struggling to break free and yelling. His words were too muffled by the hide to make any sense.

"We wrapped him up in a horsehide and brought him back here," Boone went on. "We weren't able to get close to the camp, but questioning one of them will get us the information we need."

"Let's take a look at our guest," Spartacus proposed.

Boone nodded at the rider, who unceremoniously dumped his cargo onto the hard earth.

The man in the horsehide uttered an audible grunt.

Boone walked to the hide and began unraveling the lariat securing the prisoner.

Spartacus covered the figure while the Cavalry riders watched. Boone had done well. This man would talk, or Spartacus would use him for a pincushion.

That was when he finally noticed.

"He's wearing moccasins," Spartacus noted. "I thought that the soldiers all wore black combat boots."

Boone was still undoing the rope. "Maybe he was a scout. I hear they sometimes wear civilian duds."

The man in the horsehide had quieted.

As Boone continued to undo the rope, the folds of the horsehide loosened. The lower edge flapped in the wind, exposing the form underneath to the waist.

"He's got a gun!" one of the riders cried in alarm.

Actually, he had two. A pair of pearl-handled revolvers, one in each hand.

Boone rose and started to draw his .44 Magnums.

"I don't think those will be necessary," Spartacus said.

Boone paused and glanced at Spartacus, puzzled. "What do you mean?"

"Take a good look at those revolvers," Spartacus suggested.

Boone knelt and stared at the handguns. It took a minute for it to dawn on him. He looked up at Spartacus. "It can't be!"

"You know it can't be," Spartacus said, "and I know it can't be. But . . ." He walked up to the hide and leaned over the prone figure, placing his mouth up to the hide in the general vicinity of the man's head. "Hickok? Is that you?"

The form in the horsehide exploded, jerking and thrashing in an attempt to free himself. A string of barely audible, colorful phrases punctuated his effort.

"Calm down!" Spartacus advised. "We'll have you out in a jiffy."

Boone quickly finished removing the lariat from the thick hide. He grabbed the bottom edge and lifted, pulling the hide clear of the man inside and stepping back.

Just in time.

His face a livid red, his blond hair a mess, his buckskins disheveled, the Family's preeminent gunfighter surged to his feet, caught in the glow from the lanterns placed in the nearby wall. He glared at everyone and everything, his knuckles white on the grips of his Pythons. He glowered at Spartacus, then Boone, then at the Cavalry riders. Even their horses were included in his baleful scrutiny. He had the menacing air of a man eager to shoot someone or something, anyone or anything. All it would take was the right provocation.

Boone broke the ice. He smiled wanly and gave a little wave. "Howdy, Hickok."

It was all the opening Hickok needed.

The gunman advanced on Boone, furious, gesticulating with his revolvers. "You dang-blasted, dimwitted cow chip! Didn't you know it was me?"

"How were we supposed to know?" Boone replied. "It was too dark."

"I could of suffocated in that smelly hide!" Hickok bellowed. "And do you realize what all that bouncing around did to my kidneys?"

"I'm really sorry, Mr. Hickok," said the Cavalry rider responsible for dropping the hide on the gunman.

Hickok faced the rider. "You did this to me?" he growled.

The hapless rider blanched and gulped. He simply nodded.

Hickok twirled the Colt Pythons into their respective holsters.

"I want all of you to listen up!" he shouted, his hands hovering near his revolvers.

Spartacus suppressed an impulse to laugh. The Cavalry riders appeared to be in a state of shock. Hickok's formidable reputation had that effect on people.

"I know you hombres were just doin' your job," Hickok declared, "which is the only reason I don't blow you away here and now! But if one word of this gets out, just one word, I'll be lookin' you up to talk this over real personal like. Do you get the drift?"

Everyone nodded or otherwise acknowledged they understood.

Boone was grinning.

"What are you doing here?" Spartacus inquired. "Why aren't you with Blade and the others."

The mention of Blade immediately sobered the gunman and soothed his intense embarrassment. "I plumb forgot," he mumbled.

"What happened?" Spartacus asked.

"Blade sent Geronimo and me back in a truck," Hickok explained. "We were bringin' Bertha and Josh back to the Home so the Healers could tend to 'em."

"Bertha and Josh? Are they hurt?" Spartacus questioned him.

Hickok nodded. "Bertha is hurt bad. She might not make it. Josh is hangin' in there, though."

"What about Blade?" Spartacus probed. "Are Samuel and the Doktor still alive?"

"We won't have to worry none about the Doktor," Hickok revealed. "Last I knew, Blade was makin' for Denver. Geronimo must still be back on Highway 59. We were spying on the Army camp when these nincompoops jumped me."

"We can't leave Geronimo out there alone," Spartacus stated.

"He's got a Cavalry guy named Morton with him," Hickok disclosed. "But you're right." He stared at Boone.

"Do you want us to go after him?" Boone inquired.

"Yep," Hickok responded. "You'll have to stay with him, because Bertha and Josh are in no shape to be ridin' a horse. And there's no way you're gonna get that troop transport past the Army convoy."

"I'll leave half of my men here," Boone offered.

"Thanks," Spartacus interjected. "We can use them." He looked at Hickok. By rights, and according to the established chain of command, the gunman was now in charge of the defense of the Home. Spartacus felt mixed emotions: on the one hand, he was relieved the burden had been lifted from his shoulders, but on the other, he experienced a faint resentment Hickok was taking over.

Boone walked to his horse and swung up. "We won't let anything happen to Bertha and Joshua. Just make sure nothing happens to you." He paused. "Do you want me to send a messenger to Blade for help?"

Hickok shook his head. "The convoy will be here tomorrow. A rider could never reach Blade in time."

Boone nodded his understanding. A man on horse-back would take weeks to reach Colorado. "Take care," he said. He quickly selected half of his men, choosing the ones to go by pointing at them.

Spartacus watched as Boone and ten of his men vanished into the night.

Hickok strode up to Spartacus. "Give me the low-down."

"I think we're all set," Spartacus detailed. "All our arms have been distributed. I placed our youngsters and elderly in the cabins. Everyone from the Clan who can fight has been housed in F Block and D Block—"

"The Clan is here then?" Hickok interrupted.

"Yes," Spartacus confirmed. "We have two hundred and sixty-five fighters, not counting the ten Cavalry men. I've divided them up and assigned them to a wall."

"What about the Warriors?"

"Seiko and Shane will hold the north wall," Spartacus divulged. "Carter, Ares, and Gideon have the south wall. I gave the east wall to Crockett, Samson and . . . Sherry."

"You were plannin' to take care of the west wall all by your lonesome?"

"I didn't see where I had a choice," Spartacus said.

"Sounds like you did a right proper job," Hickok complimented his fellow Warrior.

"You're welcome to change whatever you don't like," Spartacus commented.

"There is one thing that needs changin'," Hickok commented.

"What?"

"You won't be alone on the west wall," Hickok informed him. "I'll be joinin' you."

"What about Sherry?" Spartacus asked.

"What about her?" Hickok responded defensively.

"Do you want her moved to the west wall with us?"

Hickok studied Spartacus for a moment. "Thanks, but no. You assigned her to the east wall and that's where she'll stay."

"But you're in charge now," Spartacus stated. "You can do whatever you want."

"I've gotta do what's best for the Family," Hickok said. "Having at least three Warriors on the east wall makes sense."

"You could transfer me to the east wall and have Sherry by your side," Spartacus suggested.

"Nope." The gunman sighed. "I can't be showin' any favoritism. You've already committed her to the east wall. If I change her post, the other Warriors are gonna get hot under the collar. We'll leave things just the way you have them."

"As you wish," Spartacus said.

"And as far as me being in charge goes," Hickok went on, "I ain't lettin' you off the hook that easy."

"But according to the chain of command—" Spartacus began.

"Hang the chain of command," Hickok declared. "This is all-out war. I'll make the decisions, but I want your input on everything. And I mean everything. We can't afford to make any mistakes."

"Don't I know it," Spartacus agreed.

Hickok glanced at the ten Cavalry riders. "Get some shut-eye. Be up at sunrise. I want you ready to ride if I give the word."

"Where do you want us?" one of the riders asked.

Hickok pointed at the nearest Block, C Block. "Wait on the far side of the infirmary."

"We'll be ready," the bearded rider promised. The ten Cavalrymen rode off to get some sleep.

Hickok looked at the three Family men manning the drawbridge mechanism. He gestured upward with his right hand. They proceeded to elevate the wooden bridge, the massive chain rattling and clanking as it moved the gears.

"I'm glad you're here," Spartacus commented.

"I wish Blade and the rest of the Freedom Federation Army was with me," Hickok commented.

"Do you have any idea how many we're up against?" Spartacus inquired.

"Two thousand," Hickok answered.

"Two thousand," Spartacus repeated. "Our estimate was right."

"That ain't the worst of it, pard," Hickok declared.

"What could be worse?"

"They've got a tank," Hickok told him.

"A tank!" Spartacus couldn't keep his shock from showing.

"Things are gonna get hot around here," Hickok predicted.

"What are we going to do to stop their tank?" Spartacus asked.

"Beats me," Hickok replied. "The Founder didn't leave us any antitank guns or heavy explosives."

"Then what will we do?" Spartacus queried, aghast at the idea of pitting puny automatic-rifle fire against a tank.

"We'll do what I always do," Hickok stated. "We'll play it by ear. Trust me."

"But a tank!" Spartacus exclaimed.

"Calm down, pard," Hickok advised. "Don't let it get you in an uproar."

"How can you be calm," Spartacus retorted, "knowing two thousand soldiers and a tank are going to attack our Home?"

"What good would it do me to lose sleep over it?" Hickok countered. "You should have a philosophy of life like mine."

"You have a philosophy of life?" Spartacus asked in amazement, emphasizing the first word.

"You bet your boots!" Hickok affirmed. "You've got to take what comes your way in life and make the best of it."

"That's your whole philosophy?"

"And don't sweat the small potatoes," Hickok amended his statement.

"A tank is small potatoes?" Spartacus rejoined.

"Look at the bright side," Hickok recommended.

"What bright side?"

"They ain't plannin' to nuke us." Hickok yawned. He stared to the east. "Is Sherry in our cabin?" he inquired.

"As far as I know," Spartacus responded. "She wanted to pull guard duty tonight, but I told her to get some sleep."

Hickok gazed into his friend's eyes. "Thanks. I appreciate that."

"She's supposed to be on the east wall by dawn," Spartacus said.

Hickok smiled. "Dawn is hours away. I reckon I'll mosey on over to our cabin and let her know her heart-throb has returned."

"You go ahead," Spartacus said. "I'll be waiting for you here, on top of the wall. I don't think I could get any sleep anyhow."

Hickok started to amble off. "Give a yell if you need me."

"I will," Spartacus promised. He waited until the gunman was obscured by the night, then he turned and climbed the stairs to the western rampart.

How did Hickok do it? He always remained so cool and confident, even when confronted by the gravest danger. Nothing seemed to bother the gunfighter. Or did it really affect him, and he only pretended to be indifferent? Whatever the case, Spartacus was now wholeheartedly happy the gunman was back.

Spartacus wondered how he would fare in the battle ahead. He had fought scavengers, mutates, and Trolls in the past, but never a threat of this magnitude before. Neither had most of the Warriors. Their crucible of combat loomed with the rising of the fiery sun. If the Warriors proved unworthy, the Family would fade into oblivion, its memory erased from the historical record of humanity with few to mourn its passing. The wind from the north gusted again, and for the first time that night Spartacus felt the cold.

He shivered.

9

Kurt Carpenter, the immensely wealthy filmmaker responsible for constructing the survival site he dubbed "the Home," and for organizing his followers into "the Family," had wanted to make the postwar transition as smooth as possible. Carpenter attempted to forsee the Family's future needs and provide for them. He projected a breakdown of law and order, and proceeded to amass an extensive weapons collection to insure the Family's survival. He considered an enormous library essential to the Family's welfare. How else were they to obtain the knowledge crucial for maintaining the basic necessities of life? Close to half a million books were stocked in E Block: books on gardening, hunting, fishing, and metalsmithing, natural medicine, herbal healing, geography, history, and religion and philosophy, the martial arts, military tactics, and photographic books, encyclopedias, dictionaries, sundry reference books and much, much more.

Carpenter also left them the SEAL. The Solar Energized Amphibious or Land Recreational Vehicle—SEAL, as it became known—cost Carpenter millions upon millions. Of revolutionary design, it ran on solar power collected by a pair of unique panels on the roof of the van-like vehicle. Its body was constructed of impervious plastic, shatterproof and heat-resistant, tinted green and designed to prevent anyone outside the transport from seeing within. Six extraordinary batteries, each with an unlimited life span, capable of being recharged countless times, were stored in a lead-lined case under the SEAL. Four huge tires served to convey the vehicle over any terrain. The SEAL had been Carpenter's pride and joy.

The Family saw it as an irreplaceable blessing. Without it, they would not be able to travel great distances from the Home. With it, they could go virtually anywhere. Its indestructible body shielded the occupants from harm, and Carpenter's modifications turned the SEAL into an awesome dreadnaught.

Carpenter had hired several mercenaries, skilled weapons specialists, and told them to make the SEAL unstoppable. They did their best. A pair of 50-caliber machine guns were mounted on the vehicle, one under each headlight. A miniaturized surface-to-air missile, dubbed a STINGER, was fitted in the roof above the driver's seat. At the flip of a toggle switch, a roof panel would slide aside, the missile would slant upward on its launch track, and presto! A flamethrower was positioned behind the center of the front fender, an Army Surplus model with a range of 20 feet. As if all of this weren't enough, a rocket launcher was secreted in the middle of the front grill. Shielded against the heat from the flamethrower, the rocket would emerge from its concealed compartment at the flick of the appropriate switch.

When it came to offensive weaponry, Blade reflected, the SEAL was armed to the proverbial teeth. He skill-fully drove the transport south on U.S. Highway 287, avoiding the ruts and potholes in the road. The highways in the Civilized Zone weren't in much better shape than those outside the Civilized Zone; a century of neglect had taken its toll.

Rikki-Tikki-Tavi sat across from Blade in the bucket seat next to the passenger door. His katana was cradled in his lap. Behind the pair of bucket seats separated by a console was a seat running the width of the vehicle. Yama and Teucer occupied this seat, Yama behind Blade and Teucer behind Rikki. The rear section of the SEAL was devoted to a large storage space for provisions. Curled up on top of the pile of supplies, taking a snooze, was Lynx.

"Where are we now?" Blade asked. Another small town was directly ahead, and like all of the others it was deserted.

"We just passed a sign," Rikki commented. "I didn't catch the name."

"I saw part of it," offered Teucer. "Something about *The Garden Spot of Colorado.*"

Blade scanned the sparse landscape on both sides of the highway. Except for a few trees here and there, there was nothing to compare to a "garden." Which wasn't too surprising. One thing he had noted, after many hours of studying the maps and atlases in the Family library, was that the people of long ago picked the weirdest names for places, usually with no semblance of rhyme or reason. Many aspects of the prewar culture were decidedly strange, some even perverse. Small wonder the idiots had almost destroyed the world!

The morning sun was well into the sky.

Blade frowned. There was still no sign of Samuel II or his Army. Lynx had to be right. Samuel II believed the Freedom Federation had one or more thermonuclear devices and was reluctant to engage them.

The SEAL was passing through a business district. They crossed a set of railroad tracks, and Blade wondered whether the trains were still functional. He seriously doubted that they were. The Civilized Zone's industrial production was minimal. Utilizing its sparse resources to manufacture trains, when even the necessities were scarce, would be an incredible extravagance.

"Are we going to take a break or keep going?" Teucer inquired.

Blade drove past a bank, a small market, and a couple of restaurants. Ahead, to his right, was a quaint park. "We'll take a breather," he replied. "I want to stretch my legs."

There was a side street to the left.

Blade slowed and swung onto the side street. He braked the SEAL and turned off the engine. "Have them disperse around that park," Blade instructed

Rikki. "We won't be staying long." He opened his door and dropped to the ground.

The sun was bright, the air refreshingly chill and light. A raucous flock of starlings was in a nearby tree.

Blade slowly strolled along the street, his hands clasped behind his broad back.

"Do you want any of us to come with you?" Yama called out.

Blade glanced over his right shoulder.

Rikki, Yama, and Teucer were standing near the SEAL, concern on their features.

"No, thanks," Blade responded. "I'll be back in a bit."

The rest of the trucks had stopped on U.S. Highway 287. The Cavalry riders were behind the troop transports.

Blade spotted an alley to his right and walked into it. Dry, reddish-brown dirt swirled around his moccasins. He strolled past several wooden-frame homes and came to a chain-link fence bordering a low wooden structure. On an impulse, he placed his hands on top of the chain-link fence and vaulted to the other side. He followed a cracked cement walk to the front of the low structure. A door to his left was hanging open. He stepped to the doorway and peered inside. The interior was dark and gloomy. Obviously, this building hadn't been used in years and years. A fine coating of reddish dust covered everything. Sunlight streaming through two narrow windows high on the west wall revealed a wide, clear area on one side and a cluttered workshop on the other. A row of rusty tools—screwdrivers, hammers, saws, and the like—filled the top of a wooden workbench. A pair of antique sawhorses stood near the workbench.

Blade backed from the low structure and glanced at a large green house to his right. The paint on the house was chipped and worn away, particularly around the windows and the eaves. The sidewalk had buckled near the house.

Did anyone live here?

Somehow, he didn't think so.

Curious, Blade advanced toward the house. He

skirted to the left and found a large concrete porch, riddled with cracks, and a closed door. Actually, two doors. A screen door and an inner wooden door. His right hand on the hilt of his right Bowie, Blade cautiously opened both doors with his left and slid inside, surprised they were unlocked.

The house was obviously uninhabited. Dust coated everything. There was a long white counter to his right. Suspended above the counter were white cabinets. A large metallic box stood to his left. Blade's memory stirred. He remembered several of the photographic books in the Family library, and he was able to recognize the room he was in: it was called a kitchen, and the metal box was a refrigerator.

There was an archway to his left, and a doorway near the refrigerator.

Why wasn't anyone living here?

Blade took a step and froze as something rattled near his feet. He glanced down.

There was a pile of human bones lying on the floor, coated with dust as was everything else, and partially covered by the faded remnants of a green shirt and a pair of jeans.

Was this the reason the home was unoccupied?

Blade peered at the whitish skull. There was a ragged, gaping cavity where the forehead had once been. He knew what could cause such a severe wound: a close-range blast from a shotgun.

Did the bones belong to the former owner of this house?

Blade moved to the archway and discovered a living room beyond. There was an ancient sofa to the right of the archway. To the left was a wicker chair and a small oaken stand with a white telephone resting upon it. A television with a shattered screen stood on a pedestal to the right of the sofa. Against the far wall was a cabinet containing several stereo components.

The remains of four more bodies were scattered on the living room carpet, all displaying signs of having died a violent death by gunfire.

What had transpired here?

Blade walked toward a doorway on the far side of the living room, reflecting. He was fascinated by the artifacts. So this was how a typical residence had looked before the Big Blast, he thought. Quite comfy, in an ordinary sort of way.

But why all the bodies?

Blade stepped to the next doorway and found a bedroom, a smaller room harboring an unmade bed and a vanity, two wooden dressers, and a large maple cabinet. Again, on the opposite side of the room was a doorway, only this time the door was closed.

Five more skulls leered up from the beige carpet, all of them situated near the closed door.

One thing was obvious: there had been one hell of a fight in this house.

But why?

Blade approached the closed door, his right hand on his Bowie. What was beyond the door? Why had five people perished attempting to get through it?

There was only one way to find out.

Blade gripped the doorknob and turned, slowly pulling the door open. The hinges creaked as the door swung out.

More barren bones. Four skulls and a pile of bones and old clothing formed a compact heap just inside the doorway.

What a struggle this must have been!

But the paramount question still remained: why?

Blade entered, then stopped, perplexed.

This room was the smallest of them all, not much more than 8 feet wide by 20 feet long. Shelves of books lined every wall. There was a large wooden desk in the middle of the room, and on top of the desk was a green typewriter with a sheet of paper under a paper bail.

This was it?

This was what 14 people had died for?

Blade spotted a framed photograph on the wall above the desk. He moved closer. It was a picture of a man, a woman, and their children. The woman was exceptionally attractive, with an open, honest expression. The man bordered on the lean side. He wore a shiny metallic

object on his nose, and it took Blade a moment to
remember what the object was: a pair of glasses.

Were these the former owners?

He glanced at the paper in the typewriter. There was
some faint printing on the sheet. He brushed the
ominipresent dust aside and leaned over. The subdued
light from a window near the desk illuminated the
paper.

Karen and Mark and Don and Chris:
    If you're reading this, it means you've missed us and
    we are on our way to our cabin in the high country. We
    will stay there until you catch up. As you can tell by all
    the bodies, a band of looters attacked while we were
    packing. Not to worry. Ann and the kids are fine. I have
    a few scratches. Meet us at the cabin and watch out for
    the creeps!

                                                    Larry

Blade sat down in a chair alongside the desk and
gazed at the photograph on the wall. Was the man in the
picture the one called Larry? What had he done for a
living? By what miracle had he protected his family
from so many looters? Had all of this happened at the
outset of the war? Was the house now shunned because
of all the skeletons?

Watch out for the creeps, the man had said.

He sounded a little like Hickok.

They must have been extremely close-knit, this
family. The man had valiantly defended them against
superior odds. But wasn't that what familial relation-
ships were all about? Loving selfishly. Putting the
welfare of your loved ones first. Doing whatever was
necessary to insure their happiness.

Doing whatever was necessary . . .

Blade frowned. Why hadn't he seen it earlier? If you
truly love someone, they always come first. No matter
what. You do whatever you must for them, even if it's
something you don't necessarily want to do.

Like becoming Leader of the Family.

So what if he balked at the very idea? So what if he found it difficult to confront the prospect of one of the Family dying due to his stupidity or neglicence? Didn't he love them? All of them? Weren't they his friends and associates and loved ones? Then how could he refuse them?

The answer was staring him in the face: he couldn't.

Blade rose and nodded at the photograph. "So long," he said aloud. "And thanks."

The dust stirred as Blade walked through the bedroom to the living room.

"Going somewhere, Warrior?" hissed a guttural voice.

Blade froze in the doorway, startled.

Three men, dressed all in black, including black masks over their faces, were waiting for him on the other side of the living room, lined up under the archway. All three had assumed martial arts postures. All three carried long Oriental swords.

Blade had encountered a man dressed like these three before. The man had stealthily entered the Home in the early morning hours and attempted to blow up the SEAL, only a short while before Alpha Triad had departed for the Twin Cities.

"You look surprised," the speaker stated. "You shouldn't be. The Imperial Assassins have kept your convoy under surveillance since Fort Collins, waiting our chance, waiting for you to drop your guard."

"Samuel has a message for you," said the figure in the middle, a sneer in his voice.

"He sent us to deliver it," commented the third.

"Three guesses what it is," declared the first man. With that, he charged.

10

Never in all his born days had he seen a sight like it.

Hickok stood on the rampart above the drawbridge, his hands on his hips, and gawked.

"There are so many of them!" exclaimed a young Clan woman to his left.

"That's good," Hickok told her.

She eyed him skeptically. "How can it be good?"

"It means you won't have to aim as hard," Hickok informed her, grinning.

The Civilized Zone force had parked its trucks and other vehicles in the woods bordering the cleared fields. All except the tank. It rolled from the trees and parked at the edge of the western field, its engine idling, directly across from the drawbridge. The troops had followed the tank, marching four abreast from the woods. Half of the soldiers bore to the right, half to the left, until the field near the forest was covered with green figures, all of them armed with M-16's, all of them standing at attention. Some of them wore helmets, some didn't.

Either their discipline was lax, Hickok deduced, or there was a shortage of helmets.

A hand fell on the gunman's left shoulder.

"Why are they massing to the west?" Spartacus inquired. "Why haven't they deployed their troops to surround the Home and take advantage of their numbers?"

Hickok indicated the drawbridge below them. "My guess, pard, is they intend to wallop the stuffin' out of us on the first try. They know the only way into the Home is through the drawbridge. Their head honcho must reckon this here drawbridge is our weak link.''

"It is," Spartacus mentioned.

"We'll see about that," Hickok stated grimly. He focused on a pair of men walking along the front rows of the opposing army. Was one of them the commander?

"They got here much sooner than I expected," Spartacus remarked. "I didn't think they'd make it until noon."

"They're in a hurry to die," Hickok said.

"May the Spirit preserve us," Spartacus commented.

Hickok found his mind straying. He thought of Sherry, his darling wife, and the night they had shared. She'd been overjoyed to see him, and had been all over his body like a bear on honey. He had tried to convince her they should get some shut-eye, to no avail. He'd even pleaded a headache, but still she'd persisted. He sighed contentedly at the pleasant memories. When a woman was warm for your form, there was nothing to do but take the heat.

"Look at the size of that tank!" Spartacus stated.

The tank was a behemoth, a mighty metal colossus, its huge cannon fixed on the drawbridge like the baleful gaze of a steel cyclops.

"We'll have to take out that tank," Hickok said thoughtfully.

"How?" Spartacus demanded. "We don't have any explosives."

"Then we'll improvise," Hickok remarked.

"How?" Spartacus reitereated. "What will we use to stop a tank?"

"A pillowcase."

"A what?" Spartacus leaned closer to the gunman, certain he had heard incorrectly.

"A pillowcase," Hickok repeated. "Have somebody run to B Block and get me a white pillowcase."

Spartacus started to speak, then thought better of the idea. He hurried off.

Hickok scanned the western rampart, noting the

nervous state of most of the 67 men and women
manning the wall. He couldn't say as he blamed them.
That blasted tank was a whopper.

Spartacus hurried up. "I've sent for the pillowcase."

"Good," Hickok said. "Now send runners to the
north and south walls. Have every other fighter report
here on the double, but tell 'em to keep their heads
down. I don't want the soldiers to see them when they
take their posts. Have 'em crouch below the top of the
wall. Pack 'em onto this rampart."

"On my way," Spartacus ran off.

Hickok pondered the formidable odds they were
facing. He was grateful the enemy was concentrating its
initial attack on the west wall of the Home. It meant
Sherry would be spared the first assault. But sooner or
later, the Army bozos would completely enclose the
compound. Sherry would experience her baptism of fire
as a Warrior. She, and the rest of the Family and the
Clan, would be overwhelmed by sheer force of
numbers.

Blast!

Why had he agreed to her becoming a Warrior?

What did he have for brains? Rocks?

Why were women such contrary critters? Why did all
women have this peculiar notion about doing everything
their way? Why couldn't they let the men run things?
Life would be so much simpler! With the menfolk as the
ramrods, everything would be—

He stopped himself, chuckling.

No, that wasn't such a great idea. The men had been
handling things before the Big Blast. Plato had once
said men had dominated society before the war. The
men had dictated the direction of the government and
the military.

And look where it had gotten them.

Blown to kingdom come!

Maybe the best way, the only way, was to have the
government and the military run along the same lines as
a family: by couples. That way, every time some dipsy
power-monger wanted an all-out war, his wife could
slap him upside the head and tell him to go fishing until

he cooled down. There was nothing like marriage to teach a man humility.

"Here's the pillowcase."

Hickok turned to his left.

Spartacus held a white pillowcase in his right hand.

"Thanks, pard." Hickok took the pillowcase and held it behind his back.

"How is that going to help us take out the tank?" Spartacus inquired.

"You'll see," Hickok promised. "Trust me."

There was a lot of commotion near the tank. A man in green fatigues and a taller man dressed all in brown were standing near the armored vehicle. Other soldiers were forming a column behind it.

"They're getting ready," Spartacus mentioned. "I hope you know what you're doing."

"It'll be a piece of cake," Hickok assured him.

Fighters from the north and south walls were shuffling along the western rampart, hunched over to prevent their detection by the enemy troops. They quickly filled in the open spaces on the west wall, their various weapons at the ready.

Perfect.

Hickok grinned. To the Army commander, it would appear as though there were only 69 defenders on the western wall, when in reality there were now 135.

Surprise!

Hickok glanced over his right shoulder at the four men manning the drawbridge mechanism. "Get ready to lower the drawbridge!" he shouted down to them.

"Lower the drawbridge?" Spartacus repeated in astonishment. "Are you crazy?"

"Tell everyone to fire on my order," Hickok instructed him.

"What do you have up your sleeve?" Spartacus asked. "I thought you said you want my input on everything."

"I have this up my sleeve," Hickok said, displaying the pillowcase. "I aim to—"

"They're coming!" a woman nearby screamed.

Hickok looked out over the field. Sure enough, the tank was advancing toward the Home. Two to three dozen soldiers followed behind it.

"No time now," the gunman said to Spartacus. "Just have everbody set to fire when I give the word." He hurried to the stairs.

Spartacus, annoyed, turned to the man on his right, a Family Blacksmith. "Pass the word along the wall. Fire on Hickok's command."

The Blacksmith started the message down the line of anxious defenders.

What was the gunfighter up to? Spartacus unslung his Heckler and Koch HK93 from his left shoulder and checked the magazine, his gaze on the gunman.

Hickok, armed only with his Colt Pythons, the white pillowcase in his right hand, descended the stairs to the ground. "Lower the drawbridge!" he barked at the quartet assigned to the mechanism.

The four men exchanged puzzled expressions, but they promptly did as they had been told.

Hickok stood on the inner bank of the moat, grinning in anticipation. He waited as the drawbridge slowly lowered toward him, thudding to a horizontal stop across the moat, its massive wooden planks mere inches from the Warrior's toes.

The tank and its deadly entourage had reached the halfway point between the forest and the west wall of the Home. The armored titan rumbled to an unexpected halt.

Hickok deliberately backed up, placing a good ten feet between the drawbridge and himself. He raised the white pillowcase and swung the material in wide circles over his blond head.

There was a metallic clanking sound, and an opening appeared on the top of the tank as an oval hatch of some kind was pushed aside. A man wearing a green helmet popped into view, visible from his shoulders up. He stared at the lowered drawbridge and the man waving the white flag, then twisted and yelled a few words to the men following the tank.

Hickok could readily imagine their confusion. They

were wondering if the Family was surrendering. Why else would someone be signaling with a white pillow-case?

Another man in green walked around the left side of the tank. He stopped and studied the situation with a pair of binoculars.

Hickok smiled, hoping he seemed appropriately friendly enough for the occasion.

The man in green, evidently an officer, lowered the binoculars and spoke to the man on the tank.

The man on the tank nodded, and at a word from him the gargantuan engine of destruction lumbered directly for the open drawbridge.

Hickok glanced up at the rampart. Spartacus looked like he was about to lay an egg. "Get that toothpick of yours ready," he directed his confused friend, as loudly as he dared.

Spartacus, his brow furrowed in consternation, slung the HK93 over his left shoulder and drew his broadsword.

Hickok watched the tank approach, heading straight toward him. Dear Spirit, but the blasted thing was *big*! He could see its titanic treads tearing up the soft soil as it neared the west wall. Clumps of brown dirt flew off to the sides.

The man with the helmet was still visible from the shoulders up, alertly scanning the drawbridge and the rampart for any indication of treachery.

Keep coming, moron! Hickok backed up some more, flapping the white pillowcase overhead.

The sound of the tank's motor was a strident roar by the time the monster reached the other side of the draw-bridge.

Hickok grinned and waved for all he was worth.

The man in the helmet cupped his hands around his mouth. "If you make one false move, I will blow you to shreds!"

Nice guy! Hickok retreated several more feet. "Don't!" he cried in false terror. "We surrender!"

"Just like that?" the man responded skeptically.

"We can't fight a tank!" Hickok shouted. "I don't

want any of our women and children hurt!"

Helmet-head nodded. He could understand such a motive. "I am coming across! No tricks!" he paused. "Hey! Aren't you the one who raided our camp and stole one of our jeeps?"

"It wasn't me!" Hickok lied. What did he mean— stole a jeep?

Helmet-head smirked and said something to whoever was inside the tank. It rolled across the drawbridge, treading carefully, inch by inch. Helmet-head glanced up at the rampart as he passed below it, but the defenders he could see weren't pointing their weapons in his direction.

Dozens of troopers closed in on the heels of the tank.

Hickok withdrew another eight feet or so.

The tank crawled over the drawbridge, stopping when it reached the inner bank.

Hickok found himself staring into the muzzle of the cannon. He detected a slight motion to his right, and realized a machine gun was covering him through a narrow port. He also noticed an inch or two of clear space between the barrel of the machine gun and the edges of the port.

An officer, the one with the binoculars, walked around the left side of the tank, taking care not to fall from the drawbridge into the moat. He had brown hair and an angular chin. "You are the Warrior known as Hickok, are you not?" he demanded as he halted in front of the vehicle, just to the left of the machine-gun port.

"Howdy!" Hickok beamed. "I'm right pleased to meet you."

"Cut the prattle, you buffoon!" the officer snapped. "I am Captain Luther. All of you will lay down your arms immediately!"

"Say 'pretty please' first," Hickok said.

Captain Luther scowled. "This isn't a joke, you idiot! Your surrender will be unconditional and immediate!"'

"Surrender? No one said we were surrenderin'," Hickok stated.

"What?" Captain Luther was turning red in the cheeks. "Then why were you waving a white flag?"

"Flies," Hickok replied.

"There aren't any flies at this time of year!" Captain Luther almost shrieked.

"My mistake," Hickok admitted. "I meant to say vermin."

In those final fleeting seconds, Captain Luther comprehended. He tried to turn, to shout a warning to his men.

He never uttered a word.

Hickok glanced up at Spartacus, nodded once, and dropped the white pillowcase as his hands flashed to his Pythons. He cleared leather and fired before the pillowcase reached the earth.

The gunman's shots caught Luther near the right ear and exploded out his forehead, raining blood and brains on the tank.

Even as the gunfighter drew, Spartacus was in motion. He took a flying leap from the rampart, his broadsword clutched in his right fist, and sailed over the heads of the soldiers below. His feet landed on the rear of the tank, on the very lip, and he nearly lost his balance before he recovered his footing and lunged at the man with the helmet.

Helmet-head heard the pounding of a heavy object behind him and spun.

Spartacus swung his broadsword with all the power in his muscular shoulders.

Helmet-head was about to yell an order when the point of the broadsword ripped into the left side of his throat and drove out the other side in a magnificent crimson spray.

Hickok pivoted, aiming for the machine-gun port, and fired three rounds into the small open space between the barrel and the port.

There was a ghastly scream from within the truck.

"Open fire!" Hickok cried at the top of his lungs.

The defenders on the western rampart entered the fray, all 133 of them concentrating their fire on the soldiers behind the tank.

About a dozen of the hapless troopers were on the drawbridge, and they bore the brunt of the onslaught. Their bodies jerked and rocked as bullet after bullet slammed into them.

The column of soldiers on the other side of the wall suffered the same fate; they were decimated by the hail of lead.

"Raise the drawbridge!" Hickok yelled.

A few of the troopers managed to return the fire, but they were speedily downed.

The mass of soldiers in the field beyond raised their voices in a mighty whoop and charged the Home.

"Raise the drawbridge!" Hickok shouted again.

The four men handling the mechanism were doing their best, but it was difficult for them with the added weight of the dozen troopers on the drawbridge.

On the tank, Spartacus stooped and shoved Helmethead downward. The lifeless body dropped from sight. Spartacus swiftly sheathed his broadsword and unslung the HK93. He stuck the barrel into the hatch and pulled the trigger.

There was screaming from within the metal coffin as the slugs whined and ricocheted from one side of the tank to another.

Hickok raced past the tank to the drawbridge.

There were a dozen bloody forms sprawled on the drawbridge. Another two dozen were lying on the ground outside the wall. Dashing toward the Home, already halfway across the field beyond, was the bulk of the strike force.

They had to get the blasted drawbridge up!

Hickok holstered the Pythons and frantically began rolling bodies from the drawbridge. The dead soldiers struck the water with a pronounced splash.

Two, three, four bodies landed in the moat.

The strike force was getting closer.

Hickok shoved two more troopers from the drawbridge. "Keep trying to raise it!" he ordered the quartet at the mechanism.

The four men were straining to their utmost, pushing on the metal lever responsible for activating the gears and chain.

"Need some help?" Spartacus joined the gunman, flinging bodies into the water as rapidly as he could.

Some of the charging soldiers began shooting. One or two bullets bit into the drawbridge near the harried Warriors.

The defenders on the west wall blasted away at the approaching soldiers.

Only one dead trooper left to go. Hickok grabbed the man's ankles and hauled him to the edge of the drawbridge. He kicked the body with his right foot, and it toppled from sight.

The drawbridge was beginning to elevate.

"Let's go!" Spartacus urged, running for the bank.

Hickok took three steps, and then something bit into his left thigh, wrenching his leg from under him. He fell to the wooden planks, clutching at his injury, blood flowing over his fingers.

He'd been hit!

Hickok glanced over his left shoulder.

A pair of soldiers had far outdistanced their companions. Miraculously untouched by the barrage of lead from the western rampart, they were rapidly closing on the drawbridge.

The drawbridge was still rising. It was now a foot above the inner bank.

Hickok rose to his hands and knees and made for the end of the drawbridge. He had to make it! He'd be cut to ribbons otherwise!

Spartacus, already safe on the bank, spied the gunman's predicament and jumped onto the drawbridge.

"Go back!" Hickok prompted. "Save yourself!"

Spartacus ignored the injuction and ran to Hickok's side. He looped his right arm under the gunman's shoulder and hauled Hickok to his feet. "You can take a nap later!"

A stitch work pattern of bullets bit into the wood at their feet.

Spartacus twisted, the HK93 cradled in his left arm. He leveled the barrel at the pair of nearest soldiers and let them have it.

The two soldiers reacted as if they had smacked into a wall, coming to an abrupt stop, their chests erupting in red dots, as they were brutally slammed onto their backs.

The drawbridge was now three feet above the bank.

The chattering of the M-16's and the popping and booming of the other guns involved in the battle attained a deafening crescendo. Exposed in the open, realizing their vulnerability, the soldiers in the field had checked their headlong rush and many were retreating, leaving dozens of their fallen comrades behind.

Spartacus and Hickok reached the end of the drawbridge.

The ground was four feet below.

"Can you make it?" Spartacus yelled in Hickok's left ear.

"I was hopin' you'd carry me piggyback," Hickok responded, grinning. He stepped free and pushed off with his good leg, vaulting to the inner bank of the moat. His left leg buckled as he landed and he tumbled onto his stomach.

Spartacus sprang to the grass. He leaned over and assisted the gunman in rising.

"Thanks, pard," Hickok said. "I owe you one."

With the drawbridge devoid of extra weight, the four men were able to speedily lift it to a verticle position.

The firing on the western rampart was tapering off.

Spartacus knelt and examined Hickok's left thigh. "It looks like it caught you in the fleshy part on the outside of your leg," he informed the gunman.

"Then it ain't nothin' to fret about," Hickok remarked. He began reloading the spent rounds in his Pythons.

"You should see the Healers," Spartacus recommended.

"Not now," Hickok said.

"But you're bleeding!" Spartacus protested.

"Not now," Hickok reiterated. He headed for the stairs, limping. "Come on."

Spartacus reluctantly followed.

Hickok replaced the Pythons in their holsters and ascended the stairs, gripping the railing to retain his footing until he reached the rampart.

"They've turned tail!" a man yelled.

Hickok and Spartacus peered over the top of the wall.

The strike force had reassembled near the woods. A tall man attired in brown clothing was bellowing at them.

"Who's he?" Spartacus absently asked.

"Beats me," Hickok replied. "Check our people. Give me a tally."

Spartacus nodded and left.

Hickok grimaced as a spasm lanced his left thigh.

Great!

Just great!

The battle had barely begun, and here he'd gone and gotten himself hit!

Dumb! Dumb! Dumb!

What a cow chip!

Hickok stopped berating himself and counted the bodies littering the field. Some of the dead soldiers were piled on top of one another, so an accurate count was difficult. As near as he could estimate, Hickok reckoned there were close to four dozen.

Plus the dozen on the bridge.

Five dozen. Not bad, he told himself. That only left about 1,940.

Only.

But at least the tank was out of commission.

The tall man in brown was lambasting the troops.

Hickok leaned on the top of the parapet, his arms extended to waist height, and prudently slid his fingers under the strands of barbed wire lining the outer edge of the wall.

"Look!" a nearby woman yelled.

The body of troops was filing into the forest.

What were they up to now? Hickok wondered.

The tall man in brown reappeared, carrying a white flag. Without hesitation, he strode toward the Home.

"One of them is coming this way!" stated a man on the gunman's left.

What was this action? Hickok squinted, trying to clearly see the man in brown, but he was still too far off.

Spartacus trotted up to the gunfighter.

"How'd we do?" Hickok asked him.

"You won't believe it," Spartacus replied.

"How many did we lose?" Hickok pressed him.

Spartacus beamed. "Not one."

"Are you serious?"

"A few nicks and scratches," Spartacus elaborated, "but not one dead. We were lucky."

"We caught them by surprise," Hickok stated. "We won't be able to pull a stunt like that again."

Spartacus noticed the man in brown approaching. "What's this?"

"Beats me," Hickok said, shrugging. "I reckon he wants to palaver."

"It's a trick," Spartacus stated. "He's doing to us what we did to them."

"Not likely," Hickok disagreed. "He left all his men in the trees. I think he really wants to talk."

"I'll go meet him," Spartacus offered.

"Nope."

"But you're hurt," Spartacus objected.

"I can still wobble with the best of 'em," Hickok responded. "Besides, I'll have my equalizers with me." He patted his Pythons. "If he so much as blinks crooked, I'll perforate his noggin'."

"I should go along," Spartacus protested.

"You'll stay put," Hickok ordered.

"Hickok—"

"Keep me covered." Hickok walked to the stairs and descended to the ground. "Lower the drawbridge," he told the four men.

Hickok stared at one of the dead troopers floating in the moat. Those bodies would have to be removed from the water before they polluted the stream. He gazed at the immobile tank, potentially useless unless it could be driven. How hard was it to drive a tank? Was it anything like driving a jeep or the SEAL? Somehow, he doubted it would be a piece of cake.

The drawbridge clanked to the ground.

The man in brown was waiting on the other side, about 20 yards from the west wall.

Hickok nonchalantly placed his thumbs in his gunbelt and ambled from the compound. He wended his way among the scattered bodies until he was five feet from the man in brown.

"Hello, Hickok," the man said in a low voice.

Hickok studied the speaker. He was a big one, at least six and a half feet in height, and every square inch appeared to be solid muscle. His brown clothing, immaculately neat, served as a distinct contrast to the man's animalistic facial features; he had a pronounced forehead terminating in excessively bushy eyebrows, thick lips, a deformed nose, and two of his upper teeth protruded over his lower lip. His nose was deformed, almost flattened at its tip, and his skin was strangely pitted. A shock of black hair added to his bizarre aspect.

"Should I know you, gruesome?" Hickok baited him.

"No," the big man conceded. "My name is Brutus."

"So what's with the white flag?" Hickok inquired. In reality, it was a strip of white sheeting affixed to a branch.

"I wanted to talk to you," Brutus revealed, his tone low and forceful, the trace of a grin touching the corners of his wide mouth.

"We have something to talk about?" Hickok retorted.

"The Doktor wants his notebooks," Brutus declared.

"What notebooks?" Hickok answered, stalling. How had the Doktor discovered the Family had them?

"Don't play games with me," Brutus warned. "The Doktor's last radio contact concerned four blue notebooks of his. They're his journals on his research and other activities. The Doktor wants them back. He knows one of your Warriors, Yama, stole them from Cheyenne before it was nuked. He knows the Family has them. Hand them over."

"Why don't you stick that branch where the sun don't shine," Hickok told him.

"I take it you refuse to turn the notebooks over?"
Brutus asked.

"Ain't you the bright one!" Hickok stated. "You
must make your momma real proud."

Brutus abruptly clenched his brawny fists, his face
reddening.

"Touchy, ain't we?" Hickok said. Why did Brutus
react so angrily to a harmless insult? Suddenly the
answer hit the gunman: Brutus didn't have a mother.
Brutus was one of the Doktor's test-tube creatures, one
of his genetically engineered deviates.

"I will have those notebooks," Brutus vowed, "one
way or the other."

"The Doktor wants them that bad, huh?" Hickok
queried, an idea occuring to him.

"The Doktor wants them," Brutis affirmed.

"Then you'd best take your tin soldiers and
skedaddle," Hickok said, "or I'll burn the notebooks to
ashes."

Brutus smiled. "Go ahead."

"But you just said the Doktor wants his journals
back," Hickok said in surprise.

"He does," Brutus confirmed, "but he wants the
Family destroyed even more than he wants his notebooks. Go ahead and burn them."

Hickok didn't respond. He knew the notebooks were
invaluable to the Family. The Family Elders were close
to deciphering the contents, and the information
gleaned so far indicated that the cause of the premature
senility affecting the older Family members was
contained in those notebooks.

Brutus gazed up at the west wall. "I will demolish
your Home."

"In case you hadn't noticed," Hickok reminded him,
"Some other idiot just tried. The Home is still
standing."

Brutus inexplicably smiled. "Captain Luther was an
inexperienced dolt! He really believed you were going to
surrender. He thought you were terrificd at the mere
sight of our troops and the tank." Brutus chuckled. "I
knew better, of course, but I couldn't convince him. I

knew it was a trick!" he bragged. "I advised him to keep most of our men in reserve, in case it was an ambush. And the jackass fell for it!" Brutus laughed crazily.

"I take it you were rather fond of old Luther?" Hickok quipped.

"With him gone," Brutus informed the Warrior, "I'm in charge now."

"From a jackass to a horse's ass," Hickok said. "I don't see where you're an improvement."

Brutus glared at the gunman.

"I must say," Hickok went on, taunting his foe, "I'm impressed by all the fancy words you sling around. I didn't think the Doktor's pets were that smart."

Brutus resembled a beet from the neck up. "I'll make you eat those words, you bastard! I'm one of the Doktor's favorites!"

"Whoop-de-do!"

"By this time tomorrow," Brutus pledged, "you will be dead, you and the rest of your miserable Family. I will show no mercy!"

"I have a question for you," Hickok stated.

Brutus, working himself into a frenzy over the gunman's insults, was taken aback by the comment. He stared at the Warrior, flustered. "What question?"

Hickok grinned. "How are you gonna get back to them trees?"

"What do you mean?"

"How are you gonna get from here," Hickok said, pointing to the grotesque man's exceptionally large feet, "to there." The gunman pointed at the forest 130 yards off.

"I'm going to walk," Brutus said.

"Wanna bet?" Hickok's hands hovered near the pearl grips on his Colt Pythons.

Brutus' bug-like eyes blinked rapidly. "Touch those guns and you're a dead man."

"Are you gonna scare me to death?" Hickok quipped.

"I suspected you might be treacherous," Brutus stated smugly. "That's why I instructed our sharpshooters to keep me covered. If you go for your guns, they'll make a sieve out of you!''

Hickok thoughtfully chewed on his lower lip, gauging the distance to the treeline.

Brutus, plainly nervous, took a step backwards.

"Hold on there, hoss," Hickok remarked, limping forward several steps.

"Don't even think it!" Brutus hissed.

Hickok grinned, exposing his even white teeth. "But I am thinkin' about it. And do you know what I'm thinkin'?"

Brutus didn't answer; his thick tongue flicked over his lips.

"I'm thinkin' I should blow you away, ugly," Hickok said. "I reckon those soldier boys might hightail it out of here if they don't have anybody to lead 'em."

"My sharpshooters will get you!" Brutus growled.

"Maybe." Hickok nodded. "But it's a long shot for them, and I'm only twenty yards from the Home and cover." He winked at Brutus. "I think I'm gonna go for it."

"Now you hold on!" Brutus exclaimed, a tinge of anxiety in his tone. "I came over here in good faith, under a white flag."

"Nobody asked you to come."

"I wanted to tell you how it is," Brutus mentioned.

Hickok smiled. "I know how it is."

"I'm not armed," Brutus pointed out.

"So?"

"You'd kill an unarmed man?" Brutus demanded.

Hickok laughed. "You Civilized types ain't much for brains, are you?" He indicated the wall behind him "You're threatening my Home, you scumbag! You want to kill my Family! I wouldn't care if you were on your knees, beggin' for mercy. I'd still blow you away."

Brutus glanced over his left shoulder at the woods. "At least give me a running start."

Hickok, overconfident, threw back his head and laughed again.

It was all the opening Brutus needed. His right foot swept up with surprising speed, catching the Warrior in his left thigh, impacting on the gunman's wound, right on the bullet hole in his leg.

Hickok reacted instantly, his hands diving for the Pythons, and he was clearing leather when the heavy black boot struck his injury, causing an intensely excruciating wave of agony to wash over his body, doubling him over as he staggered backwards.

Brutus knew better than to try to jump the Warrior when the gunman was holding his revolvers. He whirled and raced for the forest, running a zigzag pattern, dropping the branch with the white flag.

The Family and Clan defenders on the west wall were gaping at the stunned Warrior, momentarily distracted from the fleeing Brutus.

Hickok dropped to his right knee, shaking his head to clear the pain. He saw Brutus about 15 to 20 yards out, his sturdy legs pumping.

Something struck the ground in front of the gunman, spraying dirt over his moccasins.

The sharpshooters!

Hickok struggled to his feet and snapped off a shot from his right Python, his arm slightly unsteady from the torment in his leg.

More bullets were biting into the earth around the Warrior.

"Give him cover!" Spartacus shouted on the rampart.

The Family and Clan fighters started firing at the trees.

Hickok was furious! His first shot had apparently missed! The son of a bitch was still on his feet and making for the woods. Hickok forced his mind to ignore the anguish in his leg.

He couldn't let Brutus get away!

The left Colt boomed and bucked in his hand.

About 40 yards away, Brutus stumbled and almost fell. He recovered and continued his mad sprint for the safety of the forest.

Blast!

Hickok hobbled to his right as the turf near him erupted in a shower of dirt and dry grass.

He had to hurry!

Both Pythons blasted.

Over 50 yards off, Brutus flung his long arms out and pitched onto his face.

Something tugged at Hickok's right shoulder. He disregarded a fleeting twinge and limped forward, wanting to be sure, to put a few more rounds into Brutus.

More and more dirt kicked up at the gunfighter's feet.

Brutus was on his hands and knees, wobbly, endeavoring to rise.

A squad of 15 soldiers burst from the tree line, hastening to the rescue of their leader, firing their M-16's.

He had to nail Brutus!

Hickok managed three more shots, when strong arms encircled him from the rear and bodily lifted him from his feet.

"We can't afford to lose you!" declared a voice in the gunman's ear.

"Let me go!" Hickok bellowed. "I can get him, Spartacus!"

Spartacus, flanked by six other defenders, hurried toward the drawbridge, dragging the reluctant Hickok with him.

Although his arms were pinned to his side, Hickok could still move his elbows and wrists. He angled the barrels of his Pythons and fired each revolver.

Brutus, on his feet again, spun and clutched at his right side.

Dozens of troopers had emerged from the forest and were providing cover fire.

Spartacus reached the drawbridge with his squirming friend. A young woman from the Family abruptly groaned and toppled to the hard ground, not a foot away.

"Grab her!" Spartacus directed as he crossed the drawbridge.

Hickok ceased resisting once they were in the center of the drawbridge.

"Raise the drawbridge once we're all inside!" Spartacus commanded. He reached the inner bank and released the gunman.

The defenders on the west wall were still embroiled in their fire fight.

Hickok turned, frowning. "Why'd you butt in, pard?" he demanded. "I almost had the sucker."

Spartacus placed his right hand on the gunman's left shoulder. "There were too many of them. They were getting your range. Look. You've been hit again."

Hickok glanced at his right shoulder. The buckskin fabric was torn, revealing a crimson patch underneath.

"I appreciate what you tried to do," Spartacus continued, "but killing him was no guarantee the others would leave us alone."

"It was worth a shot," Hickok disputed him.

The drawbridge was clear, and the four men working the mechanism quickly elevated it.

The shooting on the western rampart was tapering off.

"Spartacus!" a man yelled down. "They made it to the trees!"

Hickok glanced up at the speaker, a burly Clan member with a Winchester. "And what about their leader? The guy in brown?"

"He must have been hurt real bad," the Clansman replied. "They had to carry him the last f y yards."

"At least it wasn't a total waste," Hickok opined.

"Now we're going to have the Healers examine you," Spartacus informed his fellow Warrior.

"It's too bad you're not hitched yet, pard," Hickok said.

"Why's that?" Spartacus asked.

Hickok smirked. "Because someday you're gonna make some child a terrific mother."

11

Imperial Assassins?

The first figure in black crossed the living room in four strides, swinging his sword in a vicious arc, aiming at the giant Warrior's neck.

Blade reacted instinctively, whipping his right Bowie from its sheath and parrying the sword. The two weapons produced a loud clanging sound as they collided.

The man in black was well trained. He turned the parry into another strike, bringing his sword down and around, going for the Warrior's knees.

Blade lunged backward, narrowly evading the keen edge of his opponent's sword. Before the figure could recover, Blade surged in and up with all of his prodigious strength.

The man in black grunted as the Bowie was imbedded in his chest. His head lolled back and a great gush of air escaped from his lips.

Blade wrenched his Bowie free and stood aside.

The man in black tumbled to the floor.

Blade twisted to confront the other two.

They were gone.

What the . . . ?

Blade cautiously moved toward the archway separating the living room from the kitchen.

Where had they gone? Who were the Imperial Assassins? Why did they dress all in black and carry Oriental weaponry? A memory stirred in the recesses of

Blade's mind. He recalled one of the martial arts books in the Family library. What was the title of it? *Masters of Death: The Ninja.* Come to think of it, there were a number of books dealing with the ninja. These Imperial Assassins reminded him of the traditional descriptions of the ninja. Was it possible? Were these Imperial Assassins really ninja, or simply elite soldiers trained in the martial arts and dressed as ninja?

Blade's untimely speculation nearly cost him his life.

He had reached the archway and paused, glancing to his right and scanning the kitchen.

The second Assassin came at him from the left, from the doorway near the refrigerator, his sword a blur.

Blade dodged to his right, unable to block the blow.

The sword tore into the Warrior's left leg, tearing the fabric on his fatigue pants but missing his skin.

Blade kept going. He needed more room to maneuver if he hoped to pit his shorter Bowies against the Assassin's swords. He lunged for the door. The inner, wooden door was already open. He gripped the handle to the screen door, pressed and heaved. His momentum carried him through the doorway onto the porch beyond, even as another blow of the sword narrowly missed his back.

Get clear of the house! he told himself.

Blade reached the end of the porch and drew his other Bowie, about to whirl and confront his attacker.

The third Assassin unexpectedly popped into view at the corner of the house nearest the porch, his right leg extended and rigid, standing directly in front of the huge Warrior.

Blade felt a sharp pain in his ankles, and the next moment he was flying head over heels to the ground. He landed prone, the impact jarring his body.

The second Imperial Assassin emerged from the house and joined his companion. They proceeded to circle the Warrior, their swords held high.

Blade, perplexed, rolled to his feet. What was going on? Why hadn't they finished him when they had the chance?

"Samuel wants you to die slowly," the second

Assassin said, "for all the grief you've caused him."

"We're going to carve you into little pieces," vowed the third Assassin.

Blade crouched, his knives held close to his waist. He detected movement about ten feet past the Assassins and risked a swift look.

The second Assassin took a step toward the Warrior, then stopped in confusion as his foe inexplicably straightened and grinned.

"I don't suppose I could prevail on you to give up?" Blade asked them.

The third Assassin snorted derisively. "Give up? Are you insane? It's two against one. You don't stand a chance!"

"It's two against two," stated a quiet voice behind them.

The pair of Imperial Assassins shifted their positions, turning their bodies so they could keep an eye on Blade while confronting this new threat.

"You!" the third Assassin growled.

He stood at ease, his katana in its scabbard in his right hand, his dark eyes moving from one Assassin to the other, measuring them.

"You are the one called Rikki-Tikki-Tavi," the third Assassin stated.

Rikki drew his katana and dropped the scabbard to the ground.

"We have heard of you," the third Assassin said. "You are the Warrior who thinks he is samurai," he stated disdainfully.

Rikki spread his legs apart and squatted, holding his katana above his head, waiting.

"You think you can take us?" demanded the third Assassin.

Rikki glanced at Blade. "With your permission?"

Blade nodded and smiled. "Be my guest."

The third Imperial Assassin rushed at his smaller adversary, driving his sword down and in, going for the Warrior's chest.

Rikki-Tikki-Tavi's motion was an indistinct streak. One instant he was facing the Assassin with his katana angled over his black hair; the next, he was standing slightly to the right of his original position, his katana extended at chest level, its blade coated with crimson.

The third Assassin stiffened and slowly turned, revealing a cleft from his forehead to his chin. Blood pulsed from his split face. He gasped and staggered for a few feet, before finally collapsing.

The second Assassin began to back away from the diminutive Warrior.

"Going somewhere?" Blade demanded.

The second Imperial Assassin closed on the Warrior chief.

Blade easily parried the Assassin's blows with his Bowie knives, retreating a few steps as he did, the harsh clashing of their blades ringing out over the lawn. His Bowies, each 16 inches long with 9 1/2 inches devoted to the blade, sturdily withstood the Assassin's furious onslaught.

The Assassin, determined to dispatch his huge foe and make good his escape, concentrated all of his attention on his opponent, forgetting all about Rikki-Tikki-Tavi.

A ruinous oversight.

Rikki silently crept up behind the Imperial Assassin. He held his katana in his left hand, its keen edge to his rear, its point aimed downward. He did not intend to use it.

Savagely striving to break through Blade's skillful guard, the Assassin was abruptly startled by the shattering sound of a piercing kiai coming from directly behind him. He whirled, thinking he was about to be attacked.

He was right.

Rikki-Tikki-Tavi was sheer lightning in his execution: his right foot flicked up and out, catching the Assassin on the right knee, breaking it, the Assassin shrieking as a loud snapping noise greeted the blow; his right hand flashed upward in the tegatana-naka-uchi, the handsword cross-body chop, and struck the Assassin on the right side of the neck, stunning his foe. Before the Assassin could recover, Rikki performed the oi-mae-geri-age, the front lunge upper kick, his right foot slamming into the Assassin's right temple.

The Imperial Assassin staggered to one side, then collapsed in a senseless heap.

Rikki calmly turned and recovered his scabbard. He wiped the katana clean on his left pants leg.

Blade knelt by the Imperial Assassin and checked for additional weapons. He found two short knives, a derringer, and a kyoketsu-shogei—a sharp knife attached to a lengthy cord.

Rikki replaced the katana in its scabbard and joined Blade. "They were not extremely skilled," he commented.

Blade nodded in agreement. "True. But they would probably defeat an ordinary man without much difficulty. Our training has simply been more extensive than theirs."

"What should we do with him?" Rikki dutifully inquired.

"We'll let him enjoy his nap," Blade responded, "while you check this green house again and the neighboring yards. There might be more of them lurking about."

"On my way." Rikki moved toward the house.

"Hey!" Blade called after him.

Rikki paused and glanced over his right shoulder.

"Were you looking for me?" Blade asked.

Rikki stared at the dead Imperial Assassin. "I wanted to let you know the column was taking a break, as you ordered."

"Was that all?" Blade pressed him.

Rikki shook his head. "I wanted to insure you were all right. We can't afford to lose you now, and we are in enemy territory."

"Thanks."

Rikki smiled. He walked to the green house and vanished inside.

Blade absently gazed at the unconscious Assassin. Rikki certainly was an excellent Warrior, he told himself. Which would make it all the harder to select someone to become the head Warrior if he decided to assume the post of Family Leader. No one could hold both positions simultaneously. Who should he pick to succeed him? Rikki? Hickok? Geronimo? Yama? All four were outstanding Warriors and all four had considerable combat experience. Hickok and Rikki were undoubtedly the deadliest of the bunch, but Hickok was prone to making rash decisions and allowing his emotions to dictate his course of action. Hardly a desirable trait for the head Warrior. Rikki, on the other hand, was always cool and collected.

Damn. It wasn't going to be easy. But he must pick a new Warrior chief after he became—

After he became?

The realization shocked him. He had already decided to accept Plato's offer, to become the Leader of the Family after Plato stepped down. He hadn't been conscious of making such a decision, but he knew it was how he felt.

Maybe it was for the best. Blade had to face facts. He was growing tired of the constant conflict, of the perpetual fighting, of the continual bloodshed. He needed a break. As Family Leader, he could leave the fighting to the Warriors while he tended to his family—to Jenny and their future children. What was Jenny doing right now? he wondered. Probably shooting the breeze with Sherry, Hickok's wife, and Cynthia, Geronimo's mate. Taking it easy.

Blade watched a white cloud float by overhead.

Some people had all the luck!

12

Day two of the seige.

"Why haven't they done anything yet?" demanded Spartacus impatiently. "Sunrise was hours ago."

"Maybe they're aimin' to make us sweat," Hickok replied.

"It's working," Spartacus declared. "No one got much sleep last night, and everyone is jumpy as all get out today."

Hickok yawned. "Not everyone."

The two Warriors stood on the west rampart above the drawbridge. The defenders had spent the night at their posts, fearing an assault under cover of darkness. But the enemy camp had been silent the whole night.

"I wish they'd do something!" Spartacus complained.

"No need for 'em to rush," Hickok countered. "The longer they take, the better for us." He slowly moved his right shoulder in a circular motion to relieve a stiffening of the muscles. The Healers had ministered to his wounds, applying a herbal ointment and a bandage to his left thigh and right shoulder.

"How do you figure?" Spartacus said.

"I reckon the odds are in our favor the longer this set-to continues," Hickok elaborated. "I doubt they lugged a ton of provisions along. They might have enough for a few days, even a week. But if we can hold out, Blade and the others will return. Then we'll wipe these pansies out."

"You're dreaming," Spartacus stated.

"How so?"

"We don't know how much food they've brought with them," Spartacus mentioned. "They could have enough to last a month. And we certainly don't know when Blade will return. Who knows how long his campaign against Samuel will take? A week? A month? Six months? Remember, Blade vowed not to come back until the Civilized Zone was defeated. We both know Blade is a man of his word."

Hickok laughed. "Do you always look at the negative side of things?"

"No," Spartacus replied. "I'm being realistic."

Hickok cocked his head, listening. Odd noises were emanating from the forest: sawing sounds, hammering, and shouting.

"Do you hear that?" Spartacus queried.

"Sure do, Pard."

"They're making ladders," Spartacus deduced.

"Most likely," Hickok concurred.

"Shouldn't we be preparing?" Spartacus demanded, slightly irritated by the gunman's poise when the Home was faced with imminent destruction.

"I'm working on it," Hickok informed him.

Spartacus glanced over his right shoulder at the tank. "What about that?"

Hickok followed the direction of his friend's gaze. "The tank?"

"Sure. Why not? The engine died right after we shot into it, but it may still work."

"And who's gonna drive that thing?" Hickok asked. "You?"

"I don't know how to drive a tank," Spartacus stated.

"And the Founder didn't leave us any books in the library on tank drivin'," Hickok quipped. "Darn! I guess the man couldn't think of everything!"

"All right," Spartacus said. "So none of us have driven a tank before. But one of us has driven the SEAL a number of times."

"I'm the only one who's dri—" Hickok began, then

stopped.

"Exactly," Spartacus declared, grinning.

"I don't know how to drive a tank," Hickok commented.

"You could try," Spartacus urged him.

"So could you."

"Are you chicken?" Spartacus cracked.

"I ain't no chicken," Hickok responded indignantly.

"Then why not try it? What have you got to lose?" Spartacus pressed him.

Hickok stared at the metal titan. He had other notions on how to defend the Home, but the tank would definitely come in handy. If he could drive the critter. "Are those bodies still in there?"

"Nope," Spartacus answered. "I had some of the men take them out and bury them last night, along with those bodies we fished out of the moat."

"Keep a watch," Hickok directed. He walked down the stairs to the inner bank and over to the tank.

Some of the defenders on the west wall were watching him.

Blasted busybodies!

Hickok nonchalantly hooked his thumbs in his gunbelt and strolled around the armored vehicle, sizing it up. Treads. Cannon. Machine gun. What was it like inside?

There was only one way to find out.

Hickok clambered onto the massive vehicle. He stood on the body, near the cannon, and peered down the open hatch. The sunlight supplied ample illumination to reveal the interior. It looked sort of cramped way down there.

"Do you need a lantern?" one of the men manning the drawbridge called out.

Hickok glanced at the speaker, smiling. "Thanks. But I reckon I don't need one."

More of the defenders were gazing at the gunman.

Hickok peered into the tank again, frowning. Why couldn't folks mind their own business?

Oh, well.

Here goes nothing.

The gunman climbed onto the hatch, slid his lanky legs over the edge, and released his grip. He dropped to the floor and crouched, getting his bearings.

Unbelievable!

Hickok had never seen so many switches, dials, and gauges in all his born days! What the blazes were they used for?

A small seat was located near the front of the vehicle, close to a panel filled with various indicators and buttons.

Hickok eased onto the seat and examined the control bank. Let's see. How would you turn on a tank? Would it have a key like the SEAL?

There wasn't any sign of a key.

So much for that bright idea.

Hickok noticed a large black button on the console before him. Why didn't they label these things? He reached for the button, then hesitated, unsure of himself. What if the button fired the cannon? He'd wind up blowing one of the Blocks to smithereens.

Maybe he just ought to forget it!

Hickok studied another panel, situated above his head. If he was correct, then that panel activated the cannon.

But what if he was wrong?

The gunman spotted a narrow eye slit, or port, directly in front of him. He leaned forward and squinted through the opening. As near as he could tell, the cannon wasn't pointing at any of the Blocks.

So much the better.

What to do? What to do?

Frustrated by his own indecision, Hickok stabbed the large black button.

The engine kicked over, thundered for a moment, and died.

Maybe, Hickok hopefully told himself, the motor had kicked the bucket.

Undaunted, the gunfighter tried the ignition again.

The engine roared to life, and this time it didn't conk out.

Terrific!

Now what?

Hickok concentrated on a series of levers on his right. They vaguely resembled the gearshift in the SEAL.

Were these what he wanted?

Hickok gingerly took hold of one of the metal levers and attempted to move it forward.

There was a tremendous crunching and grinding noise, but the tank didn't budge.

What was he doing wrong?

Hickok scanned the instrument panel. He tried to recall every word Plato had said about the SEAL, and the directions given in the SEAL's Operations Manual. The SEAL was fitted with an automatic transmission. Hickok remembered reading about another type of transmission, one called a manual transmission. Or something to that effect.

What had the book said?

He vaguely recalled a mention of an object known as a clutch. But where would you find a clutch in a tank? Did a tank even have a clutch?

What were those funny pedals on the floor?

Hickok cautiously placed his right foot on one of the pedals. He depressed the pedal and the motor suddenly revved even louder, but the tank still didn't move.

Blast!

Annoyed, his right foot continuing to press on the pedal, Hickok pounded on the nearest lever. "Piece of junk!" he shouted, aggravated by his apparent failure.

Without any warning, and before the gunman quite knew what was happening, the tank unexpectedly lumbered into motion.

Backwards.

Straight backwards.

Toward the moat.

Hickok frantically jerked on the lever, striving to halt the huge behemoth in its tracks. The rear end suddenly tilted downward at a sharp angle, throwing the gunman from his tenuous seat onto the floor. A hard object gouged him in the back, between his shoulder blades. He scrambled onto his stomach and clawed for the lever as the front section continued to elevate, slanting the floor at a 45 degree angle.

The engine was sputtering.

Hickok's fingers were inches from the lever when the tank's movement abruptly ceased.

The motor had died again.

Hickok froze, listening. He debated whether to start the engine and drive the tank forward. The task would be a piece of cake now that he knew how to operate the lever. All he had to do was move the lever in the opposite direction. He grabbed for it under the false assumption the tank was perched on the bank of the moat.

He was wrong.

Water gushed over the rim of the open hatch, splashing over the gunman's head, cascading into the tank.

Hickok gawked at the hatch in astonishment.

He wasn't on the bank!

He was in the blasted moat!

The water was gaining in volume and intensity as the tank resumed its backward slide.

Hickok stood, resisting the pummeling of the water, and jumped toward the opening. His hands briefly clutched the edge of the hatch, but the surging water and the slippery metal conspired to knock him to the floor before he could climb from the vehicle.

Four inches of water already covered the floor of the tank. Additional gallons poured in every second.

Hickok leaped for the hatch again, and missed. He sputtered as the falling water struck him in the face, filling his inadvertently open mouth.

This was another wonderful mess he'd gotten himself into!

The steel colossus was still inching backwards into the moat.

Hickok determined to try one more time before there was too much water accumulated inside the tank and his movement was impaired. He grit his teeth and vaulted toward the hatch. His fingers gripped the edge, and he clung to the opening as the water battered his soaking body.

He had to hang on!

The force of the water was increasing.

Over six inches covered the floor.

Hickok felt his fingers beginning to slip. He tried to clamp down tighter on the hatch, but his fingers couldn't apply any more pressure.

If he didn't make it this time, he wouldn't get another chance!

Hickok attempted to pull himself up through the hatch, but the water resisted his every effort, a liquid wall of immeasurable pressure, an irresistible force impossible for one man to overcome.

But not two men.

Hickok was clinging by his fingertips, about to drop to a watery doom, when a pair of strong hands grabbed his wrists. He could feel his benefactor straining to haul him to safety. Hickok took a gamble. His rescuer would need some help. The gunman swung his legs to the left, pressing his feet against the side of the tank for extra support, and pushed, releasing his hold on the hatch as he did.

The gambit worked.

Hickok's momentum, added to the heaving of his helper, carried him up and through the hatch. He sprawled on the top of the tank, his legs within the tank, and glanced up.

"This is getting to be a habit," Spartacus remarked. He was standing on the forward section of the tank, which was still above the water line.

Hickok coughed and pulled himself from the hatchway.

The tank was lowering even further into the moat.

"Let's get off this thing," Spartacus suggested. He turned and sprang to the inner bank, not two feet from the front of the vehicle.

Hickok coughed as he slid below the cannon to the only portion of the tank clear of the water. He rose to his knees.

"Hurry it up!" Spartacus cried, waving him on. "It's going down!"

Hickok nearly lost his balance and pitched into the

moat as the tank abruptly lurched to one side. It was all the incentive he needed. His legs uncoiled under him and he bounded to safety on the bank.

"It looks like it's hit bottom," Spartacus commented.

Hickok, bent over at the waist, his hands on his knees, his breathing labored from his exertion, stared at the tank.

The armored titan had finally come to rest on the bottom of the moat. The water covered about two-thirds of the vehicle, including the top hatch. Most of the cannon and the rest of the front was angled upward only a couple of feet from the inner bank.

"Pretty slick move," Spartacus mentioned.

Hickok, certain his ears were waterlogged, glanced up at his friend. "Huh?"

"Pretty slick move," Spartacus repeated. "It almost worked perfectly."

"It did?" Hickok absently said, wondering what in the world Spartacus was raving about.

"Sure," stated his companion. "How were you to know the water would rush in there so fast? But I still think it's a great idea, blocking the entrance the way you did."

Hickok gazed at the moat, his eyes widening in amazement. He had managed to sink the tank directly in front of the drawbridge.

"I never would have thought of it," Spartacus admitted. "I've got to hand it to you. This way, even if they breach the drawbridge, they'll have to go around the tank to reach the compound. It'll slow them up considerably, and we'll be able to pick them off. Great move!"

"Thanks, pard," Hickok mumbled.

"I guess you couldn't figure out how to use the cannon, so you decided to do the next best thing, right?" Spartacus inquired.

"It was a mite more complicated than I thought," Hickok admitted.

"Weren't you worried you'd drown?" Spartacus asked.

"Worry? Me?" Hickok chuckled. "I knew it'd be a piece of cake."

13

"He's coming around," Rikki-Tikki-Tavi declared. "Finally."

The Imperial Assassin opened his brown eyes, his head throbbing. He was lying on the grass in the center of a small park, completely surrounded by his enemies. Someone had removed all of his weapons and stripped off his black mask. His aching right knee was in a splint.

"We didn't think you'd pull through," Blade said. He stood next to the Assassin's left shoulder. "Rikki kicked you a little harder than he thought. You've been out over twenty-four hours." Blade squatted, then reached down and took hold of the Assassin's curly brown hair. He brutally tugged on the Assassin's hair, compelling the prisoner to rise to a sitting position.

"Hey!" the Assassin snapped. "That's my hair!'"

"Would you like to keep your hair?" Blade demanded harsly.

"What do you mean?" the Assassin replied.

"I'm going to ask you some questions," Blade stated, "and I want an honest answer to every one."

"I'm not telling you a damn thing!" the Assassin retorted.

"I don't have time to play games with you," Blade told him.

"You can't make me talk!" the Assassin defiantly exclaimed.

Blade sighed and glanced at a tall man dressed all in blue on his left. Rikki-Tikki-Tavi stood to Blade's right.

127

"Looks like we have a tough one here," the man in blue remarked as the breeze stirred his silver hair.

"Yama," Blade said to the one in blue, "I'd like you to meet an Imperial Assassin."

Yama grinned, his eyes locking on the Assassin's. "We both deal in the same trade," he commented.

"The same trade?" the Assassin repeated.

Yama nodded. "Death."

"Are you going to cooperate?" Blade asked the Assassin.

The Assassin stubbornly shook his head.

"Suit yourself," Blade said, shrugging. He looked at Yama. "In his left ear," he directed.

Before the Assassin could grasp the implication, Yama stepped closer and rammed the barrel of his Wilkinson Carbine into the Assassin's left ear.

The Assassin instinctively tried to draw away.

Blade wrenched on the Assassin's curly hair to restrain him. "Don't move!" he barked.

The Assassin froze, gazing at Yama.

"Now, as I was saying," Blade stated harshly, "I'm going to ask you some questions. If you don't answer, or if I suspect you're lying to me, I will nod my head and Yama will put a bullet in your brain. Do you understand?"

The Assassin moved his thin lips but nothing came out. He considered himself to be an excellent judge of character, and he was profoundly impressed by the flinty glint of Yama's steely blue eyes. Here was a Warrior who would kill him without a moment's hesitation.

"I can't hear you," Blade said.

"What . . . what do you want to know?" the Assassin stammered.

"That's better," Blade said, smiling. "What was your assignment?"

"To assassinate you," the Assassin revealed.

"Be specific," Blade ordered.

"Samuel the Second sent the three of us to spy on your column," the Assassin disclosed. "We were to keep an eye out for you and, if the opportunity presented itself, to kill you. But we were to let you know he sent us, so you would know who was responsible. He wanted us to kill you slowly. He wanted you to suffer.''

"Sounds like you're one of Sammy's favorite people," interjected a furry newcomer.

Lynx and Teucer had joined the interrogation team.

"Why assassinate only me?" Blade wanted to know.

"Samuel said if we took care of you," the Assassin elaborated, "your army would retreat from the Civilized Zone.''

Blade thoughtfully stroked his square chin. "Where have all the people gone? All the people in Fort Collins and Loveland and here?"

The Assassin glanced at Yama, then cleared his throat. "They've all been evacuated to Denver.''

"Why?" Blade inquired.

"Samuel knows what you did in Cheyenne," the Assassin replied. "I heard him tell one of his generals he's afraid you will use a thermo on one of his cities.''

Blade looked at Lynx, who threw back his feline head and laughed.

"Did I say something funny?" the Assassin asked in perplexity.

"Never mind," Blade said. He studied the Assassin for a minute. "How many Imperial Assassins are there?''

"Twenty," the Assassin responded, then hastily added, "but just eighteen now.''

"What is your function?"

"We're the personal bodyguards for Samuel the Second," the Assassin disclosed. "Samuel picks us from his army commando unit. We're the very best," he said proudly.

"Then you are loyal to Samuel the Second?" Blade demanded.

"We don't have any choice," the Assassin stated.

"Why not?"

"Anyone who disobeys Samuel is put to death," the Assassin said bitterly. "Even our families are killed.''

"What's your name?" Blade queried.

The Assassin hesitated.

"What's your name?" Blade repeated.

"George," the Assassin mumbled.

Lynx laughed.

"Well, George," Blade said, "how would you like to live in a free society? How would you like Samuel the Second's tyranny to end?"

George stared at Blade, bewildered. "A free society?"

"With elected leaders of your choice running your government," Blade detailed. "Your people could set up a government similar to the one they had before the war. Only this time select your leaders wisely."

"You're kidding, right?" George said.

"No."

"But Samuel told us you intend to conquer the Civilized Zone and rule it yourselves," George declared.

Blade chuckled. "Believe me. We have no interest in ruling the Civilized Zone. The reason we are here—and I speak for the Family, the Clan, the Moles, and the Cavalry on this—is because Samuel the Second intends to subdue us and subjugate us to his will. That we will not allow."

Rikki-Tikki-Tavi spoke up. "We already know there is a sizeable segment of the Civilized Zone populace unhappy with the status quo."

"Many people are tired of the dictatorship," George agreed, "but we haven't been able to do anything about it, what with the military backing Samuel. Not to mention the Doktor."

"You won't have to worry about the Doktor anymore," Blade informed him.

George's pale features brightened. "Really?"

"Really," Blade assured him. He paused. "What kind of reception does Samuel have planned for us?"

"He has his troops manning the wall."

"The wall?"

"Sure. Didn't you know?" George asked. "The Army Corps of Engineers built a big wall around Denver, like the one they have around Cheyenne. It was built long ago, right after the war."

"How many soldiers are at his command?" Blade
inquired.

"About a thousand," George answered.

"That doesn't make sense," Blade stated. "He
should have more than a thousand."

"He does," George confirmed.

"How many? Where are they?" Blade pressed him.

"About two thousand or so," George said. "I don't
know where they are." He looked up at Yama. "Really
and truly I don't."

Blade stood and stared at the mountains to the west,
visible above the buildings bordering the park. So! He'd
been right all along. Samuel II did have more troops.
But where were they?

"What will you do with me?" George asked
nervously.

Blade gazed down at the Assassin. "We will hold you
as our prisoner until this campaign is concluded."

"You're not going to kill me?"

"No."

George breathed a tremendous sigh of obvious relief.

"What's the quickest way to Denver?" Blade
inquired.

George pointed to the east. "Take 56 east to Interstate 25. Follow 25 south into Denver."

"Get the convoy ready to move out," Blade said to
Rikki.

Rikki nodded and left.

Blade nodded at Yama, who stepped back, with-
drawing his Wilkinson from the Assassin's ear.

George rose to his feet, anxiously eyeing those around
him.

"Let me pose another question," Blade said.

"Sure," George responded.

"What would happen if Samuel was killed? If the
military rule of the Civilized Zone was overthrown?
How would the average person react?" Blade queried.

"They'd be dancing in the streets."

"You really think so?" Blade asked.

"No one likes living under a dictator," George
stated.

Blade looked at Yama. "Take him away. Place him in one of the trucks. Tie him up."

"I won't run away," George said. "I promise."

"Sorry," Blade remarked. "I can't take the chance. We'll release you after this is all over."

Yama motioned for George to start toward the parked troop transports, then followed. George moved slowly, limping, his knee hurting.

"So, big guy," Lynx said in his high voice, "it looks like the showdown is almost here."

"I just wish I knew where those missing two thousand troops are," Blade commented, worried.

"What's the big deal?" Lynx demanded. "If they show their ugly faces, we'll stomp 'em into the dirt! Who cares where they are?"

"I care," Blade replied.

"Boy, are you a worrywart!" Lynx exclaimed sarcastically.

Blade glanced down into Lynx's lively green eyes. "You think so?"

"I know so," Lynx affirmed. "Look! You've got everything going your way. Sammy is holed up in Denver, pissin' in his pants. His Army isn't at full strength. The people will probably make you a national hero if you kick Sammy's butt. And you sent that guy . . ." Lynx paused. "What was his name again?"

"Toland."

"Yeah. You sent that Toland guy from Cheyenne to spread the word that you were coming. He was a rebel leader, wasn't he?"

"Yes."

"So he's out gathering all the rebels so they can meet you at Denver. Sammy doesn't stand a snowball's chance in hell."

"I appreciate your analysis," Blade said.

"Anytime," Lynx commented. "Say, how long do you think it will take us to reach Denver?"

"I don't know," Blade answered. "We're close. Not more than fifty miles away. But we'll be moving very slowly. I won't run the risk of an ambush." He paused. "Why'd you want to know?"

"I was kind of hoping we'd run across an open post office," Lynx said, grinning.

"A post office?"

"Yeah. You know. Where you send mail and packages and stuff like that."

"We don't have post offices outside the Civilized Zone," Blade reminded his furry associate.

"Oh. Yeah. That's right," Lynx said.

"What do you want one of these post offices for?" Blade inquired.

"I wanted to send a package to Sammy."

"A package?" Blade reiterated, puzzled.

"Yep. A box of diapers." Lynx chuckled.

"Diapers?"

"Of course," Lynx stated. "I don't want Sammy to be all smelly when I rip 'im to shreds!"

14

Where in the world was he?

The eastern horizon was tinged with a touch of red and pink, indicating the dawn was not far off.

He had to keep his eyes open!

He had to!

But he was so very, very tired. More fatigued than he had ever been. His eyelids drooped lower and lower with each passing minute. And small wonder! When was the last time he had slept? Wasn't it that nap he took in the troop transport? He sighed. Maybe he should have taken Boone up on the offer to have a Cavalryman accompany him. Then again, none of the Cavalrymen knew how to drive a jeep. And—so he reasoned—the less weight in the jeep, the more mileage he could get out of each gallon of gas. His fuel consumption was crucial. He'd barely have enough to reach Denver and warn Blade as it was!

Boone and his men had arrived at the truck less than an hour before he took off in the stolen jeep. He'd been overjoyed to learn Hickok was alive and well.

He vigorously shook his head, striving to resist his overpowering impulse to sleep. Sweet sleep. Great Spirit, preserve him!

Was he still heading in the right direction? It was difficult to determine without the aid of a map. So far as he knew, he was in southwestern South Dakota, not far from what had been once known as Rapid City. Amazingly, he hadn't encountered any opposition on

his journey. Once, the day before, he'd seen about a
dozen riders on a hill to his west. He speculated they
might have been Cavalry riders, but what if they hadn't
been?

He prayed the jeep would hold up. First, it had
sputtered and died in northeastern South Dakota. It'd
taken mere minutes to realize the jeep was out of fuel
and to refill the tank using one of the spare cans
attached to the rear of the vehicle. Then, when he'd
attempted to restart it, he must have done something
wrong. The engine had coughed and belched, but
wouldn't turn over, and a pungent odor had enveloped
the vehicle. He'd tried again and again to restart it, to
no avail.

Hours later, after the odor had dissipated, he was
able to get the motor running again.

But he'd lost so much time!

And then there'd been the mutate! One of those hair-
less, pus-covered, perpetually ravenous mutations
proliferating over the landscape since the Big Blast.
He'd spotted it lying in the center of the road,
apparently sunning itself, blocking his path. He debated
whether to simply shoot it, but he was leery of attracting
unwanted attention with the gunblast. The mutate had
been huge; driving around it was out of the question.
The highway was hemmed in on both sides by dense
forest. So he'd have to wait until the mutate rose and
shuffled into the trees. He was surprised the vile thing
hadn't seen his jeep, parked 500 yards away to the top
of a low rise. The moment the creature was out of sight,
he'd gunned the engine and continued his trip. He could
have tried to run the mutate down with his jeep, but the
vehicle might have been damaged.

So here he was, on his last legs, valiantly resisting an
urge to cease defying the inevitable and accept the neces-
sity of slumber. He found his mind drifting, and he
inadvertently closed his eyes.

Seconds passed.

With a start, he opened his eyes.

The jeep was heading toward a large boulder at the
side of the highway!

He wrenched on the steering wheel, aligning the vehicle on the road once more.

It was no use! He had to get some sleep! What good would it do anyone if he crashed?

He applied the brakes and pulled to the shoulder of the cracked and pothole-covered road. Disgusted at his lack of fortitude, he twisted the key to the Off position and leaned his weary forehead on the steering wheel.

Just a little sleep.

That was all he needed.

The sun rose above the eastern horizon, and the scenic countryside was suddenly aglow in soft yellow light.

He slowly raised his head, glancing around to insure he was alone. He didn't want anyone to sneak up—

What was that?

For a moment, he couldn't believe his eyes.

Where was he, anyway?

Had he taken a wrong turn in the darkness of the night?

There were four gigantic faces carved into a towering granite cliff. Each face must have been 50 to 60 feet high. Each had been carved in remarkable detail. The one on the left had an imposing countenance, highlighted by a sloping nose and the firm set of his chin. The second from the left seemed to have his hair parted in the middle, and he had an honest, open expression. The next one in line sported a thick mustache, and the last one a beard.

Was he dreaming?

The rising sun bathed the granite cliff in its fiery light, imparting an illusion of life to the four figures.

There was something about them.

His fatigued mind sluggishly reacted to the impressive sight, struggling to remember some elusive fact.

What was it?

Why did he—

It hit him!

He knew what it was.

Some of the books in the Family library contained photographs and references to this cliff.

Mount Rushmore.

Before the Big Blast, Mount Rushmore had been a national monument. Those four faces were the visages of four Presidents of the United States of America. What had their names been? He squinted up at the cliff, racking his memory. Lincoln was one, wasn't he? But he couldn't recall the identity of the others.

Did it matter?

They were symbols of a past glory, a glory obliterated by a nuclear war, a promise of greatness eradicated before it could attain fruition. Those four men were representative of a magnificent history, of a time when the people chose their leaders based on wisdom and loyalty to higher ideals. But in the years before the war, the populace had neglected its heritage. He remembered now. How the citizens had become apathetic and ignored the tremendous trust placed in their hands. How only a small percentage of the voters had bothered to exercise their constitutional right on election day. And how the people had selected leaders according to their image instead of their intelligence.

How sad.

How very sad.

He yawned and rubbed his sleepy eyes.

Why did people do it? he wondered.

Why did they always become so complacent about the most important matters in life? Why were they so willing to trade their hard-won freedoms for baubles, for a full stomach and a life of leisure?

Why was he babbling like an idiot?

He laughed and eased back in his seat, clutching his FNC Auto Rifle in his lap.

If he kept this nonsense up, he'd begin to sound like Hickok!

He glanced at the monument again, and noticed a wide crack running down the figure with the mustache. What had happened? Age? An earthquake? Tremors caused by a nearby nuclear blast? Whatever the case, Mount Rushmore wouldn't stand forever. Like all of mankind's accomplishments, it was destined to crumble and collapse without the constant, conscientious care it duly deserved. Whether it was a noble idea, a lofty ideal, or merely a scientific or engineering marvel, it would expire if not properly nurtured.

Enough, already!

He smiled at his rambling, closed his eyes and was asleep.

15

Day three of the siege.

One hour after dawn.

"I don't like the looks of this," Spartacus commented.

"You and me both, pard," Hickok agreed, peering at the enemy line through a pair of binoculars.

"What are they doing now?" Spartacus asked.

"Nothin'," the gunman replied. "They're waitin' for the word to attack."

Spartacus pointed at a mound of dirt near the tree line 150 yards from the west wall. "What do you suppose that is? They completed it during the night."

"I reckon they're hidin' somethin'," Hickok said.

"What?"

"How should I know?" Hickok rejoined. "I can't see through a pile of dirt."

The mysterious dirt mound was situated directly across the field from the drawbridge. On either side of the mound, their M-16's in their hands, were hundreds of soldiers. The scene was the same from each of the walls; whether it was the west, north, south, or east, hundreds of troops were lined up adjacent to a dirt mound.

"Did you get that gas like I told you?" Hickok inquired.

Spartacus nodded. "Blade took most of it with him. All I could locate were three cans."

"It'll have to do. Where did you put it?"

"I placed the cans about twenty yards north of the drawbridge," Spartacus responded. "They're hidden behind a tree near the moat."

"Perfect."

Spartacus scanned the line of soldiers. "Do you think we can hold them?"

Hickok lowered the binoculars. "We'll do our best, pard."

"At least they didn't attack last night," Spartacus commented.

"Did you get any sleep?" Hickok asked.

"I tried," Spartacus replied. "But I didn't get much."

"Me neither, pard," Hickok said. He surveyed the defenders nervously manning the western wall. "Two nights in a row without much shut-eye. I'll bet ol' Brutus planned it this way. Pretty crafty of the vermin."

"You think he's still alive?" Spartacus inquired.

Hickok nodded. "Yep. I got the impression Brutus is one tough hombre."

Spartacus looked at the gunman. "Say . . ." he began.

"What?"

"I noticed you placed Blade's wife, Jenny, and Geronimo's wife, Cynthia, in C Block with the Healers."

"Yeah? So?" Hickok responded defensively. "Jenny is a Healer, you know. And Cynthia can lend her a hand."

Spartacus grinned.

"What's so blamed humorous?" Hickok demanded.

"I—" Spartacus started to speak, then abruptly stopped.

The clear, penetrating blast of a bugle punctuated the crisp morning air.

"Uh-oh," Hickok said.

Again the bugle sounded. And a third time.

"Have you passed the word to fire on my command?" Hickok queried.

"The order was given," Spartacus replied.

"They'll begin the attack any second now," Hickok

mentioned.

The ground in front of the drawbridge suddenly erupted skyward as a powerful explosion rocked the west wall. Dirt and grass showered onto the western rampart, hitting the defenders.

"What was that?" Spartacus shouted in alarm as the noise and flying debris subsided.

"Beats me!" Hickok was striving to see through the swirling smoke and dust. What the blazes were they using? Now he knew why they'd built the dirt mound!

Another blast shook the west wall, this one closer to the drawbridge.

"They're getting the range!" Spartacus yelled.

Hickok leaned nearer to Spartacus so his voice could be heard. They were standing on the rampart above the drawbridge with other defenders on both sides. "We've got to clear the wall above the drawbridge!" Hickok directed, motioning for Spartacus to begin moving the defenders stationed to their left.

Spartacus promptly complied.

Hickok turned to his right. "Move!" he bellowed. "Get clear of the drawbridge!"

The rampart over the drawbridge was quickly evacuated, the defenders bunching on both sides.

All except for Hickok.

The gunman was still standing above the drawbridge when a shell struck the wooden structure dead center. The drawbridge was exceptionally sturdy; the Founder of the Home had insisted the bridge be four feet thick, and had told those constructing it to use the stoutest wood available. Consequently, although the west wall shook and the upper third of the drawbridge was blown to smithereens, the rest of the structure survived the first hit.

Hickok felt the rampart under his moccasined feet buckle and heave. He grabbed for the vertical lip of the wall and held fast until the quaking ceased.

The air was literally choked with smoke, dust, and minute wood fragments.

Hickok lurched to his left, his speed impaired by his

injured leg.

Spartacus appeared out of the grayish-white smoke. "What are you trying to do? Get yourself killed?"

"Thought I'd get a breath of fresh air before lunch," Hickok quipped, then coughed as some of the smoke got into his lungs.

The two Warriors moved away from the vicinity of the drawbridge.

A fourth detonation wracked the west wall of the Home, another hit on the drawbridge.

Hickok crouched, shielding his face from the shards of wood propelled by the force of the explosion. His ears were ringing. The enemy was obviously going for the drawbridge in the hope of breaching the compound's defenses. Once the drawbridge was gone, the Civilized Zone troops would still need to ford the inner moat. But with the drawbridge gone, the defenders on the west wall would be subject to gunfire from outside the wall and below it, if the soldiers could achieve a foothold.

"The firing has stopped," Spartacus noted.

Hickok flattened on the rampart and peered over the inner lip. Strands of smoke billowed around the drawbridge, partially obscuring it. He waited impatiently for the smoke to be dispelled by the breeze. How much of the drawbridge was still standing?

In another moment, he got his answer.

The smoke dissipated, revealing the realization of his worst fears; except for a three-foot section at the very bottom, attached to the enormous hinges, the drawbridge was gone!

Blast!

Hickok rose to his knees.

The west wall vibrated as yet another explosion jolted the rampart. This time the enemy gunner had aimed at a section of the upper wall 20 yards from the vacant gap where the drawbridge had once stood.

Screams and cries of agony arose from injured defenders.

More and more smoke covered the west wall.

"I'll go check!" Spartacus volunteered, and ran off.

Hickok stood, gazing toward the forest to the west.

The soldiers hadn't moved; they were formed into their ranks on either side of the dirt mound.

So!

Whatever they were using, it was apparent Brutus intended to subject the Home to a bombardment before launching his final assault.

What was that?

Hickok twisted, listening. He could hear explosions coming from every direction now. The other walls were under attack! He thought of Sherry, his wife, and forced the image from his mind. He had to concentrate on the matter at hand; too many lives depended on his judgment.

Spartacus hurried up. "Three hurt," he announced. "I'm having them taken down the stairs."

"Take everyone down the stairs," Hickok ordered.

"And leave the west rampart undefended?" Spartacus asked in surprise.

"Do it," Hickok stated.

Spartacus nodded and left.

Hickok moved to the stairs and descended to the inner bank. He stared up at the rampart, debating. Except for the demolished drawbridge, the stairs from the western rampart to the ground provided the only means of crossing the moat. Huge timbers had been imbedded in the bottom of the moat to support the stairs. It might be possible for the defenders to destroy the stairs, but why should they if they could turn the stairs into a strategic advantage?

Spartacus was supervising the evacuation of the west wall. The defenders moved in an orderly fashion down the stairs and gathered behind Hickok. Three of them, two men and a woman, were carried across the compound to C Block to be treated by the Family Healers. Another blast shattered a ten-foot section of wall before the evacuation was complete, but none of the defenders were injured.

"Are you the last one?" Hickok inquired as Spartacus came down and joined him.

"Yes," Spartacus answered, then added, "I hope you

know what you're doing."

Hickok faced the 66 defenders at his disposal. He pointed up at the west wall. "I don't reckon we can hold the wall with the drawbridge gone. And I don't see any sense to our standing up there getting our fool heads blown off waiting for the soldiers to attack." He paused. Every eye was fixed on him. "I want a skirmish line formed about ten yards from the moat," he informed them. "There isn't much cover, but we won't need much anyway. When those troopers come over the wall, they'll be sittin' ducks during the time it takes 'em to get through the barbed wire, over the parapet, and onto the rampart. That's when you hit those clowns with everything you've got. Any questions?"

No one spoke up.

"Okay." Hickok smiled at them. "Don't look so worried! It'll be a piece of cake!" he assured them.

"Form a line!" Spartacus interjected. "Keep about four feet between you and the next person. Hold your fire until Hickok gives the command."

The defenders began forming their line.

Another shell struck the west rampart. Other blasts, muted by the distance, sounded from the north, east, and south walls.

"Do you have matches with you?" Hickok asked Spartacus.

Spartacus nodded.

"Good. Then you'll be responsible for igniting the moat if we can't hold them," Hickok advised him.

"Should I await your signal?" Spartacus inquired.

"I'm not gonna have time for one if the fightin' is in full swing," Hickok said. "I'll leave it up to you. If they start to ford the moat, get to the gas cans."

"I'll handle it," Spartacus vowed.

The defenders had formed their skirmish line.

Hickok moved away from the west wall as another round hit home. Brutus was conducting his barrage in a leisurely manner, to judge by the spacing between rounds, or else they were low on shells for whatever type of artillery they were using. Then again, maybe Brutus was deliberately extending the barrage as long as possible, intending to further agitate the defenders' nerves and weaken their resolve.

Yes, sir.

If he ever got another chance, he was going to damn well make sure that Brutus acquired a new nostril . . . right in the center of the prick's forehead!

16

Day three of the seige.

One hour after the barrage began.

"It's stopped!" Sherry declared.

The east wall had sustained hit after hit, and 11 of the 69 defenders had been wounded by hurtling shrapnel or chunks of brick. A wide gap had been blown out of the southern quarter of the east wall.

The three Warriors in charge of the wall stood near the gap, their anxious eyes on the cleared field beyond.

"They'll be coming now," Crockett remarked. He had exchanged his Remington for a Beretta AR-70, converted to fully automatic by the Family Gunsmiths. His buckskins were coated with dust.

"I never thought I would see the day where our Home was under an attack like this," commented Samson, his camouflage outfit also caked with dirt. His Bushmaster Auto Pistols on his hips were fully loaded.

Sherry was thinking about Hickok. They had spent a few precious hours in their cabin the night before, and she had clung to him, covering every inch of his body with her lips, wishing the night would never end. She was terrified of losing him, the only man she had ever truly loved. Life without her flamboyant gunman was unthinkable. She wanted to be at his side now, instead of being on the east wall, her brown blouse and green pants as grimy as her companions, a M.A.C. 10 cradled in her tense hands.

"What are they waiting for?" Samson asked,

interrupting her reverie.

"For the smoke to clear," Crockett replied.

The tendrils of smoke were almost gone from the eastern field.

"Are the ropes all in place?" Crockett inquired, looking at the towering Samson.

"Yes," Samson responded. "One rope every twenty feet."

Sherry nervously licked her lips. The ropes were their only means of descending from the eastern rampart. Only the west wall had stairs leading up to the rampart; all of the other walls were manned by ascending the stairs on the west wall and following the rampart around to the appropriate post. Ropes with improvised grapling hooks had been placed along the east, north, and south walls, affording the defenders a ready avenue of escape if their positions became untenable. Unfortunately, at the inner base of each wall was the encircling moat. Defenders retreating from their posts would be extremely vulnerable as they attempted to navigate the moat to the compound beyond.

"Here they come!" Crockett suddenly exclaimed.

A great shout arose from the ranks of the 500 soldiers lined up 150 yards from the east wall. They surged forward, rushing toward the east wall, dozens of them holding assault ladders.

"They'll try for this breach," Samson mentioned, hefting his Bushmaster, his long hair swaying in the wind.

Crockett raised his right hand above his head. "On my command!" he shouted. Most of the defenders were crouched below the lip of the wall.

The troopers were racing full speed for the wall, some of them firing as they ran, ineffectual shots, the bullets striking the wall or missing entirely.

"Hold your fire!" Crockett yelled.

Only 40 yards separated the leading soldiers from the wall.

"Hold!" Crockett repeated.

Sherry felt a cold sweat break out all over her body. She thought of her family, safe in far-off Canada.

Then 30 yards.

"Hold!"

Then 20 yards.

"Fire!" Crockett screamed.

The defenders rose up and fired into the mass of charging men in green fatigues.

The front rows of troopers were torn to ribbons by the initial volley from the east wall. Soldiers twitched and jerked as round after round tore their bodies apart. Dozens dropped in their tracks. But the rest came on.

Crockett moved to the left, to the north, directing and goading the defenders.

The din was deafening.

Sherry saw a dense cluster of soldiers closing on the section of wall below her position. Samson was right. The troopers were concentrating on the breach in the wall. Even with the top portion gone, 15 feet of wall remained. The soldiers would have to use the ladders.

And use them they did.

Four ladders were thrown up against the wall below the breach. Soldiers started to climb upward while their comrades provided covering fire.

Sherry took a step forward, but before she could enter the fray and rake the troopers below, Samson reached the edge of the wall.

Resembling a magnificent titan, Samson stood in the middle of the breach, ignoring the gunfire from the enemy on the ground, and cut loose with his Bushmaster, catching the troopers on the ladders in a hail of lead, blasting them from the ladders and checking the assault.

Sherry glanced along the wall. Everywhere, defenders and troopers were embroiled in life-or-death struggles. So far, the defenders had managed to prevent any of the troopers from reaching the top of the wall.

Samson stepped back from the breach. "Reloading!" he shouted.

Sherry took his place.

The soldiers below had regrouped and were frantically mounting the ladders again. Some of them aimed at the blonde woman on the wall, their M-16's chattering as they fired.

Sherry could hear peculiar buzzing noises. Her left shoulder jerked backward as something slammed into her. She experienced a numbing sensation, but no pain. Undaunted, she angled the M.A.C. 10 over the wall and pointed it at the troopers milling below. She squeezed the trigger and held on tight as the gun bucked in her hands.

One of the soldiers was almost to the top of a ladder. Her burst caught him in the face, and his eyes and nose disappeared in a crimson geyser. His arms flung outwards, he toppled backward from the ladder, landing on several of his buddies below.

Sherry swung the M.A.C. 10 in a wide arc.

Four, five, six troopers were knocked to the ground as their forms were perforated by the slugs.

"Reloaded!" Samson bellowed, and shouldered her aside, his Bushmaster belching death and destruction.

Sherry ducked behind the parapet, her left shoulder stinging. She glanced at it. The fabric of her brown blouse was torn, and a rivulet of blood was pouring from the wound. She was surprised by the absence of pain.

A horrified scream attracted her attention.

About 15 yards to the north, three troopers had reached the top of the wall. One of them was hung up in the cicular strands of barbed wire attached to the top of the wall, but the other two had circumvented the barbed wire and reached the rampart, firing their M-16's at the defenders. Even as Sherry watched, a woman was struck in the chest; she screeched as she was hurled from the rampart by the impact, her body tumbling end over end until it splashed into the moat 20 feet below.

Sherry rose and ran toward the soldiers. They were facing to the north and didn't hear her approach. For a moment she hesitated pulling the trigger; she had never shot anyone in the back before. A training session with Hickok flashed through her mind. One of the Family had told her Hickok was capable of killing anyone, anytime, anywhere, and for no reason whatsoever. She had questioned him about the allegation. After he finished laughing, he told her part of the statement was true. He could kill, and would kill, anyone, anytime, and anywhere, if they posed a threat to his loved ones or himself. He denied killing for the sake of killing. But, as he took care to explain, killing to protect the ones you loved, to defend your Family and your Home, was justified. And, when it came time for the killing, he said it didn't matter how you did it, just so you got the job done. "Get the job done," he had advised her, "or all of those who depend on you will suffer because of your failure." For once, he hadn't bothered to use his phony Wild West lingo.

Get the job done.

Sherry let the two soldiers have it in the back. Her bullets smashed into them, stitching patterns across their shoulders, a string of bright red dots, and they pitched onto their stomachs on the rampart.

The one hung up in the barbed wire still had his M-16 in his hands. He twisted and aimed the barrel at the blonde woman.

Sherry whirled and squeezed the trigger on her M.A.C. 10

Nothing happened.

The gun was empty!

She saw the trooper smile as he realized her predicament, and his finger tightened on the trigger of his M-16.

Sherry tensed, expecting to be riddled by bullets.

The trooper's smiling visage suddenly exploded as the right side of his face sprayed outwards.

Crockett ran up to her, his Beretta smoking. He gripped her right shoulder. "Are you all right? You look pale."

"I'm fine," she mumbled.

"What? I can't hear you."

"I'm fine!" she said louder.

The east wall was now a writhing mass of defenders and troopers. At least a dozen of the soldiers had reached the top and were engaged in hand-to-hand combat with the defenders.

"We can't hold the wall!" Crockett shouted to

Sherry. "There are too many of them!"

Sherry hastily replaced the empty magazine in her M.A.C. 10.

Crockett shot a soldier endeavoring to clamber over the edge of the rampart. "We'll have to fall back!" he directed her. "Get as many as you can down the ropes and across the moat to the trees. The other walls are probably in the same shape we are, so it won't do any good to retreat along the other ramparts! Move!"

Sherry nodded and ran off, downing another trooper as she did. She found herself doubting the wisdom of Crockett's decision. The other walls might be holding their own; to abandon this wall would put the others in jeopardy. Still, how could she presume to doubt his command? She was a novice Warrior, new to her position, and Crockett was her leader, the boss of her Triad, of Zulu Triad. And now was not the time to squabble over his strategy.

A soldier loomed in front of her, frantically struggling to eject a spent magazine from his M-16.

Sherry cut him in half with the M.A.C. 10 and reached a group of seven defenders involved with pushing ladders from the wall and shooting at the mass of troopers below the wall. "Get down!" she yelled at them. "Use the rope and get to the ground! Hurry!"

One of them, a tall man, eyed her quizically for a second, then ran toward the nearest rope. The others followed on his heels.

Sherry took their post at the wall, risked a hasty look-see over the parapet, and drew back.

The soldiers were packed all along the base of the east wall, five or six deep in some spots. Dozens of ladders were inclined against the wall.

Crockett wasn't kidding.

They wouldn't be able to hold the wall.

Sherry fired a few rounds at the troopers below, hoping to stall their ascent. She ran further north, telling everyone she met to climb down the ropes. The defenders had temporarily repulsed the soldiers; all of the enemy who had attained the rampart were dead.

But the ones below were eager to take their place.

Crockett approached her, skirting fallen figures as he neared. "Everyone is on their way down!" he told her. "Samson and I will hold them up here. Get below with the rest!"

"My place is with you!" Sherry retorted.

"That's an order!"

Sherry reluctantly turned toward the closest rope, attached by its sturdy grappling hook to the lip of the rampart. She didn't relish deserting her fellow Warriors.

Crockett joined her at the rope. "Get everyone into the trees! Then take them to the cabins! That's where our second line of defense will be!"

"Will do!" Sherry swung the M.A.C. 10 over her right arm by its small shoulder strap, then grabbed the rope and swung her body over the edge of the wall. She wrapped her legs around the stout rope and began descending hand over hand to the water below.

The sounds of gunfire from the outer side of the wall momentarily abated.

Sherry's feet touched the surface of the slowly flowing moat. She was thankful she was a hardy swimmer, because the moat was 8 feet deep and 20 feet wide.

"Hurry!" Crockett shouted from up above.

She glanced upward and saw him grinning at her. She smiled and waved.

Crockett's forehead abruptly disintegrated as a slug tore through his head from back to front. He stiffened, dropped his Beretta, and fell from the rampart.

Sherry opened her mouth to scream. For an instant, she thought he was going to land on her.

Crockett's buckskin-clad form crashed into the moat two feet to her left, showering her with water and causing her to bounce and sway.

Sherry released the rope and eased into the moat. She sank up to her neck, then began furiously swimming toward the far bank. There was no need to check on Crockett; his brains no longer occupied his body.

Someone was splashing about, agitating the water a few feet to her left.

Sherry paused in midstroke and surveyed the moat.

Over a dozen other defenders, members of the Family and the Clan, were in the process of traversing the moat. Some of them were poor swimmers, as evidenced by their pathetic efforts to stay afloat. One black-haired woman was simply doing the dog paddle in the middle of the stream.

"Hurry!" Sherry called to them, and struck out for the wooded shoreline.

The surface of the moat, not six inches from her face, suddenly was riddled by a series of miniature geysers.

Sherry looked over her left shoulder, up at the wall.

Seven troopers had scaled the outer wall and were rapidly firing at the helpless defenders navigating the moat.

No!

She could feel an intense pain in her left shoulder, but she suppressed the torment and pressed on, her supple form cleaving the water in smooth, even strokes.

Somewhere, a man was screeching in terror.

A woman chimed in, her plaintive cry terminating in a loud, protracted gurgling noise.

The bank loomed ahead. The top of the inner bank was three inches above the surface of the moat. Tiny wavelets, created by the commotion in the stream, washed over the top of the bank.

She was almost there!

Someone else was screaming in anguish as the soldiers on the wall maintained their withering fusillade.

Sherry's fingers touched the hard ground forming the inner bank, and she clutched at the weeds and grass lining the bank with all of her strength.

A section of earth near her right hand exploded in a fine spray of dirt and grass as a trooper on the wall tried to gun her down.

Move! she told herself.

Sherry scrambled from the moat, keeping low, crawling forward on her hands and knees, expecting at any second to feel the brutal impact of a bullet in her back. Incredibly, she reached a tangle of brush and trees and dodged behind a wide trunk.

Several slugs smacked into the tree.

She paused, gathering her breath, and gazed around the trunk at the east wall and the moat.

Bodies of men and women were bobbing in the moat, while others wildly tried to reach the bank. On the wall above, 15 to 20 soldiers were pouring lead at the swimmers. Bodies were heaped on the rampart, troopers and defenders alike. Resistance on the rampart itself had ceased.

With one notable exception.

Fascinated, astounded, and emotionally moved to her core, Sherry saw one defender still up on the wall, a stirring, solitary figure fighting with the force of ten.

Samson.

He was still striving to hold the breach. Soldiers were surging over the parapet to his right and left, but not one of them was getting through the breach. His Bushmaster Auto Rifle apparently empty, he was using it as a club, swinging it by the barrel, the stock smashing into any trooper foolhardy enough to come within range of his muscular arms.

Even as Sherry watched, Samson clipped a soldier in the jaw and sent him plunging from the ladder. He dropped the Auto Rifle and drew his Bushmaster Auto Pistols, one in each hand, and spun, firing a blast into the soldiers approaching from the north. In a twinkling, he whirled and blasted a group of troopers closing on him from the south.

Sherry pressed the knuckles of her right hand against her mouth, inwardly praying he would prevail over his foes, but knowing the odds were too steep.

Samson turned, shooting at soldiers to his north again, and at that moment, when his attention was distracted from the breach, a pair of troopers stormed over the lip of the wall, squeezing under the barbed wire, and pounced, not bothering to use their M-16's. They leaped onto Samson, one on each arm, and tried to wrestle him to the rampart. They were like chipmunks attempting to subdue a mighty grizzly. With a shrug of his broad shoulders, Samson threw the soldiers from him. He shot one of them in the face; the other he kicked in the chest, knocking him into the moat.

Sherry became conscious of other defenders crouching near her, their attention likewise riveted on the tableau on the east wall.

Samson downed four more troopers, and then the inevitable happened.

He was hit.

A soldier rose up over the top of the wall, his M-16 pressed to his right shoulder, and fired at point-blank range.

Samson was struck in the chest. The force of the bullets striking his body caused him to stumble backward. His arms waving in an effort to retain his balance, he hovered on the brink of the wall for a second, and then fell from the rampart into the moat.

He didn't come up.

Sherry, dumbstruck, backed away from the vicinity of the moat. Dear Spirit, no! Not Samson!

"What should we do?" whispered someone to her immediate right.

Sherry rapidly blinked her eyes, trying to focus, to collect her wits.

There was 10 to 15 defenders in the woods around her, all of them eagerly awaiting her instructions.

"Head for the cabins in the center of the Home," she advised them. "We're going to make a stand there."

They started to move off.

"Wait!" she commanded them.

They stopped, staring at her.

Sherry glanced over her right shoulder at the east wall, the enormity of their situation, the gravity of their danger, fully sinking home.

The east wall had fallen!

The Home was vulnerable! The soldiers could spread out, via the rampart, to the other walls.

No!

She couldn't allow that!

"Listen," she said to the defenders surrounding her, "here's what we're going to do . . ."

17

Day three of the siege.

Ninety minutes after the barrage began.

The south wall.

"Hold them!" Carter bellowed. *"Hold them!"*

So far, the defenders on the south wall had managed to hold their own. Bodies of fallen troopers were piled at the outer base of the wall. Very few of the soldiers had attained the top of the wall, and those who did were promptly shot to ribbons.

The south wall ran from east to west. Carter stood in the middle of the wall, urging the defenders on. Gideon was posted at the east end of the wall, while Ares had been assigned to the west end. As a testimony to his renowned savagery, the largest concentration of enemy dead was under his section of the wall.

"They're running!" someone shouted.

Sure enough, the soldiers were falling back to regroup for another assault. The air was filled with smoke and an acrid stench.

Ares jogged along the rampart to Carter, his Colt AR-15 in his hands, his short sword dangling from his leather belt. His crest of red hair was caked with dust.

"How is our ammo holding up?" Carter asked him.

"We still have plenty," Ares responded in his deep voice.

Carter ran his left hand through his curly blond hair, his green eyes glancing to the west and the north. "I wonder how the other walls are doing."

The sounds of battle emanated from every direction.

"Do you want me to have one of our people check?" Ares offered.

"No," Carter replied. "We need everyone for their next attack." He paused. "How many do we have left?"

"Forty-three," Ares answered.

Carter scanned the rampart. "I'm amazed we've held them this long."

Ares checked the magazine in his Colt AR-15. "If we repulse them again, they may call it quits for the day. They must have lost seventy-five to a hundred men on our side of the Home alone."

"I don't—" Carter began to speak.

"Here they come!" a woman shouted.

The troopers were making for the south wall again.

"Look!" Carter exclaimed. "They're trying a new tack."

Ares calmly gazed at the horde of soldiers descending on the Home. They evidently had a new trick up their collective sleeve. Instead of fanning out, dispersing their forces the length of the wall and clashing with the defenders on a wide front, the troopers were organized into a massive column, and the column was heading directly toward the center of the south wall. They were gambling their superior numbers would enable them to breeze up and over the wall before the defenders could rally.

The soldiers were wrong.

"Bring everyone in to the middle!" Carter ordered Ares. He raised his Springfield M1A to his right shoulder and sighted on the front ranks of the enemy. "On my command!" he yelled to the defenders nearest him.

The converging troopers were firing at the wall as they ran, an extremely difficult task, and most of their volleys were missing.

About 30 yards separated the south wall from the soldiers.

"Fire!" Carter barked.

The defenders unleashed a terrific rain of lead on the

soldiers. Screaming and stumbling as they went down, the first rows collapsed, tripping those behind them, and momentarily halting the enemy advance.

Carter aimed at a group of six troopers and raked them with a steady burst. He could see their bodies jerking as the bullets struck home.

A male defender to Carter's right shrieked as the right side of his head was blown away.

The soldiers recovered from their initial confusion and closed on the south wall. They threw 14 assault ladders up against the central section, and the troopers promptly started to climb the ladders.

Carter leaned forward, exposing himself from the waist up, and fired at the soldiers nearest the wall.

Other defenders, in response to Ares, who was moving along the wall from west to east, began to arrive at the middle portion and added their firepower to the general melee.

The troopers at the outer base of the south wall were peppering the lip of the wall with gunfire, their effectiveness diluted by the intervening parapet.

A burly soldier was almost to the top of a ladder to Carter's left.

Carter aimed the M1A and squeezed the trigger, then cursed his stupidity because the gun was empty. He swung the M1A over his left shoulder by its strap, and drew his stainless steel Guardian-SS Auto Pistols. The right Guardian bucked in his hand as he fired.

The burly soldier grabbed at his face, screamed, and toppled from the ladder.

A woman to Carter's left was hit in the chest and flung from the rampart.

More troopers were nearing the top of the wall.

Carter realized the distinct drawback to having barbed wire attached to the top of the wall; it might hinder any invaders in clearing the top of the wall, but it also prevented the defenders from reaching down and shoving the ladders to the ground.

Another soldier to Carter's right had his hands on the lip of the parapet.

Carter shot him in the ear.

The hapless trooper stiffened and fell, knocking off one of his companions on a lower rung.

Carter crouched and replaced the Guardians in their holsters. He hastily pulled a fresh magazine from his left rear pocket and reloaded the M1A.

Ares and Gideon were approaching from the east, Gideon's shorter legs having to take three steps to every one made by his giant peer.

Ares reached Carter's side first. He leaned out and blasted the soldiers with his AR-15.

The defenders were now packed along the center section of the wall, pouring their lethal barrage into the troopers nonstop.

"We're holding them!" Carter cried, elated.

Something sailed over the top of the wall, a smallish circular object, its metallic surface glinting in the sunlight.

Gideon spotted it before the rest. As a Warrior, he was familiar with dozens upon dozens of armaments. He had studied countless books in the Family library on diverse weapons, from ancient times to the years preceding World War III. He recognized the object hurtling in their direction, and he instinctively took three steps and caught it in his left hand.

Carter had identified the object too. "Throw it!" he shouted at Gideon.

Gideon started to comply, but a shot from below caught him high on his chest, on the left side, and staggered him, causing him to drop the Uzi. He lurched to the inner edge of the rampart, his moccasins hanging over the brink.

Carter dove for his friend, trying to grip Gideon's legs and yank him to safety. His gaze fell on Gideon's face, and even as he missed his grip, Gideon's brown eyes locked on Carter's green in a silent farewell. Carter's frantic fingers were an inch from Gideon's brown trousers when Gideon sank over the rim.

Gideon smiled as he fell.

"Gideon!" Carter screamed.

Gideon was ten feet above the moat when the grenade detonated. The explosion rocked the south wall.

Carter, near the edge of the rampart, felt something wet and cool splatter over his face. His ears were ringing and the left one was bleeding. He wiped his right hand across his face, and his palm came away coated with blood, bits of flesh, and tiny pieces of Gideon's green wool shirt and brown trousers.

"Are you all right?" Ares reached down and hauled Carter to his feet.

Aghast at the demise of his fellow Warrior and partner, Carter numbly nodded.

Ares stared at a growing red stain on the surface of the moat. "He died saving us," he said solemnly.

The firing along the wall was abating as the soldiers began to retreat.

"We've held them again!" Ares stated.

Carter was gawking at his right palm.

"Why haven't they used grenades before this?" Ares asked, hoping to divert Carter's attention.

"Hickok told me last night," Carter said, mumbling, "their army is . . . ill-equipped. They have a shortage of a lot of things. I think the Civilized Zone's industrial output is minimal. The area they control doesn't contain the natural resources they need . . ." He paused, his lips quivering.

"Are you all right?" Ares repeated.

Carter looked at the fleeing troopers. "You bastards!" he yelled, enraged. "You'll pay for this! I promise you!"

Ares saw a solitary soldier, 75 yards from the wall, elevate his M-16 and fire.

Carter abruptly straightened and gasped.

A ragged red hole had appeared between his green eyes.

Ares dropped his AR-15 and seized Carter by the shoulder before the blond man could plunge from the rampart. "Carter?"

Carter's mouth was twisted in a wry grin. He tried to speak, but his mouth formed soundless words. His breath expelled from his body in a prolonged, raspy wheeze, his back arched, and he died, his lifeless green eyes staring blankly at Ares.

"Good-bye, old friend," the tall Warrior said sadly. "I will miss you. Someday we will be together in the worlds on high."

"Here they come again!" a nearby man cried in alarm.

The soldiers were advancing across the field for yet another go at the south wall.

Ares gently lowered Carter to the rampart, retrieved his AR-15, and stood, his thin lips compressed tightly, his brow furrowed in mounting anguish commingled with sheer rage. He glared at the troopers in the field. They were going to pay for what they had done! They had killed his two best friends and Triad mates! By the Spirit, they were going to pay!

"On my command," Ares shouted, raising the AR-15 to his shoulder.

18

Day three of the siege.

Two hours after the barrage began.

The north wall.

There was a temporary lull in the fighting at the north wall, although the continuing sounds of combat could be heard from the other walls.

"The Spirit smiles on us," Seiko said, using a phrase frequently heard from Family members.

"How do you mean?" inquired Shane, his brown eyes watching the distant forest for sign of another assault. His black clothes were filthy from the accumulated smoke, dirt, and his own sweat. He held a Galil Model 361, which had been converted to full auto, in his weary hands.

The defenders on the north wall had successfully repulsed three waves of soldiers. Dead troopers littered the field and were piled along the outer base of the wall.

Like the youthful Shane, Seiko's Oriental-style black clothing, especially constructed by the Family Weavers using photographs in the martial arts books in the library as a guideline, was caked with dust and grime. "We have it easier than the other walls," he said.

"We do?" Shane rejoined.

Seiko pointed at a large ditch located 20 yards from the north wall. This ditch was six feet across and four feet deep. It served as an emergency runoff tributary for the stream entering the Home. The west end of the ditch connected to the stream just north of the compound.

Ordinarily, the ditch was dammed at its junction with the stream. But whenever the stream threatened to flood, whether from heavy rainfall or another reason, the narrow dam and mud and stones could be quickly torn down, allowing the excess water to flow east past the Home. When the flooding was over, the dam could be rebuilt until the ditch was needed again. It was another of Kurt Carpenter's safety precautions. "That ditch makes our job easier," Seiko stated.

Shane gazed at the ditch, uncomprehending, his mind still dazed from the ferocity of the onslaught, from all the brutal savagery he had witnessed. This was his first major conflict, and the experience had ravaged his soul. Never, not in his wildest imaginings, had he envisioned actual war as being so utterly gruesome, so supremely . . , vile.

Seiko sensed his colleague's inner turmoil. "The ditch slows them down," he went on, hoping to dispel Shane's shock by engaging him in conversation. "The soldiers can't get up a full head of steam with the ditch there. They have to slow to cross the ditch, and that gives us all the time we need to pick them off." He paused. "We have an advantage over the other walls."

Shane glanced to the west. "How do you think Hickok and the others are doing?"

Seiko shrugged. "We'll know soon enough." He was armed with a Valmet M76 with 30-round magazine and 12-inch bayonet mounted on the tip of the barrel. Tucked under his waistband in the small of his back, covered by his baggy shirt, were his favorite nunchaku. Also tucked under his waistband, but on either hip, were a pair of sai.

Shane absently gazed at the morning sun. "It seems like we've been fighting forever."

Seiko chuckled. "You will see much more fighting before your career as a Warrior is over."

"I don't know if I can take this on a regular basis," Shane confided.

"No one forced you to become a Warrior," Seiko reminded him.

"True," Shane conceded. "I became a Warrior

because I wanted to do my bit to help the Family. And because of Hickok.''

"You look up to him, do you not?"

Shane nodded, frowning.

"What is the matter?" Seiko probed, keeping his alert brown eyes focused on the treeline.

"I don't see how Hickok does it," Shane commented.

"Does what?"

"You know his reputation," Shane said. "And I've seen him in action. He's been in all kinds of battles. He's killed—who knows how many? I used to think he was the greatest. Now, I don't know. I've shot about two dozen soldiers today. Instead of feeling happy about it, I feel . . . ashamed," he confessed.

Seiko could read the torment in Shane's features. "Do you think Hickok feels happy about all the foes he has killed?"

Shane's busy brows narrowed. "I don't know," he admitted.

"I doubt he does," Seiko stated.

"But he takes it all in stride," Shane observed. "I've seen him, remember? Hickok can crack jokes in the middle of a fight."

"You think he is too flippant then?"

"Don't you?" Shane countered.

Seiko sighed. "I am not here to judge my fellow man."

"That's a cop-out," Shane said.

"Let me ask you a question," Seiko ventured. "Do you believe in the Family and the Home?"

"Yes."

"Do you believe they should be preserved at all cost?"

"Yes."

"Do you believe in freedom? In the higher concepts of truth, beauty, and goodness?" Seiko asked.

"Yeah."

"Do you believe in your right to commune with the Spirit?"

"Of course!" Shane responded impatiently. "What's all of this got to do with anything?"

Seiko smiled. "Everything." He considered for a moment. "I don't know Hickok as well as, say, Geronimo does. But I do know that Hickok, and every other Warrior for that matter, believes in all of the values we've discussed. I also know, as do you, that there are many people in this crazy world who don't believe in the values we do. Many of them would deny us our values. Many of them want us to live the way they live. Samuel the Second is a good example. He wants the Family to conform to his ideas about living. He wants to dictate the lives of those around him. We can't permit that." Seiko indicated the fallen troopers in the field. "Do you hate them?"

Shane stared at the corpses, puzzled. "I don't know. I haven't really thought about it."

"I don't hate them," Seiko said. "I see them as pawns in a cosmic struggle between good and evil. Mindless pawns, because they fight for Samuel's values instead of their own."

"But what does all of this have to do with Hickok?" Shane interjected.

"Hickok doesn't slay others because he enjoys it, because it makes him happy. He's a Warrior because he believes certain values are worth defending to the death. If he seems flippant at times, it's only because Warriors can't allow the killing to get to them. If you dwell on the slaughter, you won't be able to function as a Warrior. And then who will defend the values in which you believe?"

"I never thought of it that way," Shane acknowledged.

"Think about it," Seiko suggested, hefting his Valmet M76, "but not right now."

"Why not?"

Seiko nodded at the forest. "Because company is coming."

With a mighty clamor, the soldiers poured from the trees once again.

19

The west wall.

"Here they come!" yelled a male defender, a Family Tiller.

Hickok, standing in the middle of the skirmish line on the inner bank of the moat next to Spartacus, ten yards from the stream, raised the Daewoo Max II he was using, and sighted on the opening in the west wall where the drawbridge had once been.

So far, his strategy had worked to perfection.

Three times the troopers had assaulted the west wall, cramming into the opening and climbing over the wall. Each time, the soldiers were stopped by the moat or exposed on the rampart. Each time, the defenders showered a hail of lead on the attackers, downing dozens upon dozens and checking the enemy charge.

Hickok had to hand it to the Founder, Kurt Carpenter. By situating the moat inside the walls, he had presented a formidable obstacle for an opposing force to overcome. If the moat had been located outside the walls, it would have been easier for their foes to cross while keeping the defenders on the rampart pinned down with blistering fire. As it was, there was no way the soldiers could swim a moat and shoot their M-16's at the same time.

The carnage wrought by the defenders was incredible. Dead troopers were stacked in the opening and piled on the rampart. Over four dozen had fallen into the moat and were clogging the stream.

The soldiers appeared again, working in unison, with a row of them packing into the drawbridge opening while a dozen clambered over the parapet onto the rampart.

"Fire!" Hickok ordered.

Without adequate protection, the troopers were punctured again and again by defender fire. Some of them screamed as they were hit, their bodies thrashing and jerking as if they were performing an outlandish dance.

After a few minutes the soldiers stopped coming.

"Cease fire!" Hickok commanded.

A cloud of white smoke drifted above the stream. The moans and whimpers of the wounded formed an eerie symphony of torment.

"Make sure you are reloaded!" Hickok directed the skirmish line.

"Do you think they'll come again?" Spartacus asked.

"Beats me," Hickok responded.

"How many have we killed so far? A hundred? Two hundred? I can't believe they keep coming back for more," Spartacus commented, wiping his sweaty brow with the back of his left hand, his HR93 in his right.

"Some folks just have bricks for brains," Hickok quipped.

Spartacus gazed to the north and the south. "Sounds like the rest of the Home is still under attack. Should I go see how we're faring?"

"Wait a spell," Hickok said. "Until we're sure these yo-yos have called it quits."

"What would you do right now if you were Brutus?" Spartacus asked his friend.

Hickok thoughtfully stroked his chin. "I reckon I'd pull back my troops and wait until tomorrow to try again. Only I'd do it differently come morning."

"In what way?"

Hickok indicated the west wall. "I'd use what ammo I had left for my artillery and blast away at one wall until it was a heap of rubble."

"Why only one wall?" Spartacus asked.

"Because they could rush all their troops at us at

once. During the night they could build portable bridges or some such to get 'em across the moat. If they could get a foothold in the compound, with their superior numbers it'd be all over in an hour or so," Hickok detailed.

"Maybe Brutus won't consider your idea," Spartacus declared. "Maybe he'll assault all four walls again."

"He might," Hickok concurred, "but I doubt even he's that blamed dumb."

They waited for the next onslaught, the strain taking a toll on their already frazzled nerves.

"They're not coming," Spartacus stated optimistically after a while.

"I need someone to climb the stairs to the rampart," Hickok said. "Have 'em take a peek at what Brutus is up to."

"I'll go," Spartacus volunteered.

"Keep your head low," Hickok advised.

"You've got it," Spartacus mentioned. He hurried to the stairs and ascended to the western rampart. As he crossed above the stream he stared down at the pale faces in the water below, some of them with their eyes wide open, some with their discolored tongues protruding, some with vacant black cavities where their eyeballs had once been. The butchery nearly sickened him.

Spartacus reached the rampart and stopped, crouched at the top of the stairs.

Bodies of troopers were strewn all along the rampart. Some were still alive; they were groaning and twitching in agony.

Spartacus moved toward the parapet, carefully scanning the soldiers to insure none of them was capable of shooting him in the back. He reached the parapet and glanced over the top.

Scores of corpses littered the west field, but there wasn't a living trooper in sight. Evidently, they were all massed in the forest. There was no indication they were intending to stage another attack.

The distant firing from the north, south, and east walls was dying down.

Had Brutus given up then?

Spartacus returned to the wooden stairs and descended to the compound.

"Well?" Hickok inquired.

"Nothing," Spartacus said.

The gunman smiled. "Good. We've got a breathing spell. Take four of our people with you and check on the other walls. I want to know exactly how many casualties we've had. Tell the other Warriors to report to me after tending to their own people."

Spartacus nodded and ran off.

Hickok turned to his right. He spotted Zahner, the leader of the Clan, 30 feet away. "Zahner!" he called out.

Zahner jogged up to the gunfighter. "Yes?"

"I want you to take a detail and clear the bodies from the rampart," Hickok directed.

"What about the ones still alive?" Zahner wanted to know.

"Shoot 'em in the head."

Zahner's mouth fell open in disbelief. "Shoot them in the head?"

"We only have four Healers," Hickok elaborated. "They're gonna be hard pressed to take care of our own wounded."

"Just shoot them in the head?" Zahner reiterated, stupefied.

"Would you rather I gave the job to somebody else?" Hickok asked softly.

"No. I can do it," Zahner stated. "I'll get Bear and Brother Timothy to lend a hand."

"Watch out," Hickok warned. "Some of 'em might have some fight left."

"Will do." Zahner departed on the run.

"You!" Hickok barked, pointing at a nearby Family Tiller.

"Me?" The man stepped forward apprehensively.

"Form a squad," Hickok instructed him. "Fish those bodies from the moat."

"What do you want done with them?" the Tiller inquired.

"Stack 'em on the inner back, right there." Hickok pointed at the edge of the moat.

"You don't want us to bury them?" the Tiller responded in amazement.

"Is everybody hard of hearing today?" Hickok snapped. "No, I don't want 'em buried. Not right now, anyway. After this is over we'll form a burial detail. But right now I want you to stack them along the bank. Make a wall of their bodies."

The Tiller gulped and hurried away.

Hickok slung his Daewoo Max II over his right shoulder. He missed his Henry, and he wondered if he would ever see the rifle again. The very first chance he got, he silently promised himself, he would head for the site of the enemy's former camp and search for the Henry. He never should have left it at the base of that tree!

A raven-haired woman with a machine gun walked up to the Warrior. "Can we take our wounded to the infirmary?"

Hickok mentally berated his stupidity. "You haven't done it yet?" he countered.

"No one told me to," the woman explained.

"Hop to it!" Hickok urged her. Blast! Why hadn't he thought of them?

The woman moved off.

Hickok limped to the edge of the stream. He gazed at the bodies in the sluggish water. Was Sherry's body in the moat too? Had she survived her first battle? He involuntarily shuddered, unable to tolerate the image of her floating in the red water, her lips cold and damp, her eyes devoid of their lively sparkle.

Please, Spirit, he prayed. Please let her be all right!

The gunman frowned. Now was not the time for personal considerations. He must plan his course of action for the next assault. If he was right, if Brutus had tossed in his chips for the day, then the Warriors would have all night to prepare their defenses, to improve and improvise where necessary. How many of the enemy had they killed today? He estimated the number of dead along the west wall at two to three hundred. If he was correct, and if the other walls had done as well, then Brutus had lost about eight hundred men. Which meant the Civilized Zone strike force had twelve hundred or so left. More than enough to polish off the Family and the Clan.

Hickok surveyed the compound.

Dozens of injured were heading for C Block, the infirmary. Some were walking unassisted, but others were being carried by their friends or borne on makeshift litters. A party of ten approached the infirmary from the direction of the east wall.

Hickok squinted, but he couldn't see Sherry among them. He breathed a sigh of relief.

The gunman's mind strayed. He thought of Bertha and Joshua, lying on the barren bed of a flatbed truck, awaiting his return so they could travel to the Home and be tended by the Healers. Were they still alive? Or had they died there, all but neglected, deprived of the company of their friends except for Geronimo? They didn't know Boone or Morton that well. Who would comfort them as they departed for the higher mansions? He would never forgive himself if they died. True, he hadn't had any option but to leave them there, but it didn't make the decision any easier.

Hickok knew he needed to do something, anything, to dispel his rare bout of moodiness. He turned and walked toward C Block.

The four Family Healers, assisted by half a dozen other Family members, were hard at work, ministering to the dozens of Family and Clan defenders injured during the battle. All of the cots in the spacious structure were already occupied, and a line had formed in front of the building, over 30 people suffering from various wounds, some of them with bloody clothing, some evidently in a state of severe shock, gaping blankly at the world around them.

Hickok stopped near the doorway.

A middle-aged woman with a shoulder injury stepped aside so he could pass.

"Thanks." Hickok said to her. He entered the Block and scanned the rows of cots. Cries of anguish, wailing and moaning, filled the chamber.

One of the Healers, an attractive blonde woman, saw the gunman and hurried up to him. "Do you need something?" she inquired.

Hickok shook his head. Her name was Jenny, and she was Blade's wife. Like Sherry, Hickok's beloved, she had blonde hair and green eyes. But Jenny had longer hair and a fuller form. Her rounded chin and cheeks gave her a decidedly youthful appearance. She wore faded, patched blue pants and a discolored yellow shirt. "No," he told her. "I just came to see how you're doin'."

Jenny glanced at the people waiting in line at the front door. "We're holding our own," she stated. "But we could use some more assistants if you find you can spare a few from wall duty."

"I'll see what I can do," Hickok promised, and turned to leave.

"Oh!" Jenny blurted, as if suddenly recalling an important matter she wanted to discuss.

Hickok hesitated. "What is it?"

"We had to move the prisoners," Jenny explained, referring to two troopers and one of the Doktor's genetically produced deviates captured by the Warriors some time back while Geronimo was off in the Dakotas. All three had been hurt before their capture and had been housed in the infirmary under guard.

"Where did you move them?" Hickok asked.

"We needed their cots," Jenny detailed, "so we had them moved to D Block. They're almost fully recovered anyway."

"Who's watching them?" Hickok asked her.

"Two men from the south wall who came in with superficial gunshot wounds," Jenny answered.

"Fine." Hickok began to take a step, then paused, remembering a question he needed to ask. "How's Gremlin?"

Gremlin was another of the Doktor's test-tube creations. Initially encountered by Blade in Kalispell, Montana, Gremlin had rebelled against the nefarious

Doktor and joined the Family. Enraged, the Doktor had sent a pair of assassins to murder Gremlin for his defection. Gremlin had survived the assassination attempt, but his right leg had been busted in four spots, severe breaks extremely difficult to set and treat. He had developed an infection and spent the past month confined to a cot in the northeast corner of the room.

"He's hanging in there," Jenny said. "He's tough. He'll pull through," she predicted.

"I hope so," Hickok stated. "I'm sort of fond of the critter."

Jenny frowned at his use of the term "critter," but Hickok didn't see anything wrong with it. How else should you refer to a "man" with leathery gray skin, red eyes, and pointed ears?

"Is Sherry all right?" Jenny asked.

Now it was the gumman's turn to frown. "Don't know yet," he muttered, and departed.

More walking wounded had joined the line while he was inside.

Hickok smiled encouragingly at them and headed for the moat. The Clan leader, Zahner, was directing the removal of bodies from the western rampart, and six men were engaged in fishing floating figures from the moat.

"Hickok!" someone called behind him.

The gunman turned.

Spartacus, his HR93 in his left hand, his right on the hilt of his broadsword, raced up, slightly out of breath.

"Report," Hickok instructed him.

"The final tally on the dead and wounded isn't in yet," Spartacus stated. "We're still counting. But from the preliminary reports, I'd estimate we lost sixty to seventy, with another forty or fifty injured."

"It could have been worse," Hickok remarked.

Spartacus stared into Hickok's eyes, his own features softening, saddening, reflecting his sense of loss. "You haven't heard the bad news."

Hickok tensed, afraid to pose his next question. "What bad news? Did we lose any Warriors?"

Spartacus nodded. "Four."

Hickok's shock showed. "Four? Are you sure?"

"Runners came from each wall to tell us the enemy stopped their assault," Spartacus informed him. "Seiko and Shane held the north wall with minimal losses. Ares reports the south wall sustained considerable damage and suffered a large number of casualties, including Carter and Gideon—"

"Carter and Gideon?" Hickok repeated, dazed. They had been his friends since childhood. He reached out and gripped Spartacus by the left shoulder. "What about . . ." he began haltingly. "What about the . . . east wall?"

A large lump seemed to slide down Spartacus's throat. "We lost Crockett . . . and Samson."

Hickok closed his eyes and silently gave thanks. "Sherry is okay?" he asked huskily.

"Sorry," Spartacus apologized. "I should have told you about her right off. She took a hit, a flesh wound to her left shoulder. From what I've learned, she also may have saved the Home."

"What?"

"The runner told me the east wall fell. With Crockett and Samson dead, the rest of the defenders took cover in the woods. Sherry rallied them. They hid behind the trees and shot at the soldiers as they came over the wall, containing them, preventing them from spreading to the north and the south along the rampart. If Sherry hadn't done what she did, Seiko and Ares would have been outflanked. She saved the entire compound," Spartacus concluded.

Hickok beamed with pride. He was so happy to hear she was alive, he felt tears forming in the corners of his eyes. He coughed and made a show of rubbing his eyelids. "That blasted smoke got in my eyes."

Spartacus placed his right hand over his mouth to hide his smile. "Yeah. A lot of us have that problem."

"How's your girlfriend?" Hickok inquired.

"She's fine," Spartacus replied. "She was on the north wall with Seiko and Shane. They weren't as hard pressed as the rest of us."

"And there's no sign of activity in the enemy camp?" Hickok asked.

"All four sides are quiet," Spartacus said.

"Then maybe we will have time to regroup," Hickok declared.

"What's our next move?" Spartacus asked him.

Hickok patted the pearl handles on his Pythons. "The way I see it, Brutus has about twelve hundred soldiers left. We took a heavy toll today, but they've still got the edge. We can't let them get inside the Home."

"How can we stop them?" Spartacus asked. "Whether they attack one wall, like you said they might, or all four, there's no way we can keep them out indefinitely."

Hickok watched Zahner on the west rampart. "We need to come up with a humdinger of an idea. Somethin' that'll stop ol' Brutus cold."

"Like what?"

"I don't rightly know. Yet. But whatever we come up with, we'd best do it fast. And whatever we come up with, it'd better work right the first time out of the chute because we won't get a second chance.

Spartacus stared at the growing pile of bodies on the bank. "I can't wait to hear what you come up with," he said.

"I do have one idea," Hickok admitted.

"What is it?" Spartacus inquired eagerly.

"You won't like it," Hickok told him.

"How do you know?"

"You won't like it," Hickok reiterated.

"Try me anyway," Spartacus urged him.

Hickok nodded toward the western rampart. "I figured we could all stand up there and toss spitballs at 'em." He chuckled at his own joke.

"Spitballs?" Spartacus shook his head and snickered.

"You gotta admit," Hickok said, "it sure would confuse the heck out of 'em."

"I think I understand something now," Spartacus stated slowly.

"You do? What?"

"The reason Blade sent you back here," Spartacus quipped.

"Very funny." Hickok suddenly sobered. "I wonder how the big guy is doing?"

20

"What do you make of it?" Rikki-Tikki-Tavi asked.

"I don't know," Blade admitted.

"It's a trap," Yama warned.

"You can't trust him," Teucer added.

The SEAL was parked on a low rise on Interstate Highway 25 north of Denver, not far past the DACONO exit. To the west rose the majestic Rocky Mountains with Longs Peak prominent among them. To the east was a flat plain, farmland. Outlined in stark contrast on the southern horizon was the metropolis of Denver, Colorado, the capital of the Civilized Zone and the stronghold of Samuel II. The gigantic wall constructed by the Army Corps of Engineers was visible, as were a dozen towering skyscrapers behind the wall. A peculiar brown cloud hung over the fortress city, pollution created by the widespread usage of wood-burning stoves and vehicle emissions, an atmospheric symbol of the evil controlling the city and dominating the Civilized Zone.

The four Warriors were standing in front of the SEAL. To the rear of the transport stretched the Freedom Federation Army. Ahead of the SEAL 30 yards was a jeep with a white flag attached to its radio antenna. Three soldiers occupied the jeep, their eyes fixed on the Warriors, their expressions clearly showing their nervousness.

There was the clatter of hooves on the tarmac, and Kilrane galloped up to the Warriors on his palomino.

"What's going on?" he demanded.

Blade pointed at the jeep. "They've brought a message from Samuel. He wants to meet with me. Alone."

"You're not thinking of going, are you?" Kilrane asked.

Blade nodded.

"You're nuts," Kilrane said. "It's a trick."

"That's what we've been telling him," Rikki mentioned.

"But he won't listen to us," Yama added.

"Why does Samuel want to meet with you?" Kilrane inquired.

"Supposedly to talk about terms for a truce," Blade replied. "There's a hill a couple of miles down the road. On the other side of the hill Samuel has pitched a tent. He wants to meet me there."

"You can't trust him," Kilrane stated.

"I know that," Blade agreed.

"But you're going anyway?" Kilrane queried.

"I have no other choice," Blade said. He turned to Rikki. "Let those soldiers know I've decided to accept Samuel's invitation. Tell them we'll abide by Samuel's rules."

Rikki frowned, disgruntled. "I'll inform them," he said sullenly. He walked toward the jeep.

Kilrane leaned forward, patting the neck of his palomino. "What are you trying to prove?"

"I have to hear what he has to say," Blade said defensively.

Kilrane straightened. "I guess you do. But if the son of a bitch tries anything, if he kills you, I want you to know my men won't rest until your death is avenged."

Blade grinned. "That's comforting."

Kilrane smiled and rode off to rejoin his Cavalry.

"The same holds true for us," Yama remarked.

Blade put his left hand on Yama's shoulder. "I appreciate your concern. I really do. But I must go. You see that, don't you?"

Yama nodded. "We understand."

"Well, I don't!" interjected a new voice.

Lynx stood behind them, appearing as if from nowhere.

"Now don't you start," Blade said.

"Are you out of your gourd?" Lynx angrily demanded. "Sammy wants to get you alone so he can eliminate your buns. It's as simple as that!"

"Undoubtedly," Blade concurred.

"Then let me come with you," Lynx urged. "I have a score to settle with Sammy."

"No."

"Why not?" Lynx demanded, peeved.

"He wants to meet me alone," Blade reminded the fiery creature.

"I could sneak up on the tent," Lynx offered, "and rip the sucker to shreds before he knew what hit him."

"No."

"It's your funeral," Lynx snapped, and left.

Blade watched Rikki deliver his reply to the soldiers in the jeep. The driver said something to Rikki, gunned the engine, and wheeled the vehicle in a tight U-turn. The jeep drove due south on Interstate 25, spewing a trail of black exhaust fumes.

Rikki returned to his companions.

"What did the driver say?" Blade inquired.

"The tent is positioned between two hills. Samuel will have his army on one hill. We'll be on the other. We can send one person down to the tent to inspect it. Then Samuel will drive down and you're to join him," Rikki detailed.

"Sounds simple enough," Blade commented.

"I still don't like it," Yama groused.

"Let's get going," Blade suggested.

They filed into the SEAL.

Blade started the transport and slowly pulled out. The column took his cue and followed, the trucks traveling at a reduced speed so as not to tire the Cavalry's horses.

"Has anyone seen Lynx?" Teucer asked.

Blade glanced over his right shoulder. Rikki-Tikki-Tavi was seated in the front, in the other bucket seat. Yama and Teucer were in the wide seat. Behind them was the rear section containing their provisions, where

Lynx usually sprawled while the convoy was on the road.

Only Lynx wasn't there.

"I haven't seen him since he argued with Blade," Yama mentioned.

"Maybe he's so mad at me he decided to ride in one of the troop transports," Blade speculated.

They rode in silence, alertly surveying the countryside for any hint of a threat.

"Are you certain I can't prevail on you to take one of us with you?" Rikki inquired after the SEAL had gone a mile.

"Samuel wants to meet me alone," Blade noted. "But I'll tell you what I'll do, just to allay your fears. The driver said one of us could inspect the tent before the meeting, right?"

"Yes," Rikki affirmed.

"Then you'll do the inspecting," Blade stated.

"Thank you," Rikki responded.

The SEAL purred along Interstate 25. Off to the west was a small herd of cattle. Beyond the grazing cows loomed the imposing mountains, many of the pointed peaks wearing white caps, draped in mantles of snow.

The terrain ahead began to gradually rise, forming a rounded hill. The highway went up and over the center of the hill.

"This should be it," Rikki said.

Blade drove slowly up the hill. He could feel his stomach churning in anxious anticipation. A quick glance in the rearview mirror assured him the convoy was barreling up the hill; two of the jeeps were in the lead, followed by the half-track, then the troop transports, and a solitary jeep at the very end. Kilrane had divided his Cavalry riders; half of them were riding on the west side of the Interstate, the remainder on the eastern side.

The SEAL reached the crest of the hill.

Blade applied the brakes and placed the vehicle in park.

"There's the tent," Yama commented.

There it was, situated between two hills, exactly as

Samuel's messenger had said it would be. The other hill was a half-mile or so to the south. Waiting in formation on the far hill was Samuel's army, a thousand strong according to George, the captured Assassin. The sunlight reflected off the windshields of various military vehicles. Banners and flags flapped in the wind. And in the middle of the level area between the hills was a large green tent.

Rikki opened the door. "I will inspect the tent most carefully," he pledged.

"We'll be waiting," Blade said, switching off the engine.

Rikki, his katana in his right hand, jogged down the hill toward the green tent. His mind was deeply troubled. This had to be a trap! There was no doubt about it. But what kind of trap? Would Samuel II draw Blade into the tent and then have his troops attack? No. That made no sense. Samuel knew the Freedom Federation would immediately come to Blade's rescue. Was Samuel attempting to kidnap Blade and hold him hostage? Again, the idea was ludicrous. How would Samuel get Blade from the tent to his own forces without being spotted? Both armies were equidistant from the green tent. Neither army could reach the tent any faster than the other. Did Samuel intend to murder Blade during their meeting? If so, how? Blade wasn't an easy man to kill, and Samuel II must be in his 70s or 80s. How would Samuel overcome Blade? And what would he gain? Killing Blade wouldn't stop the Freedom Federation Army.

So what *did* Samuel II have up his sleeve?

Rikki slowed as he neared the green tent. He saw the tent was constructed of green canvas. Samuel had placed the square tent to the west of Interstate 25, not four feet from the highway. A field surrounded the tent, and there wasn't a tree or boulder or any conceivable hiding place within two hundred yards of the site.

To all intents and purposes, the location was ideal, insuring neither side could spring an ambush without detection by the armies on either hill.

So far, so good.

Rikki stopped and cautiously walked to the flap. Someone had imbedded a pole in the ground and tied the flap to the pole, leaving the front entrance wide open.

How nice of them.

Rikki paused in the entranceway. He could clearly see every inch of the interior of the tent. The ceiling was 10 feet above the ground, while the tent walls were 15 yards in length. There was ample room for 50 men, but the spacious interior was unoccupied except for a small folding table and a pair of folding chairs. Nothing else. The rough ground served as the tent's floor, with patches of grass and weeds serving as the carpet. A pitcher of water rested on the table, next to two tall glasses.

And that was it.

Rikki entered the tent, annoyed. There *had* to be more to it than this! His intuition was blaring a siren warning in his mind. But what could be wrong? The field outside the tent was deserted. The inside was empty except for the table and the chairs. The tent walls were swaying slightly in the breeze, indicating there weren't any secret passages. The roof appeared to be exactly that: a roof. Every element of the meeting place was perfectly ordinary. There was nothing to arouse suspicion.

So why did he feel uneasy?

Rikki walked to the table, studying the arrangement. The table and chairs were ten feet from the entranceway. Sparsely covered ground took up the remainder of the space. There was simply nowhere a foe could hide.

But something was wrong.

Rikki *felt* it. And he always trusted his instincts. But what was it? If he didn't find concrete evidence, Blade would laugh off his anxiety and attend the meeting.

What? What? What?

Rikki turned and exited the tent. He began walking around the exterior, examining the walls and the earth at his feet. All he found were the stakes used to erect the tent walls, neatly imbedded in the ground at regular intervals with sturdy cord extending from each stake to a metal ring affixed to the canvas wall of the tent.

That was all.

Irritated by his failure, Rikki completed a circuit of the tent and stopped at the entranceway. He would have to report the tent was safe. There was no other choice. He took a few steps, then paused, perplexed.

What was this?

There were huge tire tracks in the center of the Interstate. They ran from the front of the tent and disappeared up the hill to the south. What made the tracks so odd was their exceptionally muddy condition. Normally, a truck wouldn't leave visible tracks on the surface of a road. But this one had, apparently because its tires were so caked with dirt and mud, that it left a trail of muddy imprints behind it.

Why the mud?

Rikki glanced around. Had the truck delivered the tent to this site? Had it backed into the field? The ground was hard, and it hadn't rained in days.

So why the mud?

Something nagged at Rikki's mind, but he couldn't identify the cause of his distress. And if all he had to report was a set of muddy truck tracks, he wouldn't be able to dissuade Blade from coming.

Back to square one.

Rikki started jogging toward the SEAL. He was disgusted at his ineptitude. There was something wrong, something out of kilter with that tent, but for the life of him he couldn't determine what it was.

Blade, Yama, Teucer, and Kilrane were waiting for him near the SEAL.

"Well?" Blade asked. "What did you find?"

Rikki drew up next to them. He frowned and shook his head. "I didn't find a thing," he admitted.

"Nothing?" Yama demanded.

"Nothing I could put my finger on," Rikki stated.

"Then I'm going," Blade announced.

"Look!" Teucer exclaimed, pointing at the far hill.

A single jeep was headed down the south hill toward the tent.

"It must be the dictator," Yama conjectured.

The jeep slowed as it approached the tent, then pulled over on the east side of the Interstate. One man, and only one man, stepped from the vehicle and walked into the tent.

"It has to be Samuel," Blade said. "I'd better be going."

"What weapons are you taking?" Rikki inquired.

Blade patted his Bowies. "Just these."

"No gun?" Rikki responded, surprised.

"The driver told us Samuel would be unarmed," Blade stated. "I'm not about to waltz into the tent packing a lot of hardware. My Bowies have never failed me before. They'll suffice."

"Are you taking the SEAL?" Yama asked him.

"Nope," Blade answered. He glanced at Kilrane. "Would you have one of our jeeps driven up here?"

"On its way," Kilrane said, and departed.

"Why won't you take the SEAL?" Rikki wanted to know. "Its bulletproof body can protect you in case of an ambush."

"The SEAL stays here," Blade declared. "We can't run the risk of it falling into enemy hands. With all the firepower it has, the SEAL is invaluable to our Family." He paused. "Besides, if I do get into hot water, you can bail me out with the SEAL."

"I don't know," Rikki commented doubtfully.

"You have been paying attention to the driving lessons I gave you on the way down here, haven't you?" Blade asked.

"You know I have," Rikki retorted.

"Then what's the problem?" Blade queried him.

Further conversation was precluded by the arrival of the jeep. The driver, a brown-haired man from the Clan, parked the vehicle and hopped out, leaving the engine idling. "It's all yours," he said to Blade.

Blade walked around the front of the jeep and climbed into the driver's seat. He fondly gazed at Rikki-Tikki-Tavi. "Hold the fort until I return." He hesitated. "If I shouldn't return," he added, "then you know what to tell Jenny."

Rikki nodded.

"Give a yell if you need us," Yama advised.

Blade smiled at them and shifted into gear.

"The Spirit be with you," Rikki offered.

Blade drove toward the tent. He didn't want to alarm his friends, but he agreed with their assessment. Knowing Samuel II as he did, there was no doubt this arrangement was a setup. But if he refused to attend, the violent clash between the Freedom Federation and the Civilized Zone's army became inevitable. If he did meet with Samuel, there was always the prospect, no matter how unlikely, of resolving the conflict, of settling the war, without the further loss of lives.

Rikki-Tikki-Tavi had been right; the needless loss of life appalled him. He could kill when necessary, even ruthlessly on occasion, but not wantonly, not indiscriminately.

The tent reared its dark green shape directly ahead, its sides whipping in the wind like a ghastly green ghost.

Blade parked his jeep alongside the front one. He peered into Samuel's vehicle before climbing from his own, noting it empty. As he slid from his jeep he happened to notice a brown tarp bundled on the back seat.

The sun was almost overhead, at the noontime point in its aerial trajectory.

Blade insured his Bowies were loose in their sheaths, took a deep breath, and entered the tent.

"I was beginning to believe you wouldn't show," stated the lone occupant.

Blade scanned the interior, noting the table, the chairs, the wide empty space beyond. A disturbing thought flitted across his mind: why so large a tent for a meeting between two men?

"Did you have to bring them?" demanded the speaker.

Blade stared at the man sitting to the left of the folding table, and it was only with consumate self-control that he was able to prevent his shock from showing.

Samuel II was well on in years, and his aged body displayed every wrinkle, every crack in his dry, sagging skin. His shiny pate was bald, utterly devoid of hair, but laced with a prominent network of protruding veins. The man's face seemed to have sunk, to have turned inward on itself; his cheeks were pronounced hollows, his eyes black pools in their recessed sockets, and even his chin had a decidedly cleft aspect. His nose, a long pointed extention of flesh and cartilage, was the only elevated feature on his countenance. Thin, tight lips covered his small mouth. Not much of his body was visible owing to the ill-fitting green fatigues he wore. He raised his withered right hand and pointed at the Bowies. "Did you have to bring them?" he repeated in his raspy voice.

"I never go anywhere without them," Blade replied.

"Ahhhh, yes. Ever the devoted Warrior." Samuel II indicated the vacant chair. "Why don't you have a seat?"

Blade slowly crossed to the chair and sat down.

"Care for some water?" Samuel asked.

"No thanks," Blade replied.

"Suit yourself," Samuel said. He poured himself a tall glass and held it close to his lips. "Here's to progress," the remarked, and gulped a mouthful.

What was that supposed to mean? Blade gazed around the tent again.

"A bit nervous, are we?" Samuel inquired a trifle sarcastically.

"You wanted to discuss a truce," Blade reminded him.

Samuel tittered, his dark eyes twinkling in their sockets. Despite his advanced years, there was considerable vitality left in the man.

"What's so funny?" Blade demanded.

"A private joke," Samuel responded. "We'll talk about the truce soon enough. First, though, I'd like to get to know you a little better."

"What?"

"I thought we'd have a nice chitchat," Samuel mentioned.

A nice chitchat? Blade studied the dictator, perplexed. What kind of game was Samuel playing? Was he senile? Here they were, the Civilized Zone and the Freedom Federation, embroiled in an all-out war, and Samuel wanted to "chitchat"?

Something wasn't right.

"I must say," Samuel said politely, "your Family has caused me no end of trouble. You Warriors are a fierce bunch."

Was that intended as a compliment? Blade remained silent.

"If you don't mind," Samuel continued undeterred, "I'd like to pose a few questions your way."

Blade leaned forward in his chair. "Questions?"

"Yes," Samuel said, nodding, his skin quivering as he moved. "For instance, what have you done with the Doktor?"

Blade didn't reply.

"Is he dead?" Samuel inquired. "I haven't heard from him, and the last I knew he was heading for Catlow, Wyoming. I've received reports of a terrible battle there. Was that you?"

"We were in Catlow," Blade disclosed.

"And now you are here and the Doktor isn't," Samuel observed. "The answer to my question is self-evident." He examined Blade for a moment. "You are much younger than I expected."

Why was Samuel being so courteous? Blade was stumped. This didn't conform to the dictator's reputation as a singularly blood-thirsty individual.

"Still," Samuel went on, "I know age is no determiner of ability. You must be equally as surprised to find someone of my advanced years ruling the Civilized Zone."

"I am," Blade admitted.

"Do you know how I do it?" Samuel queried.

"I know how you do it," Blade snapped. "You rule with an iron fist and you crush all opposition."

Samuel nodded, cackling. "True. But that's only half of my secret. Do you know what the other half is?"

Blade shook his head.

"Giving the people a third of the things they think they want. You can't have them completely unsatisfied or a spontaneous revolution will develop practically overnight. No, you give them some of the luxuries of life, just enough to keep them contented and under your thumb. It works every time.'' Samuel beamed.

"And you admit it?'' Blade asked, surprised.

Samuel swept the tent with his spindly right arm. "There's no one else here. Who's to tell?''

"Your audacity astounds me,'' Blade stated.

"Thank you,'' Samuel rejoined.

"About the truce,'' Blade prompted him.

"In good time, dear lad,'' Samuel said patronizingly. "There are a few more items to cover. What happened to the Flatheads?''

"Which Flatheads?'' Blade responded.

Samuel chuckled, his eyes sparkling. "You must think I'm a doddering old fool. I assure you, Blade, I am not. I'm referring to the Flathead Indians you rescued from Catlow.''

How did Samuel know about them? Blade couldn't see any harm in divulging the truth. "They're on their way back to Montana,'' he said. "They wanted to return to their homeland.''

"Why?''

"They wanted to search for other survivors of your attack,'' Blade explained, his mind straying to his run to Kalispell and the war between the Flatheads and the Civilized Zone Army, a war the Flatheads lost. "You didn't kill or capture all of them, you know. The survivors are going to march to our Home for Star and take her to Montana if she wants to go.''

"Who is Star?'' Samuel inquired.

"The daughter of the Flathead chief,'' Blade commented. "You should remember him,'' he said, baiting the dictator. "Your men slaughtered his people and killed him. You still use some of the Flatheads as slave labor.''

"You sound like you disagree,'' Samuel remarked.

"Of course!'' Blade said angrily. "Do you expect me to condone slavery?''

"A moot point,'' Samuel declared. He took a sip of water. "Do you know who Clarissa is?''

The name didn't ring a bell. "Should I?" Blade retorted.

"Clarissa was the Doktor's assistant," Samuel elaborated. "My spies reported her traveling south through Denver over a week ago. You have no inkling of her destination?"

"How would I know?" Blade responded.

"No harm in asking," Samuel said. He straightened in his seat. "Now to the important matters. How many thermos do you have at your disposal?"

Blade suppressed a grin. So! Lynx had hit the nail on the head! The dictator believed the Family possessed some of the portable thermonuclear devices! "Why should I tell you?" he retorted.

"Then you admit you do have some?" Samuel asked, his voice lowering as he peered intently at the strapping Warrior.

"Do you doubt it?" Blade confidently replied.

Samuel unexpectedly nodded. "Yes, I do."

Blade nonchalantly reclined in his chair. Uh-oh. This was trouble. His only hope of swiftly ending the war, of preventing more carnage, lay in convincing the dictator the Family had confiscated some thermos. "We have three thermos," he lied.

"Oh, you do, do you?" Samuel said skeptically.

"If you don't think we have the thermos," Blade noted, "then why did you evacuate Fort Collins, Loveland, and the other cities?"

"Because my generals think you have the thermos," Samuel revealed. "They suspect you stole them from the Cheyenne Citadel before it was nuked."

"That's what we did," Blade stated belligerently.

Samuel's eyes narrowed as he scrutinized the Warrior. "And you have these thermos with your column?"

"Yes."

"And you plan to use them on Denver if we don't capitulate?" Samuel speculated.

"Exactly," Blade confirmed.

A smile creased Samuel's features, one more wrinkle in the sea of lines. "I . . . don't . . . think . . . so," he stated slowly.

This wasn't going as anticipated. Blade rested his hands on his Bowies. "Why not?"

Samuel calmly placed his elbows on the table top and cradled his chin in his palms. "I consider myself to be an excellent judge of character. You don't stay in power as long as I have if you can't distinguish your friends from your enemies, or potential enemies. You become extremely adept at reading people, at assessing their character. My newly appointed generals believe you have thermos. They pressured me into this meeting. The fools are afraid you will nuke Denver." He paused, smiling. "I agreed to this meeting on the remote possibility you might, indeed, possess thermos. But one look at your face convinces me you don't have them. You're a rotten liar, Blade."

Blade frowned, annoyed at himself. He never could lie well.

Samuel cackled at his triumph. "Don't feel so bad. Honesty is, by its very nature, transparent."

"So now we go to war," Blade stated regretfully.

"Perhaps not," Samuel said.

"You're willing to forget your goals of conquering the territory formerly controlled by the United States of America?" Blade asked in disbelief.

"No."

"I didn't think so," Blade muttered. "Then there will be a war, after all. The Freedom Federation is not going to stand by and watch you subdue the entire country," he declared. "We won't forsake our freedom for a dictatorship. We will use everything in our power to stop you."

"One step at a time," Samuel cryptically commented.

"What do you mean by that?"

"I mean," Samuel said, leering, "you learn to take life one step at a time when you reach my age. I'll dispose of the rabble comprising the so-called Freedom Federation presently. First, though, I will dispose of their commander-in-chief."

Blade glared at the dictator. "I won't be easy to dispose of," he growled, his resentment toward this smug, sanguinary megalomaniac growing by the moment.

"Not easy," Samuel agreed, "but not impossible either."

"I can't wait for you to try!" Blade snapped.

Samuel laughed. "I'm not crazy! I wouldn't think of trying to kill you myself." He paused, smirking. "I'll leave it to them." He waved his left hand in an arc.

Blade glanced to his right, then froze, dumbfounded.

There were 17 of them, all dressed in black, their faces covered by black masks, all armed with sharp Oriental swords. They completely encircled the folding table and the chairs.

How?

Samuel chuckled, delighted by the Warrior's astonished reaction.

Blade suddenly perceived the brilliance of their strategem. They had dug holes in the ground large enough to accommodate a man, 17 holes spaced at ten-foot intervals, aligned along the inner walls of the tent, invisible from the outside and imperceptible inside. An outstanding job of camouflage.

"You won't leave this tent alive," Samuel predicted.

Blade tensed, about to draw his Bowies. The odds were too great against him. His only consolation would be to take out Samuel before the Imperial Assassins got him.

"There's one more question," Samuel casually mentioned.

Blade started to ease his Bowies from their sheaths.

"Do you miss your father?" Samuel asked.

The unforeseen query startled Blade. His father? What did his father have to do with anything?

Samuel was grinning, obviously relishing the emotional torment he was causing the Warrior. "How many years has it been now? Four years since your father was killed?"

"Leave my father out of this!" Blade said, his tone low and threatening.

Samuel ignored him. "Do you remember how your father was killed?" he taunted.

Blade's face was turning red.

"Of course you do," Samuel answered his own question. "Your father was killed by a big cat. Did you ever wonder where that big cat came from?"

Blade felt as if he would explode. "I know where the cat came from! The Doktor sent it to kill my father!"

Samuel's white eyebrows arched upward. "Oh? You know that, do you? The Doktor must have told you the cat was one of his earlier genetically engineered creations. A test-tube animal. Did you know the Doktor developed the cat from a mountain lion embryo? He raised the animal from a kitten. It would do whatever he wanted."

Blade's mind was spinning. Why was Samuel reminding him of all this?

"Actually," Samuel resumed as if lecturing a student, "the animal was a consequence of the Doktor's research with test-tube produced mutations and his work with the chemical clouds."

Blade's rage was almost uncontrollable.

"You must hate the creature responsible for your father's demise," Samuel remarked.

Blade slowly stood.

"Would you like to meet it?" Samuel innocently asked.

Blade couldn't seem to find his voice. "What?"

"Would you like to meet it? I thought a reunion might be in order," Samuel said. He nodded at one of the Imperial Assassins.

Four of the Assassins immediately lowered their swords and slid them into their scabbards. The four moved to a spot eight feet from the folding table. They formed a line, knelt, and felt along the ground with their hands. Satisfied, they rose as one and began walking to the right, pulling a section of the "ground" after them.

"Take a look," Samuel urged Blade. "It's an old friend of yours."

Blade, bewildered, moved around the table.

The quartet of Assassins had uncovered a circular pit 20 feet in diameter.

So!

This explained why the tent was so large.

The pit had been covered by a heavy tarp, and the tarp coated with a layer of earth and clumps of weeds and grass.

But what had held aloft the tarp?

Blade walked to the edge of the pit and glanced down.

There was a thin, clear sheet of plastic covering the pit. The plastic sheet was half an inch thick and attached to the edge of the pit by a series of huge metal clamps. Apparently, one end of each clamp was shaped like a stake and imbedded in the upper wall of the pit. The clamp portion was secured to the plastic sheet, supporting it. Small holes had been drilled in the plastic sheet for ventilation purposes.

"A person could walk on that plastic without breaking it," Samuel commented behind the Warrior. "It's incredibly strong."

Blade barely heard the words. His eyes were riveted on the creature reclining on the earthen floor of the pit, the creature responsible for ripping his father to shreds.

The monstrosity was eight feet in length, not counting the two-foot tail. In general, its contours resembled a mountain lion. But there the resemblance ended. Its skin wasn't smooth like a cougar's; the texture was scabrous, with clumps of its light brown hair missing and replaced by festering sores. The creature's ears were large and tapered to a point; its eyes were vivid green orbs, slanted at an angle across its forehead; its upper teeth protruded over its red lower lip; and saliva was drooling over his chin.

"The Doktor gave it to me as a gift after he tired of it," Samuel was saying. "He named it Beelzebub."

The deformed genetic deviate—Beelzebub—rose to its feet. Its paws were immense. A studded leather collar encircled its neck.

Blade's body erupted in a cold sweat.

"You have no idea how much effort was entailed in arranging this touching reunion," Samuel said. "But it was all worth it! I vowed to seek revenge for all of the trouble you've caused me. For what you did in Fox and

Thief River Falls, for the disruption of my meticulous timetable in the Twin Cities, for Kalispell, and for the nuking of the Citadel at Cheyenne. For all of them!'' The dictator's voice was rising in intensity.

Blade ignored Samuel. His eyes were locked on Beelzebub's. The cat was staring up at him and snarling.

"After I've disposed of you,." Samuel was raving, "I will return to my army. We will withdraw to Denver and await the coming of spring. I will consolidate my empire and inscript more civilians into my military. Then, when we outnumber your pitiful Freedom Federation force by five to one, I will attack." He giggled inanely. "So much for the Freedom Federation."

Blade's hands were on his Bowies. He absently gazed at the floor of the pit, 12 feet below.

"By the time your people on the hill realize something is wrong and hurry down here," Samuel gloated, "I will be safe with my troops. My Assassins will secret themselves until your army departs."

Beelzebub suddenly roared, glaring fixedly at Blade, instinctively sensing the animosity, the sheer fury, welling up within the human.

"As I was saying before," Samuel stated gleefully, "that plastic can sustain a man's weight under normal circumstances. If you're walking on it or standing on it you'll be safe." He snickered. "But I wonder what would happen if someone fell on it?"

Blade, his attention arrested by the killer of his father, realized his danger too late.

A pair of hands slammed into the Warrior's back, hurtling him forward, over the edge of the pit and onto the sheet of plastic. He managed to brace his impact with his hands, but it wasn't enough to reduce the shuddering shock to the plastic. The abrupt collision rocked the sheet, vibrating the plastic, causing it to bounce, to sway violently, to tremble and crack, and finally split in two.

Samuel screeched in delight.

Blade felt the plastic sheet give way. He slid through the gap, trying to retain a tenuous grip on part of the plastic. His left side bore the brunt of the impact. One half of the sheet thudded into the earth an inch from his head, almost decapitating him.

"Pull!" the dictator was bellowing. "Pull! Pull!"

Blade found himself on the ground in the middle of the pit. The two halves of the plastic sheet had caved inward, their inner rims digging into the floor of the pit, their outer rims pressed against the pit top.

Beelzebub was unscathed, but pinned behind one of the plastic sections.

The Imperial Assassins were grouped around the pit, bent over. They had hold of one section of plastic and were laboriously heaving the slab to the surface.

The section imprisoning Beelzebub was still in place. Evidently they were saving the best for last.

"Pull! Pull!" Samuel was dancing and prancing in ecstasy.

With a united effort, the Imperial Assassins were able to lift the first section over the rim of the pit and slide it aside.

"The other one!" Samuel goaded them. "The other one!"

Blade rose to his feet, drawing his Bowies., He began backing away from the plastic section restraining the incensed feline.

The second section slowly climbed upward as the Assassins strained to clear the pit.

Beelzebub snarled and clawed at the plastic sheet.

Blade clutched his Bowies and waited.

The second section was a foot above the dirt floor.

Beelzebub pawed at the receding edge of the sheet, growling.

Blade's mouth felt dry. He struggled to compose his whirling thoughts. Be calm! he told himself. You'll lose it if you can't concentrate! He had to forget this thing was responsible for slaying his father. His acute hatred would impair his skill, would make him fatally careless. Concentrate! his mind screamed. Concentrate!

The second section was four feet above the floor.

Beelzebub watched the plastic sheet, fascinated by its ascent.

"Kill him!" Samuel shouted down. "Kill him!"

The Assassins raised the second section above the lip of the pit and deposited it near the first.

"Kill him!" Samuel cried.

Beelzebub finally focused on the human in the pit. It rose on all fours and roared.

"Kill him!"

Blade inched backwards. His body made contact with the pit wall.

"Kill him!"

He was trapped! There was nowhere else to turn.

"Kill him!"

Beelzebub hissed and charged.

Blade met the rush head-on. He drew his right Bowie back and plunged its keen blade in Beelzebub's chest as the creature pounced. The force of the cat's attack drove Blade into the pit wall. His breath was expelled from his lungs in an audible whoosh. He grunted and recovered, slicing his left Bowie into Beelzebub's thick neck as the deviate slashed and raked with its six-inch claws.

Beelzebub shrieked and snarled, trying to bury its teeth in the human's throat.

Blade knew his arms and legs were being torn to ribbons. He had to break free or the loss of blood alone would be his undoing. He jammed his right elbow into the cat's neck, pressing those razor teeth from him, and swept his left Bowie up and in, hoping his hasty aim would hit the mark.

It did.

The Bowie stabbed into Beelzebub's right eye.

Roaring in shock and agony, Beelzebub bounded to the left. Its right eye was split open, streaming a greenish-red fluid down its furry cheek and over its chin.

Samuel II was gaping at the fight in amazement, unable to believe his champion was hurt.

The 17 Imperial Assassins ringed the pit, watching expectantly.

Blade staggered aside, putting distance between the cat and himself. Blood was pouring from his arms and legs; fortunately, the deviate had missed his abdomen.

Beelzebub crouched along the far wall, licking its face.

Blade gripped his Bowies tightly and stopped. What would be the best killing stroke? To the neck? To the heart? To the head? The cat wasn't—

Something sharp lanced into Blade's right shoulder. He twisted to the right as a lancing spasm tore through his arm.

What?

Samuel was laughing.

Blade grit his teeth and glanced at his right arm. A throwing knife was sunk to the hilt in his shoulder. He looked up at the pit rim.

Samuel II was patting an Assassin on the back.

Now what? Was Samuel expecting him to fight Beelzebub and the Assassins simultaneously? Blade slid his left Bowie into its sheath, reached across his broad chest, and wrenched the throwing knife from his shoulder. His right arm became a river of blood.

Samuel leaned over the edge of the pit. "What's wrong, Warrior?" he baited Blade. "Where's your vaunted proficiency now? I was misled. My men told me you were deadly, someone to be feared. Yet all I see is a pathetic muscle-bound clod!" He giggled, rubbing his boney hands together. "Did you really think you could defeat me? *Me?*"

Blade saw Beelzebub crouching for another spring. Taking on the deviate and the Assassins at the same time was impossible. He needed a distraction, something completely unexpected, something to divert the Assassins while he dealt with the cat.

But what?

Samuel's smirking visage provided the answer. He was still leaning over the pit, reveling in his impending victory.

"You're forgetting one thing!" Blade shouted, keeping his eyes on Beelzebub.

"What's that?" Samuel replied, scoffing.

"An old saying we have in the Family," Blade stated, dropping his left arm to his side.

"Well, what the hell is it?" Samuel demanded.

Blade slowly smiled. "Never count your chickens until they're hatched."

"I don't get the point," Samuel said, puzzled.

"You will." Blade's left arm flashed upward. The throwing knife streaked straight and true, the result of innumerable hours spent in practice.

Samuel's eyes widened in startled wonder as the throwing knife penetrated his throat and stuck fast. He gagged, dribbling blood from his mouth, and reached for the knife in an attempt to draw it out. His body quivered, then pitched headlong into the pit.

Just as Beelzebub charged again.

Blade ducked to his right, avoiding those raking claws, and the cat reached the wall and whirled to confront its foe.

Samuel's body thumped to the dirt floor a foot to the left of the deviate.

Beelzebub spun, automatically facing in the direction of the sound, thinking the noise was produced by another opponent.

Blade made his move. He leaped, diving for the cat, his arms outstretched, the Bowies angled outwards. Before Beelzebub could react, Blade was on him, plunging the Bowies home. The left Bowie drove into the cat's right ear, even as the right speared into its left eye.

Beelzebub went into a frenzy, its body contorting and writhing, jerking spasmodically, wildly jerking and twisting in every direction.

Blade was tossed from the uncontrollable deviate, unable to withstand the animal's death throes. He felt his head smack against a hard surface, and the world reeled before his eyes. Vertigo engulfed him and he fell to his knees.

Get up!

On your feet!

His mind was screaming at him to stand! The Assassins would use him for a pincushion if he didn't get to his feet! Blade struggled to stand. He heard a loud cry arise overhead, followed by the clanging of metal upon metal. A machine gun burped. He shook his head, his vision clearing.

Beelzebub was lying on the floor, flat on its stomach, the Bowies protruding from its head, dead.

There was a confused blur of activity on the rim of the pit. Swords swinging. Guns blasting. Yelling.

Blade thought he saw Rikki-Tikki-Tavi cut an Assassin from chin to navel with his katana. And wasn't that Yama, scimitar in hand, taking the arm off another man in black? His mind was rambling. What had he hit his head on?

One of the Assassins jumped to the pit floor. He raised his sword and closed on the Warrior.

The last sight Blade saw before losing conscious was that of a brown, furry form leaping onto the Assassin and bearing him to the ground.

Who the . . .

21

Day four of the siege.

Dawn.

Hickok stood on the bank of the moat directly across from the opening in the west wall. He surveyed the pile of bodies lining the bank, then glanced to his right and left. Formed in a skirmish line were 25 defenders in each direction—50 fighters in all. It would have to be enough.

The rest was up to Spartacus.

"How much longer do you think it will be?" Sherry asked. She was standing to the gunman's left. Her left shoulder was bandaged.

"Soon," Seiko answered. He was five feet to Hickok's right. "Very soon."

Spartacus and Ares, as well as 138 other defenders, were absent from the line. So was Shane.

"I pray your plan works," Seiko said to Hickok.

"You and me both, pard," the gunman responded. He licked his lips and listened for the inevitable sound signaling the onslaught.

During the preceding evening Brutus had regrouped his forces, moving almost all of his troops into the forest on the west side of the Home. Only a handful remained to the north, east, and south, enough to serve as lookouts in case the defenders attempted to escape. The night had been moonless and tranquil, and shortly before dawn the sentries had joined their comrades in the trees.

"Don't fire until I give the word!" Hickok reminded them.

Brutus wasn't wasting any time. The section of the rampart above the ruined drawbridge suddenly exploded in a shower of brick and dust.

"Get ready!" Hickok shouted.

Two more rounds hit the west wall near the ruined drawbridge, widening the rift even further.

Hickok wondered what type of artillery they were using. He couldn't hear the shattering blast of a cannon and their tank was now a home for the fish in the moat. So what was it? What could easily fire a projectile 150 yards, and with such relative silence.

Another shell smacked into the west wall.

The gunman mentally reviewed the military books in the Family library. He ticked off a list: siege artillery, howitzers, mortars, rocket laun—! Hold it! A mortar would fit the bill. The 81-millimeter mortar could fire a 12-pound shell close to 2500 yards.

More and more rounds were striking the west wall, sending large chunks crashing to the ground or into the moat.

Hickok nodded. Brutus was using all four mortars on the west wall. Good. The bastard's predictability would be his downfall.

The barrage lasted for half an hour. The 53 defenders on the inner bank were untouched by the zinging debris. The gap in the center of the wall widened and widened.

It took a moment for Hickok to realize the bombardment was over. His ears were ringing, and his nostrils were stinging from the dense cloud of smoke hovering above the wall, the moat, and the bank. He was thankful Brutus had limited the barrage to the walls instead of lobbing shells into the compound at the blocks. But then, what good would it have done Brutus to destroy a block or two if he couldn't get past the outer walls? There was a method to Brutus's madness.

"I hear them," Seiko announced, raising his Valmet M76 to his shoulder.

Hickok heard them too. The pounding of hundreds of feet on the hard earth beyond the west wall.

This was it.

Brutus was throwing everything he had at the breach in the west wall.

"Here they come!" Hickok barked.

"Take care, lover," Sherry said tenderly.

The gunman glanced at her. She was staring at him lovingly, her affection reflected in her green eyes. "You take care," he told her. He opened his mouth to say more, to let her know he loved her.

He was out of time.

The Civilized Zone soldiers surged through the breach in the west wall, a horde of green intent on the total destruction of the Home, the sunlight glinting off their M-16's and their bayonets. A tremendous shout arose from the troops as they saw the defenders standing on the other side of the five-foot wall of bodies on the inner bank.

"Fire!" Hickok commanded.

Mayhem ensued.

Although the swirling smoke limited visibility, both sides could distinguish each other. The defenders opened up, pouring shots into the green mass in the breach, downing dozens.

For their part, the soldiers returned the fire as best they could. Some of them carried crude wooden platforms, actually small rafts. They tossed the rafts into the moat, one after the other, while others scrambled onto the platforms and frantically began lashing them together into a makeshift bridge. Their task was faciliated by the stacked wall of bodies on the inner bank; the defenders couldn't see into the moat unless then ran up to the bodies and peered over the top, exposing their heads and shoulders.

Even as one group of soliders constructed their bridge, five platoons were scaling the west wall, using ladders to reach the parapet and scramble under the barbed wire to the rampart. The first dozen were immediately slain by the defenders, but as more and more of them reached the rampart, they spilled from the rampart onto the wooden stairs over the moat. Eight of them reached the top of the stairs and were promptly perforated with bullets. But the rest kept coming, and within minutes a steady stream of troopers was racing down the stairs to the inner bank. The wall of dead soldiers ran behind the stairs, posing another obstacle. Horrified at the sight of their deceased companions callously piled on the rough ground, the troopers hesitated, balking at the idea of touching the bodies. But the only avenue of approach to the defenders was over the wall of corpses, and after their initial hesitation the soldiers rallied and started over the bodies.

The defenders blasted them as the troopers clambered over the corpses. For every soldier shot, two more took his place.

In the moat, the troopers had hastily finished their crude bridge. It wobbled and swayed in the stream, but by angling the platforms past the tank and securing several of them to the armored vehicle, they erected a functional bridge four feet wide.

Brutus was in the Home.

Hickok had emptied his Daewoo Max II into the attackers. He clutched the gun by the barrel and ran up to the wall of bodies.

A soldier was climbing over the stack of corpses.

Hickok swung the Daewoo, catching the trooper on the right cheek, splitting it open and knocking the soldier to the far side. He glanced in both directions.

The defenders were now fighting a containing action along the wall. Many were embroiled in hand-to-hand combat.

One of the troopers was striving to lance a bayonet into Seiko. His Velmet empty and discarded, Seiko held a pair of sai in his hands, trident-like bladed weapons twenty inches in length. He dodged a stab of the bayonet and twisted, ramming his left sai into the soldier's neck. Without missing a beat, he wrenched the sai free and went after another soldier.

"Look out!" a woman screamed.

Hickok turned toward the wall of corpses, dropping the Daewoo.

A trooper was aiming his M-16 at the gunman, but he

never pulled the trigger. The top of his head vanished in a burst of crimson, hair, and flesh.

Sherry reached the gunman's side. "Are you trying to get yourself killed?"

Hickok drew his Pythons and sent a slug crashing through the brain of a soldier almost over the wall of bodies.

The onrushing troopers were beginning to knock openings in the corpse wall. Some of the more enterprising soldiers bore to the right and the left as they crossed the moat. They realized that the wall of their fallen comrades only extended for 30 yards along the inner bank, and decided to take the path of least resistance and charge around the ends of the wall rather than take on the defenders in the middle.

Hickok saw he was being outflanked and smiled.

Perfect!

It was all going according to his plan!

Now for the hard part.

"Fall back!" he yelled, waving his arms. "Fall back!"

The defenders, with only 31 left of the original 53, sprinted to the east, abandoning the corpse wall, firing as they ran.

The soldiers, on seeing the defenders retreating, gave a great shout and rushed forward, swirling over the wall of bodies and surging around both ends.

"Hurry!" Hickok goaded his fighters.

The compound was partially obscured by the haze and gunsmoke. Several of the defenders tripped as they ran.

One of them was Sherry.

Hickok heard her cry out and spun.

Sherry was on her knees, her left leg twisted under her, her back to the charging troopers.

One of them was almost on her. He was drawing back his M-16 for a lunge with his bayonet when Seiko appeared out of the smoke. He blocked the thrust of the bayonet and countered with his right sai, sinking it to the hilt in the soldier's chest.

Hickok was already in motion. He reached Sherry's

side and hauled her to her feet. "Come on!" His eyes caught Seiko's, and in that fleeting instant he conveyed the depth of his gratitude with the expression on his face and the relief in his blue eyes.

Seiko smiled and nodded . . . and staggered as a bullet penetrated his head from behind, exiting his cranium between the eyes.

"Seiko!" Sherry screamed.

Seiko stiffened and fell.

Hickok, his left arm supporting the woman he loved, spotted a trooper 15 yards off, an M-16 pressed to his left shoulder. The gunman fired his right Python as the M-16 cracked, and Hickok felt his right sleeve tugged by an invisible hand.

The soldier was flung backward to the unyielding turf.

"Let's go!" Hickok hurried now, forcing his injured left thigh to cooperate with his body.

The troopers had knocked over the corpse wall, and hundreds of them were running pell-mell after the fleeing defenders, bearing due east.

How many yards more? The smoke hid the earthen breastwork from view, but Hickok knew the hastily constructed, breast-high dirt fortification couldn't be more than ten yards ahead. Hickok had kept the defenders up all night working on the breastwork, digging in shifts, and none of them had slept a wink.

Where the blazes was it?

Bullets were buzzing by overhead.

The smoke abruptly dissipated and there it was, 80 yards in length and 4 1/2 feet in height, covering the ground like a giant reddish-brown snake.

Hickok never slowed. He placed both arms around Sherry and jumped, reaching the top of the breastwork in one bound.

Bullets spattered into the mound of dirt.

The gunman rolled, bearing Sherry with him. They slid over the top and tumbled to the ground on the far side. Hickok rose to his knees, scanning to his right and left.

Spartacus, Ares, and the remaining 138 defenders

were ready, their guns in their hands, crouched below the rim of the breastwork.

Hickok glanced over the top of the earthen mound.

Hundreds of soldiers were crammed into the open space between the breastwork and the moat, the nearest ranks only 15 yards away. There was nowhere they could hide, nothing they could use as cover. They were caught in the open, completely unprotected, utterly defenseless.

Now!

"Fire!" Hickok commanded at the top of his lungs.

In unison, the defenders rose up from behind the breastwork and fired. Their firearms, a mixture of automatics, lever and bolt actions, and shotguns, belched death and thundered annihilation upon the soldiers.

The troopers reacted as if, en masse, they had slammed into an invisible barrior. Many were arrested in midstride, their green uniforms dotted with bright red holes. The soldiers in the rear, unaware of the devastation in front, pushed forward, preventing the forward ranks from escaping.

The defenders fired and fired and fired.

Their ranks ravaged by the fusillade, the troopers wavered, then broke, fleeing back toward safety, toward the moat and the makeshift bridge.

Hickok tensed, waiting for the coup de grace. If Shane was in position, and if none of the soldiers had spotted him, and if he had emptied the gas cans into the moat as instructed. . .

The soldiers were clustered on the inner bank, climbing the stairs, and darting across the bridge when the moat went up. A veritable inferno of flame fried them to a crisp, burning the bridge and setting the overhead stairs afire. Cries of suffering and torment filled the air.

Hickok swept the defenders with his gaze. "Charge!" he ordered, and vaulted the breastwork. He closed on the hapless troopers, his Pythons booming, downing two, three, four in swift succession.

Spartacus was at his side every step of the way.

Caught between the flaming moat and the onrushing defenders, the troopers were ruthlessly butchered, game to the last man, resisting with their dying breath. Their bodies were piled in heaps.

The gunfire gradually tapered off as fewer and fewer of the soldiers were able to oppose the defenders.

Hickok stopped, endeavoring to see through the acrid smoke. Fatigue-covered forms overspread the ground.

"Hickok!" someone roared to his right.

The gunman whirled, his Pythons held at waist level, his fingers on the triggers.

It was Brutus.

The hulking brute was seven yards away, his left hand holding a stout branch and using it as a crutch, while his right held an automatic pistol. Brutus grinned, knowing he had the gunman, knowing the best the gunfighter could hope was to tie him and even then Hickok was dead.

With a resounding, deafening detonation, the nearby tank exploded, its ammunition and shells ignited by the blaze in the moat.

The concussion knocked both Hickok and Brutus to the earth, a gust of hot air spurting past them.

Hickok rose to his knees first, and he fired both Pythons as Brutus heaved erect, he fired again as Brutus lurched backward, and again as Brutus attempted to lift his pistol.

And then Spartacus was there, appearing beside Brutus out of the smoke, his broadsword grasped in both hands. He swung the blade with all of his might, putting his entire body into a gleaming arc as the broadsword cleaved the air and connected with Brutus's neck.

Hickok saw Brutus's head leave his body, soaring upward end over end, trailing a crimson plume. The head seemed to move in slow motion as it attained the apex of its flight and plummeted to the earth, bouncing twice and finally coming to a rest at the gunman's feet.

"Are you okay?" Sherry asked from the gunman's right.

Hickok nodded. The gunfire had ended. He stared at

the grisly trophy of his victory, fascinated.

"Are you sure you're all right?" Sherry persisted.

Hickok abruptly felt as if every muscle, every bone in his whole body, ached, had been stretched to its limit and far beyond. "I'm fine," he mumbled.

Ares joined them, exulting in their triumph. "We did it!" he gloated. "We beat them! We saved the Home!"

Hickok absently gazed at the hundreds of bodies around him, many of them near the moat charred beyond recognition. "Yeah," he said dryly. "We did it."

Ares glanced at Sherry and Spartacus, puzzled. "I don't get it. What's the matter with you?" he asked the gunman.

Hickok wearily holstered his Pythons and looped his left arm under Sherry's right shoulder. "Nothing," he replied, leading her off.

"Hey!" Ares called after them. "What do you want us to do? Where are you going?"

Hickok paused and looked back. "I want you to form a detail and clean up this mess. Scout the forest and make sure none of them are left. Allow some of our people to rest. Work them in shifts."

"But what about you?" Ares inquired.

"I'm going to have the Healers tend to my wife," Hickok responded, "and then we're going to enjoy some heavy kissy-wissy in our cabin."

"Are you serious?" Ares queried.

"I promise I'll shoot the first son of a bitch who interrupts us," Hickok vowed. "Is that serious enough for you?"

"Sounds pretty serious to me," Ares admitted.

Hickok and Sherry strolled off, arm in arm.

Ares glanced at Spartacus. "Now what was that all about?"

"I think Hickok just told you something," Spartacus said, wiping his bloody broadsword on his left pant leg.

"Like what?"

"Like," Spartacus stated thoughtfully, "maybe, instead of flapping your gums over our great win, you should be giving thanks you're still alive."

Ares surveyed the battlefield, the dead and the dying, the pools of blood, and the charred and ruptured bodies. "Oh," was all he could think of to say. Then once more, very softly, "Oh."

22

Blade was dreaming. He was lying on his back in a soft, plush bed, his head propped on a comfortable white pillow. The bed was ornate, with four wooden posts at each corner and a blue canopy overhead. This fancy bed was unlike any the Family owned; theirs were plain and Spartan compared to this luxurious resting place. Yes, he knew he was dreaming, so he didn't become alarmed when a brown-haired man with a kind face, but wearing a military uniform, entered his dream through a door situated beyond the foot of the bed. He wasn't particularly concerned as this soldier walked around the bed and approached him. After all, what possible harm could a figment of his imagination do?

Consequently, the Warrior chief was flabbergasted when this apparition smiled at him, took hold of his right wrist, and spoke. "You're awake!"

It wasn't a dream!

He'd been captured by Samuel!

Blade came up off the bed in a rush, his right hand lashing out and clamping on the soldier's throat.

"Help!" the man screamed. "Help!"

Blade applied more pressure on the soldier's neck, striving to crush his windpipe before his cries brought the guards.

He wasn't successful.

The bedroom door flew open and in ran Rikki-Tikki-Tavi, his katana in its scabbard clutched in his right hand.

Blade gawked, confused. Had Rikki come to rescue him?

"Blade! Release him!" Rikki came up to Blade and took hold of his right arm. "Let him go!" he urged.

Perplexed, Blade reluctantly relaxed his fingers.

The unfortunate soldier staggered backward, gasping for breath. "He . . . nearly . . . killed me!" he wheezed.

Blade suddenly realized his arms and legs were covered with cuts and gashes. Some of the larger wounds had been stitched up. His body was naked except for a skimpy pair of white shorts. "What's going on?" he blurted. "Where am I?"

Rikki was grinning. "Congratulations. You almost throttled your doctor," he said, unable to suppress a chuckle.

"My doctor?" Blade repeated, puzzled.

Rikki nodded at the puffing physician. "This is Dr. Edmonds. He's the man who saved your life."

Blade's complete consternation was displayed on his face.

"You lost a lot of blood," Rikki elaborated. "The cat slashed you forty-three times. You would have bled to death without a transfusion. General Reese offered the services of the best doctor in Denver."

"I'm in Denver?" Blade asked. He couldn't believe it. Maybe he was dreaming all of this.

"You are in Denver," confirmed a deep voice from the doorway.

Blade looked at the speaker.

The newcomer was about six feet in height with a lean build. He wore a neatly pressed uniform with gold insignia on the shoulders. His hair was black, his eyes brown. His clean-shaven face reflected his inner sense of honesty, of trustworthiness. He smiled and extended his right hand as he walked up to the bed. "I'm pleased to meet you. I am General Reese."

Blade absently shook hands.

"You're probably wondering what you're doing here," General Reese said. "Do you remember what happened in the tent?"

Blade nodded.

"We saw some of your friends, your fellow Warriors, drive down to the tent in that vehicle you call a SEAL. We waited for awhile, then I drove down under a flag of truce. Your men had slain all of the Imperial Assassins and pulled you from the pit. Samuel and his damn pet were both dead. You were bleeding profusely, and I called my medics to examine you. It was agreed you would die unless you received a quick transfusion. Your men lacked the equipment and the blood. I suggested we should bring you here. Dr. Edmonds performed the transfusion and has been watching over you for two days."

"I've been here two days?" Blade mumbled, stunned.

"Your army is encamped outside the walls," General Reese explained. "We have supplied them with food and other provisions."

"Wait a minute," Blade said, struggling to comprehend. "Do you mean to tell me you're one of Samuel's generals?"

General Reese nodded. "I *was* one of the bastard's generals," he corrected the Warrior.

"Then why didn't you try to save Samuel?" Blade inquired suspiciously. "Why didn't you send down your troops when you saw the SEAL heading for the tent?"

General Reese grinned. "You must understand something. Samuel appointed myself and two others as his generals after his previous generals were killed in Cheyenne when you nuked the Citadel. None of us bore Samuel any great affection. Actually, we hated him. We wanted to see him die. His old officers had been with him for decades, and they were an integral part of his corrupt regime." He paused and proudly straightened his shoulders. "We owed no loyalty to Samuel. Our allegiance is to the people of the Civilized Zone. Many junior officers have wanted to rebel for years. But any revolution while the Doktor and Samuel were alive was out of the question. The Doktor's genetic deviates and Samuel's senior-grade officers would have nipped any revolt in the bud. We had to bide our time until the circumstances were favorable."

He beamed at Blade. "Thanks to you, we were

handed the perfect opportunity on a silver platter."

"Then we've won?" Blade said, amazed.

"Rikki-Tikki-Tavi has told me you don't intend to use a thermo on Denver," General Reese mentioned. "He also informed me the Family does not plan to install one of your own members in Samuel's place. Is all this true?"

"We won't use a thermo unless forced. We only want peace."

"And yet your Federation declared war on the Civilized Zone," General Reese said, studying Blade's expression.

"As Rikki also probably told you," Blade stated, "we declared war as an act of self-preservation. We knew all about Samuel's grand scheme to reconquer the former territory of the United States, and we weren't about to let ourselves be dominated by a dictator."

General Reese nodded. "I believe you," he said. "And, on behalf of the people of the Civilized Zone, I formally offer our surrender."

Blade glanced at Rikki. "Have you heard from Toland, the rebel leader?"

"I can answer that," General Reese interjected. "Yes, we have. He's on his way to Denver and should arrive today. I've already granted him total amnesty."

"Will you agree to work with him in the formation of your new government?" Blade demanded.

"Better than that," General Reese said. "I will place my entire command at his disposal."

Blade slowly nodded. "I trust you, General Reese. But I must make one thing clear to you. If you should change your mind and attempt to take over the government, or if the military balks at the prospect of holding popular elections, I will return to Denver with the Federation Army."

"There will be no need for that," General Reese assured Blade. "We are sincere. And once the people have tasted true freedom there will be no turning back."

"That's what they believed before World War III," Blade reminded the officer. "Look where it got them."

"We will diligently preserve our newfound freedom," General Reese vowed.

"I hope so," Blade commented. "For your sake."

Dr. Edmonds moved closer to the Warrior. "If you don't mind," he stated, "and if you promise to let me live, I'd like to examine your stitches and apply dressing and bandages."

Blade laughed. "Be my guest," he said. "And I apologize for what I did to you."

"I'll have some food brought," General Reese mentioned. "If you feel up to it, tomorrow I'd like you to address our people at Mile High Stadium."

"You want me to speak to your citizens?" Blade responded.

"We have already announced Samuel's death," General Reese revealed. "You have become something of a hero to the populace. They would be thrilled to hear from you personally."

"I don't know," Blade equivocated.

There was an abrupt commotion outside of the bedroom. A figure dressed all in blue darted into the chamber, his Wilkinson in his left hand, his normally controlled features registering his severe anxiety. It was Yama. "Blade!" he called, and dashed to the bed.

"What is it?" Blade asked apprehensively.

Yama was short of breath. "Geronimo . . . Geronimo is at the camp," he announced. "He reports the Home is under attack."

"By whom?" Blade inquired, quickly sliding from the bed.

"Geronimo says two thousand troops from the Civilized Zone were about twelve miles from the compound when he stole a jeep and came to warn us," Yama replied.

Blade glared at General Reese.

The general's surprise was self-evident. "I didn't know!" he assured the Warrior. "Believe me! I didn't know! I knew some of our troops were missing, but Samuel wouldn't say where they were."

"I believe you," Blade stated.

"I'll do anything I can to help," General Reese proposed.

"I'll need to borrow a set of fatigues," Blade said. "My address to your people will have to wait. We're leaving immediately." He contemplated a moment. "I could use gasoline for my convoy."

"It's yours," General Reese pledged.

"Then let's get this show on the road!"

23

The Freedom Federation Army halted at the edge of the woods on the west side of the Home.

"We're too late!" Geronimo exclaimed in an agonized tone. "I didn't reach you in time!" He pounded the steering wheel in frustration.

The drawbridge and a sizeable portion of the west wall were missing. Heaps of rubble lined the outer base of the wall.

"Where are all the bodies?" Blade asked. "There should be bodies."

Geronimo was driving the SEAL. Blade, his arms and legs swathed in herbally treated bandages under his fatigues, sat in the passenger-side bucket seat. Rikki, Yama, and Teucer occupied the middle seat, while Lynx had reclaimed his customary post atop the provisions in the rear section.

"For that matter," Yama said, "where is the Civilized Zone Army?"

"There's one way to find out," Blade stated, and nodded at Geronimo.

The SEAL raced toward the compound. Behind it, the other vehicles in the convoy lumbered from the trees and braked in the field, disgorging the Clan and Mole fighters. They hurriedly formed into their designated squads, weapons at the ready.

"Looks like your west wall has been blown all to hell," Lynx mentioned.

Yama turned in his seat and glared at Lynx.

"Hey, chuckles, don't blame me!" Lynx said. "I didn't do it!"

Geronimo brought the SEAL to a stop ten yards from the wall.

Rikki leaned forward, pointing. "Someone has built a bridge over the moat."

Sure enough, a massive wooden bridge had been erected over the stream.

"Where did *they* come from?" Blade demanded of no one in particular.

They all knew what he meant. Dozens of military vehicles, troop transports and jeeps, were parked in neat rows along the inner bank of the moat.

Geronimo opened his door, grabbing his FNC Auto Rifle from the console. He leaped to the ground.

The others quickly joined him.

"Be careful," Blade warned. "It could be a trap."

"And you're an expert on traps, right?" Lynx sarcastically remarked.

They reached the bridge and paused.

"Do you hear laughter?" Rikki inquired.

"And singing?" added Teucer.

"It's coming from the other side of those vehicles," Blade declared.

Cautiously, the six crossed the bridge and stopped at the edge of the bank.

"Hold it!" someone barked.

They whirled to their left, in the direction of the voice.

Geronimo was the first to recover. He lowered the FNC, chuckling. "I should have known."

Hickok was leaning against a nearby jeep, his arms casually folded across his chest. "You hombres ain't goin' nowhere unless you know the password."

"Password?" Blade repeated.

"Yep," Hickok said. "We've been havin' a dickens of a time lately with varmints comin' in whenever they felt like it. So now nobody gets in unless they know the password."

Blade's temper flared. "Password!" He stalked toward Hickok. "I'll give you a password!"

Hickok straightened and extended his arms, palms outward. "Whoa, big fella! What's got you all in a tizzy?"

Blade's face was turning red. "Do you have any idea of what we went through to get here? We thought you were under attack!"

"We were," Hickok hastily stated. "Where do you think all of these vehicles came from? They don't sprout from seeds, you know."

"Then where's the Civilized Zone Army?" Blade demanded.

Hickok slowly drew his right index finger across his throat.

Blade blanched and stared in the direction of the blocks. "How many did we lose?"

"A bunch," Hickok replied. "I've got a complete list for you."

"Jenny—" Blade began.

"Jenny's fine," Hickok revealed. He looked at Geronimo. "So is your missus, Cynthia. Plato is okay. But we lost four Warriors."

"Which four?" Blade asked.

Hickok frowned at the recollection. " Seiko—"

Rikki-Tikki-Tavi sadly bowed his head.

"—Carter, Gideon, and Crockett," Hickok said, finishing the list. "We thought we lost Samson too, but he was found on the southeast bank of the moat. He was shot up a mite, but the Healers say he'll pull through. The lug is built like an ox."

"What happened?" Blade asked, eager for details.

"I'll give you a rundown," Hickok promised, "but first you gotta give me the scoop on your mission."

"Samuel the Second is dead," Blade detailed. "His generals surrendered to us and agreed to hold elections within three months. The dictatorship is destroyed. Toland, the rebel leader, has been appointed interim leader until the elections are held."

"They rolled over without a fight?" Hickok queried.

"Not exactly," Blade replied. "They're afraid we'll use a thermo on Denver if they don't comply. Besides which, I think just about everybody was tired of living under a dictator. They can't wait to establish a representative form of government again.''

"I just hope they don't muck it up like they did the last time," Hickok remarked.

Lynx, silently standing to the rear of the group, chimed in. "There was one fight worth mentioning."

"Oh?" Hickok noticed Blade averting his eyes.

"Yep," Lynx continued. "Blade managed to get himself trapped by Sammy. He was on his last legs when we pulled his fat out of the fire." He paused, grinning. "Blade owes his life to me!" he bragged.

"That true, pard?" Hickok asked.

Blade reluctantly nodded. "Lynx hid in the back of my jeep, and he signaled Rikki, Yama, and Teucer when I needed them the most."

"You realize Lynx will never let you hear the end of it?" Hickok mentioned.

Blade rolled his eyes skyward. "Don't I know it."

Hickok glanced at Geronimo. "And what the blazes happened to you?"

"I stole a jeep and headed for Denver," Geronimo disclosed. "I looked all over for you before I left, but all I found was your rifle."

"You found my Henry?" Hickok exclaimed happily.

"It's in the SEAL," Geronimo said. "Boone and his men arrived a little while before I took off, so I knew Bertha and Joshua were in good hands." He hesitated. "How are they, anyway?"

Hickok smiled. "The Healers say they'll both pull through."

"Thank the Spirit," Geronimo stated in relief.

Hickok gazed at the west wall. "We've been busy rebuilding. The bridge was our first job."

Blade draped his right arm over his friend's shoulders. "You can tell us all about it. Later. Right now, I want to see Jenny."

"And I must see Cynthia," Geronimo mentioned.

They started to walk away from the stream. Hickok stepped to one side and looked back, over the bridge. "Shouldn't one of us let your men know it's safe to come in?"

Blade laughed. "I almost forgot about them!"

"Some commander you are," Hickok quipped.

"I'll let them know," Teucer volunteered, and ran off.

Blade stretched. "It feels good to be at our Home again."

"I'll echo that," Geronimo concurred.

Rikki nodded knowingly. "We should give thanks for our deliverance."

Yama suddenly sniffed the air. "Is that roast venison I detect?"

"You're just in time for a shindig we're throwin'," Hickok said.

They threaded their way through the rows of military vehicles.

"Say," Hickok remarked, struck by a thought. "Where the blazes is Kilrane?"

"He's in South Dakota with the Cavalry," Blade answered. "His horses couldn't keep pace with our vehicles on a long haul, so we came on by ourselves. We plan to hold a summit meeting in a month."

"Jenny and Cynthia will be tickled pink to see you," Hickok predicted.

"How is Sherry?" Blade inquired.

"She was injured during the attack," Hickok informed them. "But she's okay. Actually," he said, and lowered his voice so only Blade and Geronimo could overhear, "we've been busy making babies."

Geronimo stopped so abruptly the others almost ran into him. "You've been doing what?" he demanded in a loud tone.

Hickok placed his right index finger over his lips. "Shhhh! Not so blamed loud, pard! Do you want the whole world to know?"

Geronimo cupped his hands around his mouth. "Hickok and Sherry are baby-making!" he shouted.

"Shhhhhh!" Hickok frantically motioned for Geronimo to pipe down.

"Beware, world!" Geronimo cried. "I don't think you're ready for another Hickok!"

The gunman feigned outraged indignation. "You

dang-blasted, mangy, good-for-nothin' Injun! I should of known better than to tell you! You're a regular gossip, you know that? The Elders ought to appoint you as our official town crier!"

Blade smiled. Things were back to normal. And, for the first time in months, he felt genuine happiness pervading his soul. This was what it was all about, he told himself. The Home, the Family, his loved ones and friends together, sharing their lives, their joys, and their sorrows, encountering life's difficulties and emerging from their trials even closer than before.

It didn't get any better than this.

And he wouldn't have it any other way.

Epilogue

A year passed, a time of relative tranquility.

Toland was elected President of the Civilized Zone, and a representative legislature was duly installed. A constitution was drafted insuring everyone their fundamental rights.

The Flathead Indians were freed from their slave labor in the Civilized Zone and returned to Montana. A delegation arrived at the Home and, after considerable soul-searching, Star, the Indian princess, decided to rejoin her tribe. Before leaving, she signed a treaty between the Flatheads and the Home.

Months were required, but eventually the Home was completely rebuilt. A new drawbridge was installed, only this one was designed to open by swinging outward instead of inward, this enabling the Family to preserve the new bridge.

Joshua, Bertha, Samson, and Gremlin all recovered. Joshua became the undisputed spiritual sage in the Family. Samson again took up his duties as a Warrior. Bertha received the highest honor she could imagine: she was relegated to Warrior status to replace one of the four lost. Three other Warriors were also selected: Sundance, Helen, and Marcus.

By deciphering the Doktor's four blue notebooks, the Elders discovered the source of the premature senility: the Doktor had poisoned their water supply, the stream, by installing time-released chemical canisters in the stream above the moat. The notebooks detailed the location of the seven canisters, and specified the antidote for the senility.

Plato recovered his vitality and strength and, to Blade's relief, retained his position as Family Leader.

Both Blade and Hickok became fathers to newborn sons during the course of the year. Hickok assisted in the delivery of his, and Sherry afterward claimed she hardly noticed her labor because she was too busy laughing at Hickok's antics.

About a year after the siege, the Family, the Civilized Zone, the Clan, the Moles, the Cavalry, and the Flathead Indians held one of their periodic conclaves. The respective heads unanimously agreed the time was propitious for discovering the fate of the rest of the country after World War III. Accordingly, they decided to send an expedition east of the Mississippi to ascertain if the terrfiying rumors they had heard were true. Because of its impervious body and its lethal armament, the SEAL was chosen as the appropriate vehicle. Volunteers were called for, and all of the Warriors offered to go on the mission.

Three were selected.

But that is a tale for another day.